Enduring
Love

SYDNEY COVE, BOOK 3

Enduring Love

BONNIE LEON

Revell

a division of Baker Publishing Group
Grand Rapids, Michigan

© 2009 by Bonnie Leon

Published by Revell
a division of Baker Publishing Group
P.O. Box 6287, Grand Rapids, MI 49516-6287
www.revellbooks.com

Printed in the United States of America

Library of Congress Cataloging-in-Publication Data
Leon, Bonnie.
    Enduring love / Bonnie Leon.
        p.   cm. — (Sydney Cove ; bk. 3)
    ISBN 978-0-8007-3178-6 (pbk.)
        1. Young women—Fiction. 2. British—New South Wales—Fiction. 3. New
    South Wales—Fiction. I. Title.
    PS3562.E533E53 2009
    813′.54—dc22   2009000245

1

Love can overcome anything, thought Hannah Bradshaw as she stepped out of the modest theater and looked down the street toward the center of Sydney Town. It had only been three years since that terrible winter in 1804 when she'd first set foot in this community as a prisoner. It felt like a lifetime ago.

New South Wales was growing up. The town bustled with activity. There were clothing shops, apothecaries, bakeries, a bank, and even a fine restaurant. A carriage moved past, its inhabitants hidden inside. Glancing up at her husband, Hannah thought, *Life is perfect.*

"What a splendid day," John said. "Even if it is unseasonably cool for autumn."

"I'm almost afraid to feel this happy." Hannah rested a hand on his arm, liking the feel of his wool coat. She leaned against him; thankfulness for his enduring devotion enveloped her in warmth. Although they'd begun their journey together under dire circumstances, they'd managed to find love and, together, had stood resiliently against the world's storms. He smiled down at her and Hannah felt her heart quicken—John still had the power to take her breath away.

She looked at her friends. So much had happened since coming to New South Wales. She'd met Lydia onboard the prison ship and they'd been chums since. And then there was Perry who had grown up on the streets of London but stood with John through the excruciating days onboard the ghastly ship and then the terror that met them in Sydney Town. Perry's new bride, Gwen, had been employed at the Athertons' when Hannah had joined the household, and she'd welcomed her right off, brightening her days there. Even David, who'd been raised among the well-to-do in London, was a valued friend. He'd become Parramatta's physician and Lydia's husband. And was a gift to them all.

Perry pulled Gwen protectively under one arm. He smiled down at her. "How did I manage to get along without ye?"

Her eyes alight, Gwen snuggled in close to her husband. "I don't know." She giggled. "How did ye?"

Lydia tucked an arm into David's. "Love is grand. It conquers all. Don't ye agree, husband?"

"I do at that." David startled her by brushing her lips with his.

A rare blush colored her cheeks. "David! We're in public."

"You two behave as if you're still newly wed," John said with a laugh.

"We are." Lydia gave David a tender look. "It's been a scant two months since we said our vows."

Perry nuzzled Gwen's neck and she giggled. He pulled her closer. "And for us, two days." He grinned devilishly. "How 'bout we go back to the hotel, luv?"

Blushing, Gwen leaned against him.

Hannah smiled at her friends, their ardor reminding her of how it had been for her and John in the beginning. Her passion and John's love had taken her by surprise.

"We'll see ye later." Perry grasped Gwen's hand and the two hurried toward the hotel.

John's arm went around Hannah. "Remember?"

"It's not been that long ago." She gave him a playful squeeze.

"So, luv, what did you think of the play?" John asked.

"I think Shakespeare is a masterful playwright."

"That he is. And *The Merry Wives of Windsor* was quite amusing."

"It was at that." Hannah met his hazel eyes. "With all the tomfoolery, I was beginning to wonder if Anne and Fenton would end up together. I'm glad they did. They were meant for each other." Admiring the way John's dark curls framed his strong angular face, she was tempted to brush a strand of untamed hair off his forehead, but she refrained.

His attention moved to something across the street. The color drained from his face.

"John. What is it?" Hannah followed his gaze, searching for whatever was distressing her husband. Nothing seemed out of the ordinary. Normal foot traffic moved up and down the street, and a woman stood outside the boardinghouse. Although quite handsome, there didn't seem to be anything unusual about her. Reddish brown hair had been tucked up beneath a stylish hat. Eyes so dark they were nearly black found John and stared back at him. A look of surprise touched them, then changed to delight.

Hannah felt a thump of alarm. "John?" She grabbed his arm. He seemed unaware of her.

"What's gotten into ye? Do ye know her?" Lydia folded her arms over her chest and stared at the stranger. "Who is it?"

John made no reply, but Hannah could feel the tension in his body.

"John?" Hannah tried to draw him closer, but he was unyielding and she let loose of his arm. "Who is she?" Her fear mounted. Why did this stranger have such a profound effect on her husband?

After glancing up and down the street, the auburn-haired stranger crossed and walked purposefully toward John. She moved with confidence, her arms swinging freely at her sides and her hips swaying. Hannah's insides churned. Something was terribly wrong. Who was this woman? And why was John staring at her as if he were seeing an apparition?

He took a step away from Hannah. Holding his back rigid and his jaw locked, he waited as if for an assault.

The woman was close now. Smiling, she showed off perfect teeth. "John, I can barely believe my luck at finding you so quickly." She took his hands in hers, stood at arm's length, and gazed at him.

John's eyes were hard and accusing.

"After all this time, I'd think you'd have something to say. Aren't you happy to see me?"

"Margaret," he whispered.

Like the roar of a cannon, the name reverberated through Hannah's mind. Margaret was his late wife's name.

"Why are you looking at me so?" the woman asked.

"I thought you dead."

"Dead?" Shock flashed across Margaret's face. "I can assure you I'm very much alive. Although I nearly died from a stomach ailment . . . after you disappeared." Sorrow creased her face. "I needed you so badly." She dabbed at her eyes with a handkerchief. "By the time I was recovered enough to search for you, you'd been transported." Tears pooled and spilled onto her cheeks. "I thought I'd lost you forever." She managed a tremulous smile. "But I've found you. It's like a miracle. I've been searching so long."

John's expression remained harsh.

Margaret's eyes went to David and Lydia and then rested on Hannah. "Don't you think you ought to introduce your . . . friends?"

As if waking from a trance, John looked at his companions. With a nod he said, "This is David and Lydia Gelson." He moved closer to Hannah and rested a hand on her back. "This is Hannah . . . my wife."

Margaret pressed her fingers to her lips. "Your wife?" She turned dark eyes on Hannah as if looking at something fearful, and then looked back to John. "Then . . . who am I?"

Hannah could feel her pulse throbbing throughout her body. Trying to keep her voice from trembling, she asked, "John?"

Without looking at Hannah, he squared his jaw and said austerely, "This is Margaret."

"I've heard her name before, but *who* is she?"

John didn't answer.

Margaret's gaze returned to Hannah's. "I'm his wife. I've been trying to find him since he left London." She turned to John. "And now I have and . . . and . . ." She seemed to fight to control her emotions. "And you're married to someone else?"

Lydia stepped forward. "This is some sort of horrible trick. John can't have another wife. He's married to Hannah."

"Lydia." David took her arm. "Perhaps you and I should go to the hotel and give John and Hannah and . . . Margaret time alone."

Alone? Hannah thought. *There are three of us. How can we be alone?* Her heart thrummed so hard she wondered if it might

9

fly out of her chest. She stared at the woman and then looked at John. "You said she had died."

"I thought she had. That's what I was told." His eyes implored Hannah to believe him.

Feeling as if she might shatter into pieces, Hannah grabbed for something solid to hang on to and finally pressed a hand against a storefront wall. She looked at Lydia, who could not conceal her shock and sympathy. Hannah took a step back. Blackness enveloped her and she thought she might be sick. "I . . . I'm going to our room." She looked from John to Margaret, unable to believe what she was seeing, and then turned and hurried toward the hotel. *Don't faint. Don't faint*, she thought, keeping a hand on the wall and walking as swiftly as she could manage.

She stepped into the hotel lobby. *Lord, how can this be? What am I to do?* She fought back tears, not wanting anyone to see her anguish.

"Hannah, wait." John's voice carried through the hotel lobby.

She hurried her steps. She couldn't look at him, couldn't speak to him. He was married . . . to someone else. *Dear Lord!*

His steps echoed behind her, moving closer. "Hannah. Please. Wait. I didn't know. I didn't know."

Hannah walked faster. "Leave me be. I can't speak to you now." She kept her eyes forward and continued walking. She could barely see and felt as if she were moving through a dark tunnel. "Go away."

"Hannah, please listen. I thought she was dead. And now . . . that she's not, it changes nothing. I'll have naught to do with her. She betrayed me—she and Henry. They took everything of value to me. I want nothing to do with her. I love only you. Please believe me."

Standing behind the dressing panel, Hannah shivered as she slipped her sleeping gown over her head. She hugged herself, not wanting to step outside of the protective shield. John was there, morose and silent. He shouldn't even be in her room. He had another wife.

Trying to slow her breathing and quiet her trembling, Hannah moved from behind the panel and crossed to the bureau. Releasing her dark hair from its pins, she gave it several strokes with a brush. Without a glance at John, she moved to the bed and slipped between cold sheets. She lay down and pulled the blankets up over her, holding her body stiff and still. The window had been left open and a chill breeze ruffled the curtains.

John sat in a straight-backed chair, his arms pressed against his thighs, hands clasped as if in prayer. He stared at the floor.

Hannah knew he anguished just as she did, but she couldn't think of anything to say. She put out the lamp and the night enveloped them. Lying on her back, she remained still, staring at the ceiling hidden by the blackness. Night sounds carried in from outside—a frog chirped and someone's growling cough carried up from the city street; distant voices chatted. And then it was quiet.

Hannah was thankful for the refuge of the darkness. *God help me. I don't know what to do.* She closed her eyes and Margaret's handsome face popped into her mind. Trepidation and misery pressed down on her. *Did she have to be so stunning?* Hannah felt plain in comparison.

The chair creaked, and Hannah heard the sounds of John

undressing. He draped his shirt and then his pants over the chair, then crossed the room. Hannah couldn't see him, but she knew he stood beside the bed . . . for a long while. She waited, breathing shallowly. The mattress gave and John lay down, lying motionless.

Hannah remained still. *How can we live like this? It's impossible.* Knowing the question had to be raised, she asked, "What are we to do?"

For a long moment, John made no reply, then he whispered, "I don't know."

He reached for Hannah's hand, but she withdrew, unable to bear his touch.

"I'll divorce her."

"Divorce is not a solution. You know it's almost never allowed."

"She deceived me. She and my cousin Henry took my company, the business my father built, and every penny I had. She's not my wife. She never was, not really. What wife would treat her husband so? It was all a sham."

Hannah didn't want to defend Margaret, but she and John must face the truth. "How do you know she did those things?"

"I just know. She was seen leaving our home with Henry. They went away together, and then the money disappeared from my bank account. I was told Henry made the withdrawal."

"Henry, not Margaret." Hannah pushed up on one elbow, facing John. "If she dishonored you that way, then why would she come here now? Perhaps you've misjudged her." Hannah didn't want to voice what was in her mind, but it must be said. "I saw love in her eyes, John. Love for you."

Silence, like a dark presence, spread through the room. When

John spoke, his voice was heavy and thick. "Even if that's true . . . it doesn't matter. I don't love her anymore. You're my only love. You're my wife."

"You're already married, John. Don't you see? We're not husband and wife."

"We are." John's voice was resolute.

"No, John, we're not."

2

Lydia and David led the way. John followed Hannah. His eyes grazed the room crowded with early morning breakfasters, mostly families. "How 'bout next to the window?" He tried to keep his voice light. He noticed two business acquaintances sitting near the back. The elder gentleman, Mr. Phelps, nodded. John lifted his hat to him, then tucked it beneath one arm. With a glance about the unpretentious restaurant, he was thankful to see no one else of consequence. He wasn't up to polite conversation.

"Perfect," Lydia said. "The clouds have gone, and the morning sun will feel good." She moved toward the front of the room, with David hurrying to keep up.

Perry followed, Gwen on his arm. "It'll probably be hot by the time we start for home."

His hand pressed lightly against Hannah's back, John steered her to the table. Beneath his palm, he could feel the tightness of her muscles. Pulling out a chair, he chanced a glance and saw tightly pursed lips and dark, unhappy eyes. She didn't look at him. He took the seat beside her.

Perry leaned back in his chair and, taking a big breath, expanded his narrow rib cage. "It's a fine day." He sounded overly cheerful.

Gwen laid a hand on Perry's arm. "It is." Her eyes went to Hannah, then quickly moved to Lydia. She smiled. "I wish we could stay longer."

Lydia pushed back loose hairs that had fallen onto her face. "Me too. And that dreadful road—I don't look forward to it." She placed her hands on the table in front of her and leaned toward John and Hannah. "So . . . I suppose we can ignore your predicament and go on with our breakfast as if nothing's changed, but that wouldn't be right."

Hannah looked at Lydia, surprise in her eyes.

"What are ye two going to do?"

Hannah pressed her lips more tightly together and glanced at John.

He shook his head. It was just like Lydia to steer straight into trouble. He closed his eyes, wishing the whole matter would disappear. He didn't want to discuss it. Margaret was a part of his life he wanted to forget.

What Henry and Margaret had done glared at him from the past, and he couldn't look away. Revulsion and fury roared through John. His mind rewound and he felt as if he were still in prison and just learning of their treachery. They'd done to him what no person had the right to do to any other. Margaret had defiled their marriage bed by lying with Henry, and then while he was suffering in prison, they'd stripped him of his business and his assets. Everything he and his father had worked for had been taken.

John clenched his teeth. He thought he'd put all this behind him, forgiven the wrongs done . . . but when he'd seen Margaret, he'd again tasted bitterness and rage.

15

Lydia unfolded her napkin. "It's unbelievable Margaret thinks she can simply saunter up to you after all this time and act as if nothing has happened. The nerve . . ." She dropped the napkin on her lap then fixed her eyes on John. "So, what are ye going to do?"

David rested a hand on Lydia's arm. "Luv, I'm sure if he wanted us to know, he'd have said."

Lydia glanced at David's hand. "I simply thought we might be of help."

John needed to say something. He looked at Hannah, hoping for encouragement, but she stared at clasped hands in her lap. He looked back to Lydia. "As far as I'm concerned, Margaret is dead. I don't intend to give her the time of day. We shan't see each other again, I'm certain of that."

"A decree of divorce should be forthcoming then, eh?" Lydia pressed.

"Not easy to do." Perry leaned his elbows on the table. "I knew a bloke once who tried to divorce his wife; he had good cause, but he never managed to get one. He lived the rest of his life with the wench on one side and her father on the other, musket ready." He chuckled.

Gwen jabbed him in the side with her elbow.

"What? What did I say? It's the truth." His smirk disappeared. "I've never known one person who managed to free themselves, not unless their spouse went off with someone else."

"I doubt anyone would want a woman like her," David said.

"If it were the right bloke, he'd take her," said Lydia. "What 'bout that newly widowed constable? He might be looking for a wife. She is comely. Perhaps we ought to inquire."

John felt a flicker of hope. "Do you think it possible to divorce if she has another suitor?"

16

Lydia shrugged. "Maybe. I'm wondering if she came because there's a need for wives in New South Wales. There are a lot of men without women." Lydia rested her chin in one hand.

"Not likely," Perry said. "She wouldn't have any trouble finding a husband in London, treacherous or not."

John studied a brilliantly colored butterfly fluttering against the window. It tried again and again to get inside, its delicate wings trembling. "I've just cause for divorce—after what she and Henry did."

"I should say you do." Lydia's tone was heated. "That woman was more than unfaithful, she—"

John held up a hand to shush her. "Enough." He didn't want to hear more. And he could see all this talk was upsetting Hannah. She'd turned ashen. He took her hand and squeezed it gently. "I shall apply for a divorce."

"As Perry said, it's not so easily done." Hannah's voice quaked.

"That may be so, but I'm determined. It shall be accomplished whether she has another suitor or not." The fear and hurt in Hannah's voice pierced John's heart. This wasn't fair to her. His rancor intensified. It was so like Margaret to do what pleased her with no thought to anyone else.

"Not to worry, luv. I'll see to Margaret. She'll not have her way." He lifted Hannah's hand and kissed the back of her fingers. "Trust me."

Hannah nodded, but she barely looked at him.

A cranky-looking woman, wearing an apron blemished with spatterings of the morning's fare, set platters of eggs, toast, and hot porridge on the table. She returned a moment later with a stack of plates and a handful of utensils. "I'll be back with tea and coffee, if ye like."

17

"We do." Lydia picked up a plate, dished a helping of eggs onto it and a slice of toast, and set it in front of David. Gwen did the same for Perry, then scooped out a bit of hot cereal for herself.

John picked up a plate. "What would you like, luv?"

"Nothing. I'm not hungry."

John studied her a moment. "The eggs look fresh."

"No. Tea is all I want."

"All right, then." John served himself eggs and toast.

The woman returned with tea and coffee, placing them on the table. "Anything more I can get ye?"

"I think we're fine," David said.

With a nod, she moved away.

Hannah lifted the kettle and poured herself a cup of tea and then stirred in a bit of sugar.

"It will be a long trip home." John leaned closer to Hannah. "You'd best have something to eat."

"I said . . . I'm not hungry." Hannah's tone was sharp.

"Just meant to help."

Hannah flashed him a heated look. "There's nothing you can do to help."

John's natural response would be to defend himself. Instead he returned to his breakfast and his thoughts. *There must be a solution*. He took a bite of egg. It was tasteless. He poured himself a cup of coffee and took a drink of the dark brew. He looked into the cup. *Bitter, like my life.*

Conversation came in fits and starts and finally died altogether. When the meal was nearly completed, the woman who had served them returned. "Is one of ye John Bradshaw?"

John set down his fork and wiped his mouth with his napkin. "That would be me." She handed him a small envelope and walked away.

He looked at it, turning it over and over in his hands. He knew it was from Margaret. He glanced at the others.

Lydia set her spoon aside. "Well, are ye going to read it?"

John slipped an index finger beneath a wax seal, opened the envelope, and lifted out a note. He didn't want to read it. Margaret couldn't possibly have anything to say that he wanted to hear. Still, his eyes dropped to the note. He immediately recognized the florid script.

My dearest John. I am at a loss to explain my feelings, but I will do my best. I am delighted to have finally found you, and yet my heart is breaking over your austere reception. I have dreamed of our reunion and what it would be like. Your rebuff confuses me. I can only guess at your reasons.

It seems we have much to talk about, especially upon learning that you've remarried. I understand why you would take a wife when believing me to be dead. However, I must point out that your present marriage is invalid since you are still married to me.

John felt the hard thrum of his heart. It was true—Hannah was not his legal wife.

Please come to me at the boardinghouse so we can talk. I will do my best to explain all that has happened since your arrest. You must believe it was never my intention that you be imprisoned and sent to this godforsaken country. I love you. I always have. Yours sincerely . . . Margaret.

John reread the note. Was it possible he had misunderstood the circumstances of her disappearance? He tucked the letter back into the envelope, then looked at his companions and at Hannah. "It's from Margaret. She wants to speak to me. This is all quite a mess. I must go."

If it were possible, Hannah's skin became even more ashen. Her chin trembled and she fought tears. John took her hand. "We must sort this out so we can go on with our lives. Try not to worry, luv. Everything will be fine. I promise."

"Of course it will be." Lydia smiled encouragement. "The Lord wouldn't bring ye together to allow something like this to separate ye, especially after all ye've been through. Ye'll stand against this, like all the other troubles ye've faced before. And the Lord's not forgotten Thomas. He's in the midst of this too."

"Lydia's right," David said. "I'm sure you'll find a solution." His tone belied the words.

Hannah stood. "I'm going to our room. I'll wait there." Her brown eyes sought out John's and held them for a moment before she turned and walked away.

"Poor Hannah," Gwen said. "I can't imagine." She looked at John. "I'm sorry.

Perry laid his fork on his plate. "Ye'll find a way to solve this, I've no doubt."

John stood. "Of course, you're right. Though this is shocking and seems a mess, I'm confident it's not out of God's control. Just as you've said, he'll sort it out. I'll speak to Margaret and then to the governor. I'm sure he'll understand I have good reason to divorce her."

John wished he felt as confident as his words sounded. If while living in London Margaret truly hadn't meant him any harm, then speaking to the governor would do him little good.

***

Shoulders back, spine straight, John left the café. Inside he quailed. What could he say to a woman he'd hated for years and

20

had believed dead? He imagined telling her what he thought about what she'd done, and he could feel the pleasure of retribution.

Unaware of his steps, he kept moving. A wagon rolled past and a dog barked, but they seemed part of another world. Everything around him seemed blurred. There were people, horses, drays loaded with supplies, but they moved by like vague shadows. A woman twirling a parasol sauntered past and smiled. John barely noticed. His mind was with Margaret. What would she say? No matter what it was, he didn't want to hear. If giving all his worldly possessions could keep him from this meeting, he'd have offered them gladly.

He stopped in front of the boardinghouse. Its white walls shouted at him, the spotless windows winked malevolence. He stared at the door. When it opened suddenly and a man stepped out, John's pulse picked up. The man brushed past with barely a glance.

He forced his hand to reach for the knob, grabbed and turned. Opening the door, he stepped onto a carpeted entryway and pulled the door closed behind him.

A doorway to his right led to a parlor, where Margaret sat on a divan sipping tea. She didn't see him, seemingly entranced by a book she was reading.

She wore a gown made of lavender linen with long sleeves and a rather revealing neckline. John felt familiarity. She was more handsome than when he'd last seen her. She wore her auburn hair caught back, allowing thick tresses to cascade onto her shoulders and down her back. It shimmered in the sunlight. Her dark eyes were lined by heavy lashes, and when she lifted the cup to her mouth, her full lips seemed to caress the rim.

John was captivated and for a brief moment transported back to their first meeting. He'd been instantly smitten and thrilled when she seemed interested in him. Their courtship had been heated and brief. They were married soon after that first encounter.

John tugged at his waistcoat and stepped into the room. Margaret looked up. Was it adoration he saw in her dark eyes? He dare not think on it.

"Margaret, you wished to speak to me?"

"Yes. I'm grateful you've come. I was afraid you might not."

"It seems I have no choice." John kept his tone impersonal. "We're still married, and that means we've matters to discuss."

Margaret looked wounded. "I should think so."

Removing his hat, John crossed to a cushioned chair and sat. Sliding the brim through his fingers, he held his angry thoughts inside and waited for her to speak. After all, she'd summoned him.

Margaret set her book aside. She offered John a loving gaze. "It's wonderful to look at you. There were times I feared I'd never see you again."

Her voice was soft as rose petals, and John felt a stirring in his heart, remembering how he'd once loved her. He'd always been enraptured by her voice.

"It seems we've a bit of a problem. You've taken a wife, yet you're still married to me."

"We've no problem." John fought to keep his voice resolute. "We'll divorce."

Shock tightened Margaret's features. "Divorce? How can you suggest such a thing? After all I've done to find you? I've come so far. I thought you loved me." Her hands trembled and she set her saucer and cup on the table beside her. "Have you no feelings for me at all?"

"I did . . . once. But that was a long time ago."

"What cause have you to divorce me?"

"Cause? You ask me for a cause?" John was taken aback. "After what you did?"

"What I did?" Margaret tugged a handkerchief out from beneath the cuff of her sleeve and dabbed at tears.

"You act so innocent." He could barely hold back a sneer. "I was in prison because I defended Henry in a fight at the pub. And then you and he went off together and took my fortune with you." He set his jaw and glared at her, enjoying the sense of reprisal.

Margaret looked bewildered. "That's not how it was at all. I can't believe you'd entertain such an idea."

"Henry told me how it happened. You weren't innocent."

"I am innocent of this. You know how I loved you . . . there has never been anyone else. Henry forced me to go with him. He held me captive, and . . . I had no choice or lose my life." She gazed at her hands, seeming to relive some sort of horror. "While holding me prisoner, he told me of his scheme and how he'd taken the business and its assets. I anguished for you, John. Please believe me."

John was not convinced. "A neighbor saw you leave together. He made no mention of your being in distress—quite the contrary."

"That's how Henry wanted it to look. He held a pistol to my side every moment we were traveling. And then . . . he . . ." She twisted the handkerchief. "He ravaged me." A sob escaped and she buried her face in the handkerchief.

John didn't know how to respond. All this could be a ruse, but for what purpose?

"I became ill and Henry left me. By the time I made my way back to London, you'd already been transported."

"If you were so distraught about my going, why did it take you so long to find me? It's been three years."

"How is a woman alone to undertake such a journey? I had no means. When I returned to our home, it had been sold and there was not a farthing left in the bank. Henry took everything."

John stared at her, hoping to discern the truth. How could he trust her?

"Please, John, you must believe me." Margaret moved from the settee, dropping to her knees in front of him. "All this time, I've thought only of you and the life we could have. I've prayed I'd find you. And now I have."

John didn't know what to believe.

"Why would I come all this way, if not for love?"

He could think of no reason. Even with the additional property he'd purchased, he had only a fledgling farm and very little cash. He gazed into her dark eyes, trying to read what was there. He was stunned by what he saw—devotion. "Why not a letter, then?" he asked.

"I did write. If you didn't receive word from me, it is the post that is to blame."

John knew gaolers cared little about the prisoners or the mail. What if he'd been wrong all this time? He pushed out of the chair and offered Margaret a hand up. The two stood almost toe to toe.

Remembering Hannah, John turned abruptly and walked to the window. Looking out on the street, his eyes moved to the hotel. Hannah was there . . . waiting for him. If Margaret were speaking the truth, what would that mean for him and Hannah? Pain swelled in his chest like a cruel fist squeezing his heart.

He turned and looked at Margaret. "I'll think on what you've said." John couldn't allow her to see his emotions. He moved toward the door. "We'll speak again."

"John, please. What shall I do?"

He didn't want to hear her velvet voice plead. He wanted to hate her. "I'll think on it. That's all I can do. I promise nothing." He walked out of the room, knowing that under these circumstances a divorce would never be granted.

3

Hannah stood at the window of her hotel room and watched the street below. Two women, both with children in tow, greeted one another, chatted for a few moments, and then went on their way. A shopkeeper swept the sidewalk in front of his store, then stopped to study a wagon roll past, which raised more dust that would need to be cleaned away. Two dogs barked at him from the back of the wagon, which seemed to be overflowing with children. How odd that the world went on as it always had while her life had been turned upside down.

John had been gone a long while. She couldn't imagine what he and Margaret could be talking about all this time, or perhaps she was afraid to imagine. Finally, she moved to the mirror. She looked dreadful, her eyes puffy and red-rimmed. Removing the pins from her hair, she allowed the dark tresses to fall to her shoulders, then pulled a brush through the fine strands. John often caressed her hair, saying it was soft as silk.

What could be taking so long?

After pinning her hair back in place, she splashed her face with cool water and returned to her position at the window. She caught her breath when she saw John cross the street. He walked with purpose, his fists clenched and his brow furrowed. Clearly, he was distressed. Hannah suddenly felt sick.

She watched until he disappeared beneath the hotel eaves, then turned and faced the door. He'd be there any moment. Noticing a wrinkle on the bedspread, she moved to smooth it, then quickly returned to her place at the window. What would he say? What had Margaret told him?

Muffled footfalls moved down the hallway toward her room. *It must be him.* Just outside the room the paces stopped. The door didn't open. *He's just standing there.* Hannah knew that whatever had taken place must be bad. She held her breath.

When the knob finally turned, Hannah hugged herself about the waist. *What if he still loves Margaret? What shall I do? I can't bear it.* She shushed her runaway thoughts, reminding herself of John's devotion to her. How many times had he assured her of his love—more than she could count. And hadn't he always said he would love her forever? She clung to the tender memories.

The door opened and John stepped into the room. At first he didn't look at her, but when his hazel eyes settled on her face, she saw his anguish. She sucked in a breath and pressed a hand to her stomach.

He closed the door. Silence hung between husband and wife.

Hannah couldn't bear to hear, but she must know and finally asked, "What's happened?" Wishing she could take back the question, she turned to the window and stared at the street and its people who happily went about their daily errands. "No. Don't tell me." She wanted to be one of those people—the one's whose lives weren't ruined. If only she and John could go on with theirs, as if nothing had happened.

"Hannah, we must talk." John's voice sounded tight, as if he were being strangled. He moved to her, but she didn't turn to face him. Resting his hands on her upper arms, he pulled her close.

Hannah didn't respond. She couldn't.

"It would be best if you sat down."

She could hear the death knoll in his voice. Feeling the heat of tears and the rending of her heart, she moved to a writing desk and seated herself. Laying trembling hands on the desktop, she stared at them. What had happened? Barely able to breathe, she forced herself to look at John. "Tell me."

He paced while telling her about his meeting with Margaret. Every time Hannah tried to break in with a question, he'd hush her and hurry on with the story as if getting it all out at once made it less devastating. When he'd finished, he stopped his striding back and forth and gazed at Hannah.

She loves him. I've lost him. Holding back tears, she looked at her husband. "Do you love her?"

"Of course not. Is that what you think?" He moved toward her.

"Don't. Please." She pushed to her feet and backed away.

John stopped abruptly. "I don't love her. I love only you."

Hannah clasped her hands tightly, as if holding on would keep her world in order. She looked at the door; she needed to get out—to get away.

"Hannah." John's voice entreated her to remain.

"It seems she never meant you any harm. Henry is your enemy, not Margaret. She was a victim, just as you were."

"That doesn't change anything. I don't love her. I'll file for a divorce."

"Why? It won't be granted. You know it's impossible except under the most severe circumstances."

"These are severe."

Hannah wished she could agree with John, but she knew pretending was useless. "Margaret's done you no harm. In good faith she traveled from London, all the while believing you to be imprisoned, yet willing to stand at your side." Suddenly like a dark wave, understanding of Margaret's desperate situation and her devotion toward John swept over Hannah. "She must love you very much."

"I'm not convinced of that."

With hopelessness seeping into her soul, Hannah dropped her arms to her sides. "I wish it weren't true, if only it weren't, but we've got to see things as they are, not as we want them to be."

She met John's eyes, their light dimmed by grief. "You must free yourself from what you've believed these past three years and see the truth of the circumstances. Margaret risked a great deal to come here." Hannah returned to the window and pressed a palm against the glass. "If what she says is true, you and I have no marriage. And there's nothing that can be done about it."

In three strides John was beside her. "You can't know that. I love you. You love me. And we *are* married."

Hannah turned and faced him. He was so close she could feel his breath. She placed her hands against his chest. "How is it possible for a man to be married to two women at the same time?"

John didn't speak right away. "There must be a law that can sort out a situation like this."

"If so, I've never heard of it." She waited, hoping that he might remember a similar situation or something that might help restore their life.

He said nothing.

"That's it, then."

"I can't be married to you and Margaret at the same time. It's impossible."

"That is our dilemma and our tragedy."

John tried to pull Hannah to him, but she resisted. "Where are we if we've not got each other?" he asked. Again he tried to draw her close.

Needing his strength and the warmth of his arms, Hannah relented, allowing the embrace. She pressed her face against his shirt, breathing in the scent of him. She could no longer hold back the tears. Wrapping her arms about him, she allowed herself to weep. A barren future rushed at her. "How can I live without you?"

"You won't have to." John's voice trembled. "We'll speak to Reverend Taylor. He'll know what to do. There must be a way."

Hannah held him more tightly. "I pray you're right."

<hr />

John didn't hurry the team as the wagon moved through Parramatta. Hannah felt as if she were part of a funeral procession. David and Lydia stood in the doorway of the apothecary and nodded encouragement as they passed. Mrs. Atherton stepped out of the mercantile and lifted a hand in a small wave. "All will be well. Have faith."

Hannah wanted to believe her, but she knew it would take more than human determination. This difficulty required a miracle.

The closer they came to the rectory, the more she trembled.

The quaking moved from her insides to her limbs and then to her lips. She couldn't keep her hands still in her lap and noticed that even John moved the traces from one hand to the other again and again.

He slapped the reins. "Thomas said he'd see to the stock. He's a good lad."

"That he is." Hannah could still see the dread in Thomas's eyes as they'd driven off. With Jackson at his side, he'd stood on the veranda, gripping the railing until they'd moved out of sight. All morning he'd peppered Hannah and John with questions. But they had no adequate answers, nothing to offer comfort or hope, only more questions.

"I'm afraid for him," Hannah said. "He's already been through so much—losing his sister and his mum and dad. Although we've become his family, something like this could destroy him. Don't you remember how hard it was on the poor lad when he came to us?"

"He'll be fine. We'll be fine."

"John, he's terrified. I could see it in his eyes and in his manner. And he's a right to be."

"We don't know that. I'm sure the reverend will have good news for us." John turned the horses off the main road and onto the drive that led to the rectory. In the shade of a large gum tree he pulled the team to a stop. After setting the brake and tying off the reins, he climbed down and offered Hannah a hand. "I'll just give the animals a drink before we go in. It's a bit hot and they're likely thirsty. I'd hoped for cooler weather by now, but it seems summer will stay for a while longer."

Why is he prattling on over the mundane? Our life is over. He won't allow himself to see the truth. She watched John dip a bucket into a water trough, then lift it out. "I remember March in London. When the winter cold lifted, it felt like a time of renewal, the earliest flowers would be up and the grasses turned a vibrant green." She missed the beauty, more now than she could remember since leaving.

Glancing about, her eyes and her spirit took in the thirsty trees, drooping bushes, and grasses burned to a pale brown. Everything seemed dead. It suited the way she felt. What if John was wrong and they had no future together? *I couldn't bear it.* She closed her eyes. *Lord, give me strength. Offer us a merciful solution.*

John carried the bucket to the horses and gave each a drink, then set the bucket back in its place beside the trough. He moved to Hannah and took her arm. "You ready, then?"

"No."

John offered a reassuring smile, gave her arm a gentle squeeze, and then guided her toward the rectory.

Reverend Taylor stepped onto a small porch. He smiled warmly, but his eyes were troubled. "I've been expecting you." He gripped John's hand. "Welcome." Nodding at Hannah, he added, "It's grand to see you." His tone turned grim. "If only it were under more pleasant circumstances." He stood aside, opening the door wide.

Hannah had been in the reverend's house only once before. Nothing had changed. It was still sparsely furnished and spotlessly clean. The only thing cluttered was a desk piled with books and papers. Hannah knew that must be the place where he composed his sermons.

"Please, sit," he said. "Can I offer you some refreshment? It's a bit warm today."

"Water would be nice." Hannah's mouth had gone dry.

"I'm quite all right," John said.

32

She settled on a settee with John beside her. They held each other's hands tightly.

The reverend returned from the kitchen carrying a glass of water. "I brought it up from the spring just a bit ago, so it's still cool." He gave it to Hannah, then sat in a cushioned chair opposite the settee.

Hannah sipped the water. "It's quite refreshing, thank you."

The reverend smiled and ran a hand over the fabric on the arm of the chair. "Only piece of furniture I brought with me from London. It belonged to my mum. It's all I have left of her, except memories, of course. This was her chair. When she told stories, she'd sit here and gather me and my brothers onto her lap." He patted the arm. "Good memories."

He puffed out a small breath and set serious blue eyes on Hannah and then John. "Perhaps we ought to pray before we begin, eh?" He bowed his head. "Our Father in heaven, we thank thee for thy presence and for thy consolation. We ask thee to give us an extra measure of comfort in these troubled times. And might thee bestow upon us wisdom and strength greater than our own as we sort out this plight. Help us to trust in thy holy and judicious sovereignty, always remembering that there is nothing that touches our lives that thee has not allowed. We thank thee for thy love and for thy mercy—in thy Son's name we pray. Amen."

He looked up. "Now then, tell me what's happened. I've only heard rumors."

"I suppose there are a lot of those floating about," John said, taking a stab at levity.

"You tell him," Hannah said.

John released Hannah's hand and leaned forward, resting his arms on his legs. "As you know, I've been married before, while living in London. After my arrest, I learned that my wife Margaret and my cousin Henry had betrayed me. My understanding was that they'd run off together and then stolen my property. And later I was told Margaret had died. I left London believing myself to be a widower."

"I do recall hearing about that. Wasn't Henry caught in a swindle here in Sydney Town?"

"Yes. He was."

"He's in prison?"

"Newcastle."

"And as I understand, you had a hand in his capture?"

"That's right."

The reverend nodded. "All right, now what's happened?"

"Hannah and I were in Sydney Town for a short holiday with friends when Margaret approached me."

The reverend sat back. "That must have been quite a shock, eh?"

"Yes, and more." John cleared his throat and glanced at Hannah. "It was and it is devastating for us both."

Hannah could feel the staggering blow of the meeting as if it had just occurred.

"What happened then?" The reverend pressed his palms together and steepled his fingers.

"Margaret asked to meet with me, and so I went to the boardinghouse where she's staying. She explained that she'd never left willingly with Henry, but that he'd taken her prisoner, and soon after, she became gravely ill. He left her, took my properties, and disappeared." John leaned back, resting an arm on the settee. "By that time I'd been transported."

The reverend nodded. "And why has she come here now?"

"She says she loves me and wants to be reunited."

34

Tears blurred Hannah's vision. How had her dream come to this?

"Before you were imprisoned, had she ever been disloyal or corrupt in any way?"

"No. Not that I know of."

"And her only reason for coming now is to reconcile?"

"That's what she says." John glanced at Hannah. "I don't know that I trust her completely, but she certainly couldn't be out for financial gain. The farm is doing well, but we're still just getting on our feet."

"What gives you cause to doubt her now?"

"Nothing, really. But I've thought for so long that she betrayed me, and it's hard to believe anything else."

The reverend nodded thoughtfully. "And why didn't she write all this time? That would seem the customary and easiest way of contacting you."

"According to Margaret, she did write but didn't get a reply." John shrugged. "I didn't receive any word from her."

The reverend cleared his throat. "I don't suppose that's so unusual, prisoners often don't get their mail."

A hush spread through the room like a dark vapor.

"Have you any reason to disbelieve her?"

"I don't know. At first I thought her a liar. Now I'm not sure what I believe. When I saw my cousin, he never mentioned Margaret."

"Yes, of course. But your cousin would have had no reason to tell the truth in this instance. That would have implicated him in another serious crime."

Hannah held her glass with both hands and could feel the coolness of the water. She sipped but could barely swallow past the tightness in her throat.

The reverend leaned forward in the chair. "What is it you'd like to do?"

"I was hoping to get a decree of divorce . . . after all, I'm married to Hannah."

With a nod, the reverend looked at Hannah. "And you, are you in agreement?"

Hannah didn't know how to answer. She wanted this all to go away; a divorce could make that happen. But what would God think of such an action? "I love John and can't imagine life without him. But I have a fear of the Lord. In my understanding of Scripture, God does not take marriage lightly . . . nor should we. I don't know what's right."

"What's right is for us to remain married." John stood. "Hannah and I *are* married. Tell her, Reverend." When the minister didn't answer immediately, John continued, sounding desperate. "You know we are. We stood at the front of your church and vowed to cherish and to love one another until our last breath. You presided over our vows."

"Yes, John, I remember. Calm yourself. Please, sit." The minister kept his tone soft and steady. "I'm certain that when you took your vows, you gave them in earnest, on that matter we have no differences." He straightened. "I've never married. Years ago I chose to devote my life to God only. But I can imagine the anguish you both must feel." He rested his arms on his thighs and leaned toward John and Hannah.

"As I understand God's Word, it seems clear to me that he sees divorce as a grave sin. And allows it only under the strictest of circumstances . . . none of which you've described to me. That is, as long as Margaret is speaking the truth."

Hannah steeled herself against what he would say next. She wished it were possible to close out his voice.

He continued, his expression mournful. "The church cannot sanction divorce under these circumstances."

Hannah thought her heart might stop. She'd known what to expect, but to actually hear the words from the reverend's mouth was more dreadful than she'd imagined. She looked at John—the truth penetrating her soul like a stake being driven into her heart.

"What are we to do?" John demanded. "I can't be married to two women at once."

His forehead furrowed, the reverend studied his hands, then looked at John and Hannah, his expression firm. "When you said your vows, John, you were already married, which means those vows are not binding."

4

With her hands clasped tightly in her lap, Hannah sat on the wagon seat and tried not to think. John kept his eyes forward, his jaw set. Neither spoke as the wagon rolled homeward, rattling over fissures and cavities in the dry road.

Raucous calls of rosellas and cockatoos fractured the stagnant, humid air. Hannah barely noticed the discordant songs. Her mind kept repeating the reverend's words, *Your vows are not binding . . . not binding.* She would lose John. The idea sucked the breath from her. How was it possible?

She could see Thomas's sweet, trusting face as they'd left the station that morning. She'd promised him all would be well.

Hannah stared through a haze of unshed tears. When Thomas had come to live with her and John months before, life had already betrayed him. How would he survive yet another injustice? The sting of tears burned and she swallowed past the tightness in her throat. *Lord, what will become of him?*

They turned onto the drive leading to the house. Hannah fidgeted, and John rested a steadying hand over hers. "It will be all right."

"No, it won't. It can't be. Nothing will ever be right again."

John stared at her and said nothing.

"You speak as if you believe, but your words are empty, John. There's nothing to be done."

"We'll find a way."

Hannah wished he'd stop pretending. It only made her feel worse. Her eyes moved to their home. She remembered the morning when their friends and neighbors had shown up with materials and with willing arms and backs to lend. In days the house had risen from the dirt. The ache in her chest became sharper. It had all been for naught.

Thomas stepped onto the porch, jumped to the ground, and ran toward them. How could she tell him that, once again, his life was about to be torn asunder? And that the home and family he'd grown to love would exist no more.

Blond curls fell onto a furrowed brow. "Mum? Dad?" He gazed up at them, using his hand to shield his eyes from the sun.

Jackson loped toward them, his tongue hanging and tail waving.

John climbed down, gave Jackson a pat, and then assisted Hannah. She couldn't look at Thomas. He'd know. John rested a hand on the boy's head for a moment, then without a word, he walked toward the barn, his steps heavy.

Thomas stared after him, then looked at Hannah. "Mum?"

She forced herself to look at him. What could she say?

"What's happened? Tell me." His voice was strident, demanding.

Hannah gently squeezed his shoulder. "We don't know for certain." She watched John slide open the barn door and disappear inside. Why had he left this to her?

"What did Reverend Taylor say? Ye told me things would be all right."

Hannah kept her eyes on the barn.

"What did he say?"

She glanced at Thomas and then stared at the house, needing to avoid his gaze. "He said . . ." She could barely believe the reverend's counsel; how could she repeat it? "He told us that your father and I aren't . . . married . . . that Margaret is his wife."

"No. That can't be. Ye had a wedding. Yer married . . . and . . . and . . ." He balled his hands into fists, and tears washed into his eyes. "It's not true. Reverend Taylor's wrong. Talk to someone else."

Jackson trotted up to Thomas and nuzzled his hand. Silent tears spilled onto the boy's cheeks, and his chin quivered. Ignoring the dog, he shoved the toe of his boot into the dry earth.

Feeling as if her heart would break, Hannah bent and pulled the boy close. If only there were a way to restore his life, his hope—her life and her hope.

He buried his face against her shoulder. "What will become of us?"

Hannah didn't have an answer, at least not one she could speak of. "We'll work out something. The Lord hasn't forgotten us." She caressed his hair. It felt hot and damp. Gently placing a finger under his chin, she lifted his face and smiled at him. "Now, will you be a good lad and fetch me some cheese from the springhouse?"

Thomas wiped at his tears, leaving dirty smudges on his cheeks. He stood for a long moment staring at her, then with his hands in his pockets, he scuffed his way down the track leading to the river.

Hannah watched, anguish permeating her soul. *God, this is not justice. He deserves better than this. He's already lost so much. How can you take another family from him?*

Fighting for control, she straightened and, with a glance at the barn, walked up the steps and into the house. It needed a good cleaning. Hard work had often set things to rights for Hannah. She counted on it now.

She swept the floors and then scrubbed them. But this time, no matter how hard she scoured the wooden boards, there was no relief, no balm to soothe her. She scrubbed harder, determined to lift away every fragment of grime and hurt.

Rather than there being a quieting in her spirit, she felt a boiling over of emotions and a rising wave of agony and fear, until it all became a flood of tears she couldn't stop. They washed from her eyes, ran down her cheeks, and dripped from her chin, mixing with the soapy water on the floor. Sobs like great heaves of agony rose from inside Hannah. Dropping back onto her heels, she let them come. "I've lost him . . . forever."

She sat there for a long while, and when there seemed to be no tears left, her mind turned to Lydia. She needed her friend. In the past Lydia had always been there, making the bleakest moment feel tolerable. *I've got to go.*

She pushed to her feet, leaving the bucket and scrub brush as they were. Her eyes stinging and still wet, she was barely able to see as she walked outside. Dabbing at the moisture with the edge of her apron, she strode to the barn. John and Thomas were cleaning stalls. Pitchforks in hand, they stared at her. "I'm going to see Lydia. I'll be home before dark."

His expression cheerless, John asked, "You all right, luv?"

Hannah stared at him. *Of course I'm not all right.*

When she didn't answer, John moved toward her.

"No. Stay where you are. It's not you I need now."

He stopped and stared at the barn floor. "It'd be best if I slept out here from now on." He shoved the tines of the pitchfork into the ground. "I'll move my things out before you get back."

Feeling as if she were suffocating beneath the weight of anguish, Hannah couldn't respond. John was right.

"So then, do you agree?"

"It's the only thing to do," Hannah managed to say before turning and walking back to the house.

Although thinking she'd cried herself empty, there were more tears to be shed, and Hannah wept nearly all the way into town. However, when she drove through Parramatta, she managed to put on a pleasant expression, even nodding and saying hello to those she passed. When she reached the apothecary and surgery, Hannah pulled the wagon to a stop. Drained and feeling weary, she tied off the reins and climbed down. Stepping into the apothecary, the pungent odor of herbs and medicines stung her nose. No one seemed to be about. *They're most likely in the surgery.*

"Lydia," she called softly. When there was no answer, she called again. "Hello. Is anyone here?"

A door leading to the back of the building opened. Lydia emerged, wearing a bloodied smock. "I thought it sounded like ye." Her smile faded almost instantly. "Hannah, what's happened? Ye look terrible."

"I need to talk to you."

"I want to help, luv, but I'm needed just now. Can ye wait while we finish with a surgery? We're nearly done."

"Yes. I'll wait."

"Good. I shan't be long. I promise."

As Lydia stepped back through the door, Hannah envisioned

42

a patient lying on the surgical table exposed and helpless, his body being invaded by the doctor's hands. She would gladly have changed places. The invasion of one's body was more tolerable than the invasion of one's soul.

Unable to abide waiting in the small shop with its noxious smells, Hannah stepped outside. It was hot, so she sat on the bench beside the office door. A merchant on the opposite side of the street cleaned the window of his establishment. He turned and, with a smile, nodded at her. She wondered if he knew. How many knew?

Hannah couldn't sit still, so she walked the quiet streets of Parramatta, wishing something would distract her from the anguish roiling inside. Two boys chased after a rolling hoop. They'd catch it and then send it off again, using a wooden rod to control its direction. An old man walked slowly toward her, following a dog that appeared to be even older than his owner. The man nodded as he hobbled past.

Hannah turned and watched him, wondering what it would be like to be old. Would the hardships of life feel less painful? Did the old look forward to death? If death were to come to her now, it would be a relief.

The voice of a little girl called, "Hannah."

She turned to see Lottie running toward her. She wore her usual bright smile, but when she approached, she sobered and threw her arms around Hannah's waist. "I heard. I'm so sorry, mum."

Hannah pulled her closer and stroked the little girl's red hair, fighting tears.

Lottie stepped back and looked up at Hannah, her brown eyes grief-stricken. "Is there nothing to be done?"

Hannah gazed back down the street. "I don't believe so."

"But God can do anything, mum. Ye remember how he took care of us on the ship and got me a mum and dad, then brought us back together again. He can do anything. I just know he'll fix this too."

Poor Lottie had lost her mother while onboard the prison ship. Alone, she found Hannah. They'd needed each other and for a while it had looked like they would be a family, just the two of them. A fresh wave of grief swept over Hannah. She'd lost so much. Forcing down the rush of emotions, she knelt in front of the little girl. "Of course God can do anything, but sometimes our desires aren't the same as his. And then we simply must trust him."

Lottie's eyes brimmed. "I know, mum, but I don't think this is what God wants. He loves ye too much for that."

Hannah pulled her close again, feeling renewed strength as the little girl's arms tightened about her neck. "We'll just have to give this mess to him and know that he'll see us through." She held the little girl away from her and smiled. "Perhaps we can have a picnic soon, just you and your mum and me and Thomas. Would you like that?"

"Oh yes, indeed."

Hannah straightened. "Where is your mum?"

"She's at the millinery shop, trying on hats. I truly don't like shopping for a new hat; it's not interesting in the least. Mum said I could take a stroll 'bout town. But I'd best get back. She'll be wondering after me."

"You wouldn't want to worry her." Hannah smiled. "I'll see you soon. Say hello to your mother for me, eh?"

"I will." Lottie gave her another quick hug. "I love ye." With that, she trotted off down the street.

Hannah turned back the way she'd come. *Perhaps they've finished.* She ambled toward the apothecary.

When she was barely more than a block from the mercantile, the door opened and Margaret stepped out. She didn't notice Hannah. A man followed closely behind her. He said something that must have been humorous, because Margaret laughed. She didn't seem a bit distraught. *Of course she wouldn't be. She's certain of who she is—John's wife.* The thought rolled over Hannah like a dark, burling cloud.

The man was stocky and rather good looking. He placed a hand on Margaret's back as they set off up the street. He acted rather too familiar. After all, Margaret was a married woman.

I wonder who he is. I don't recall John mentioning that she had brothers. Hannah watched them until they moved out of sight, then continued to the apothecary. *It was foolish of me to come. There's nothing Lydia can do. There's nothing anyone can do.*

No longer wearing the bloodied smock, Lydia stepped onto the street. She moved toward Hannah and, without saying a word, pulled her into strong arms. "I'm sorry to have kept ye waiting."

"Oh, I don't mind. I probably shouldn't have come."

Lydia held her back a bit. "Of course ye should have."

"Is your patient all right?"

"Yes. He'll be fine, but what a mess. He drove a spike into his leg."

"Oh, my word. Who was it?"

"The smithy. Good thing he has another man working with him. He'll be off his feet for a while."

"Sounds ghastly. I'm not sure how you do it."

"I rather like it. David says I have a natural way in surgery."

She moved toward the door. "Would ye like some tea? I've made some."

"Thank you. That would be nice."

Lydia walked indoors.

"I'll wait out here." Hannah glanced inside. "The odor is a bit much for me today."

"Really? I barely notice it anymore." She smiled and disappeared inside.

Hannah sat on the bench and watched the street. The heat felt oppressive, and she longed for a cooling breeze.

Lydia reappeared a few minutes later, carrying a tray. "This ought to do it, then." She sat on the bench and set the tray between her and Hannah. "I thought a lemon tart might be nice. It's my first try at them. I hope they're not too bitter."

"They look good." Hannah didn't feel much like eating, but to be polite she picked up a tart and took a bite. "It's quite good. You're not only talented in the surgery but the kitchen as well."

Lydia smiled. "If I recall, ye like just a bit of sugar with yer tea."

"Yes, if you have it."

"I do." Lydia lifted the lid off a small container, spooned out a chunk of sugar, and added it to Hannah's tea.

Taking the beverage, Hannah stirred until the sugar dissolved, then set the spoon on the saucer. She wasn't sure what to tell Lydia now that she had the opportunity. When she left the station, she'd only known she needed her friend.

"So, did ye speak to the reverend?"

"We did."

"And . . . ?"

Hannah sipped her tea. Even with sugar it tasted bitter. *Ap-*

46

propriate. Hannah worked to keep her emotions in check and her tone impersonal. "Reverend Taylor said John is married to Margaret and that our marriage is invalid."

Lydia sucked in a breath. "That can't be true."

"It is, I assure you." She set her cup on the saucer. "When John inquired about a divorce, the reverend asked if there was just cause. There isn't, and so there is no way John can divorce her."

"But what about all that happened in London?"

"It seems John misjudged Margaret. The trouble was all his cousin's doing."

Lydia broke off a piece of tart. "He'll still seek a divorce, won't he?"

"He's going to try . . . but Reverend Taylor is certain any request will be denied."

"She doesn't deserve him."

"She does. She's his wife, and she traveled all the way from England to find him." Hannah shook her head. "That's the awful thing . . . I can't hate her."

"Just the same, John ought to ask her if she'd agree to a divorce. He loves ye."

Hannah stared at the street with its dust and rising heat waves. The situation felt unreal. If only it were a terrible dream and she could wake up.

"It's not right. There must be a way for ye to repair this thing."

Hannah sighed. "I've prayed. I don't know what else to do."

"Ye could talk to Margaret. She might understand. John doesn't love her, he loves ye. Why would she want a man who is in love with someone else?"

47

"Even so, that doesn't change the fact that they're married."

"John must convince her to release him."

"He's an honorable man. He won't go against the law." Hannah wiped at a stray tear. "That's one of the things I love about him—his integrity."

"But what about ye, Hannah? John cares 'bout ye too."

"He'll abide by the law. And although he's going to pursue a divorce, the law is the law." Hannah brushed a crumb off her skirt. "I won't be a party to destroying a marriage. And I won't live with a man who is married to someone else."

Lydia's eyes teared. "Oh, but Hannah . . . what will ye do, then?"

She set the tart on the tray. "God hasn't forgotten me. He'll show me what I'm to do." Her words sounded convincing, and although Hannah was certain God was looking out for her, inside she quailed at what lay ahead.

The shopkeeper across the street draped a rug over a railing and then beat the dirt from it. "I'm like that rug. God uses what he must to accomplish his will within the hearts of his children—to clean them and shape them. I'm being changed by this." She choked back tears. "I trust that he'll do what's best."

"He doesn't intend to beat ye. Ye have no need of that." Lydia took Hannah's hand. "I want to help. Please tell me what I can do."

"There's nothing now. Except to pray." Hannah compressed her lips, barely able to continue. "John's moving out of the house."

"Where is he going? How can ye make a go of it out there all on yer own?"

"He's living in the barn and will continue to work the farm."

"And what of Margaret?"

Hannah couldn't let her mind travel to the next step. The image of John sharing a life with another woman was more than she could bear. But of course that's what was coming . . . and soon. The hurt inside twisted like a knife ripping through flesh.

"I don't know just how it will happen, but he and Margaret will have to learn to share a life again." Holding back tears, she said, "Please pray for us, for me and Thomas—he's hurting terribly. And for John. This is dreadful for him." She let her cup and saucer rest in her lap. "We must pray for Margaret as well. This can't be easy for her, either." Hannah remembered how happy Margaret had seemed. Was this truly a trying time for her?

Studying the golden liquid in her cup, she said softly, "I saw her. She's here in town."

"Really? Do ye suppose she's going to set up a home here, then?"

"I should think so. Her husband lives here."

The sun rested just above golden hills, turning the sky pink and then red. John laid his arms on the top rung of the stock pen and gazed at the bronzed fields. They looked like soft yellow velvet, but the beauty of it didn't touch him. Nothing could break through the brittle exterior of his wounded heart.

Quincy rode in and pulled his horse to a stop in front of John. He climbed out of the saddle. "We've a bit of trouble." He led the horse to the water trough.

"More trouble is something we don't need."

49

Quincy set his hat on a post and then scooped water from the trough and splashed his face, dumping some over his head. Pushing back wet hair, he turned to John. "Know ye don't need any more worries, but . . . I found the remains of a couple lambs. Looks like a dingo, maybe more than one." Quincy combed his wet hair with his fingers and resettled his hat on his head. Water ran in dirty rivulets down his face and neck.

"How far out?"

"Half a mile, I'd say. Down in the draw."

"We can't leave the beasts to dine on the flocks. We'll set up a watch tonight and hopefully put an end to them." John glanced at the house. "I'll tell Hannah." Wishing he could avoid her, he hesitated. Conversations between them had become awkward.

"Ye want me to tell her?" Quincy asked.

"No. I'll do it." John strode to the house and stepped onto the porch. Instead of walking in, he knocked and then waited.

Her cheeks flushed and dusted with flour, Hannah opened the door.

She looked almost childlike, and John was taken aback for a moment. He struggled to find something to say. "Bit hot to have the door closed."

"It's either the heat or the flies." She gazed at him. "What can I do for you?"

"Just thought you ought to know Quincy and I will be out tonight. Dingoes took a couple of lambs."

Thomas pushed past his mother and onto the porch. "Can I go?"

"I don't see—"

"Of course not," said Hannah. "You'll be out much too late, and we've studies to see to in the morning."

50

"I'll still do me schoolwork. I promise." He gazed up at Hannah, hope making his blue eyes brighter than usual. "Please, Mum."

"I don't like you out and about at night."

"I'll be with Dad and Quincy—no harm'll come to me. One day I'll need to know how to take care of trouble like this."

Hannah folded her arms over her chest.

"I'll see that he's safe," John said. "And I figure there's no reason he can't do his studies later in the day."

Hannah didn't answer immediately, but finally said, "All right, then. Go ahead."

Thomas grabbed a hat, said a quick thank you, and hurried out the door.

"I expect him home in one piece."

John tipped his hat. "No worries. He'll be fine." He wanted to kiss away the hurt he saw in Hannah's eyes. But that was no longer possible. Instead, he walked away. "I'll get him back as soon as I can," he called over his shoulder.

***

With Jackson tied in the barn and the sun disappearing in a fiery display on the horizon, John, Quincy, and Thomas rode through pale yellow grasses.

"Ye think it'll take long to find them dingoes?" Thomas asked, his voice lit with excitement.

"Can't know. Just have to wait and see." John looked at Quincy. "It'd be a good idea if we kept an eye out for the other mob we've got out on the flats."

"True."

"All right, then. I'll take the mob in the draw, and you go

along to the batch we've got grazing east of here." John glanced at a clear sky. "Moon ought to be of help."

Quincy reached into his pack. "Brought some bread and some tack. Figured we'd be hungry before the night's through." He handed a portion to John.

"If I hear you fire your musket, we'll come your way, and you do the same for us."

"Right." Quincy rode off, quickly blending into the darkening landscape.

John and Thomas moved on, riding toward the gully. Long before they could see the flock, the baaing of sheep settling in for the night carried over the hills toward them. When they reached the mob, John stopped, dismounted, and tied his horse to a tree. Thomas did the same.

"Ye think we'll have to wait long?" Thomas squatted in the dry grass beside his father.

"No telling." John stared into the darkness searching for dingoes but thinking of Hannah. She'd be lighting the lamps and settling into her chair for the evening, her sewing basket in her lap. He longed to be with her. *Lord, there must be a way . . . something we can do.*

"Ye figure I ought to have me own musket soon?" Thomas asked, breaking into John's thoughts.

"You've a way to go—your shoulders need to broaden some and you need more height. A musket's not meant for a boy." Thomas seemed especially young and vulnerable in the shimmer of moonlight. "You'll need a couple more years yet."

"I'm big for me age."

"True enough. And you're stout. But you're not yet ready . . . maybe soon."

Stillness settled over the land and the murmuring and rustling of the sheep quieted.

"Why'd ya move into the barn?" Thomas asked.

"Your mum and I decided it was best."

"Why? You're married. I thought married people lived in the same house."

"They do . . . usually, but things are different now." John searched his mind for a reasonable answer.

"It's Margaret, isn't it?" When John didn't reply, Thomas pushed. "Do ye love her instead of Mum?"

John took in a breath. "I don't love her, but . . ." How could he explain?

"I don't like her. I want her to go away."

"You don't even know her, Thomas. And I can't tell her to leave . . . she's my . . . wife."

Silence, like a long slow blink, hung between father and son. Finally Thomas asked, "How can she be yer wife? Yer married to Mum."

"Yes . . . but I was married to Margaret a long time ago . . . when I lived in London . . . before I knew your mum."

"That doesn't change nothin'. I don't want her 'ere."

John wished he could quiet the desperation he heard in Thomas's voice. He placed the butt of his musket on the ground. "It's not as easy as that. She wants to stay."

"I don't understand how ye can be married to Mum and to her."

"It's complicated."

"Complicated how?"

John pressed fingers to his forehead and closed his eyes before looking at Thomas. "According to the law, Margaret's my wife because I married her before I met your mum."

"Then why did ye marry Mum?"

"I thought Margaret was dead."

His voice quiet, Thomas asked, "Can't ye pretend she's dead?"

"Can't. Wouldn't be right." But John couldn't help wishing it was possible or that Margaret had never found him.

"What's right 'bout leaving Mum alone?" Thomas sounded angry.

"I'm not going to leave her. I'll take care of her . . . and you."

"How ye going to do that?"

John gazed at the dark sky with its countless stars. "I don't know . . . not just yet anyways."

5

Hannah added hot water to the half-filled laundry tub, set the bucket aside, and lifted a pair of Thomas's trousers from a basket of clothes. She dunked them into the water, then using a bar of soap, worked the cloth against a scrub board.

How in heaven's name does he manage to find so much dirt? She considered his active life and smiled. How could he not get dirty? There wasn't a tree he didn't think needed climbing, nor a lizard or rabbit that didn't need chasing. He spent a fair amount of time digging for worms to dangle from his fishing pole, plus he often worked alongside his father.

In spite of the tragedy that had befallen the family, Thomas had managed to push aside the turmoil and had attempted to go on as usual. Was it possible their lives could remain as they were? Hannah knew it wasn't. Change would come, but just how soon she couldn't guess. When it did arrive, what would happen to her and Thomas? Possibilities swirled through her mind, and sorrow brought a swell of despair.

This isn't fair, Lord. Not for me, nor for John, and especially not for Thomas. He's made a place for himself here, he has a family.

Since Margaret had invaded their world, Thomas had been quieter than usual. Everyone was. An oppressive cloud hung over the farm and over their lives. Hannah dropped the pants into a basket and picked up another pair.

She scrubbed harder as her mind worked on their troubles. Soon her arms and her back ached. She didn't mind—physical pain relieved some of her mental anguish. When she'd completed Thomas's clothes, she lifted the basket and, resting it against her hip, walked toward the river where she would rinse them.

Thomas leaped out from within a grove of eucalypts and galloped toward her. "I'll carry that for ye." He met her, smiling, and squinted against the morning sun. "And I'll rinse them too."

"Why thank you, Thomas. That will be a great help." Hannah handed him the basket. "I've still more wash to do." She tousled his hair. "You're growing into a fine young man."

His eyes registering gratification, he turned and headed toward the river.

With her heart twisting, Hannah watched him go.

Her mind flashed back to the day he'd first come to them, orphaned and hostile. He'd made it clear that John and Hannah would never be his parents. If not for John's unfailing commitment to the boy, he'd have gone his way.

Shame washed over Hannah as she remembered how harsh she'd been. John had believed in God's power and authority, while she'd feared failure. In spite of her faithlessness, they'd become a family, and now . . . now only God knew what would become of them. Even though John continued to state that all would be well, she understood that his bravado was a façade. There would be no easy answer to their dilemma. But was this too much even for God?

These days John kept mostly to himself and spent little time in the house. She missed his presence. She longed for the quiet evenings they'd once shared in front of the hearth reading or working—the dangers of the world shut outside their sturdy home. She slept poorly and sometimes in the night would lay her hand on the place where John used to lie beside her. She'd imagine he was still there, his muscles warm and supple beneath her fingers.

A sound came from the barn and Hannah turned to look. John stood outside the door, balancing a wagon wheel against the ground. His eyes rested on her. Feeling as if he could read her thoughts, her face burned.

He smiled but was unable to disguise his sadness before turning his attention to Thomas. His look of sorrow deepened as he watched the lad move toward the river. With only a glance toward Hannah, he rolled the wheel toward the tool shop.

Hannah returned to the washtub and lifted one of John's shirts, and with a glance toward the shop to make sure he wasn't watching, she pressed it to her nose. She loved the smell of him, even the odor of sweat and toil.

She plunked the garment into the water and scrubbed at it, holding back negative thoughts. No matter how painful the circumstances, things were what they were, and there was nothing she could do about any of it.

She worked the fabric against the washboard, adding more and more soap as if she could wash away the sorrow and resentment. Finally, with the shirt as clean as she could manage, she sat back on her heels, gripping the washboard. She wanted to cry, needed to, but she'd already shed more tears than she knew she possessed. Would the time come when they stopped, a time when the hurting ceased?

Although John usually took his meals alone, she'd invited him to join her and Thomas for dinner that night and had planned something special, one of his favorites—roasted beef with cabbage. She'd also prepared custard for dessert. Maybe a good meal would spark a little of the old happiness.

She knew such an idea was silliness. Food couldn't fix this problem. It would take a master—The Master. She closed her eyes for a moment. *Lord, if it is not your will for John and me to share our lives, then I ask that you remove my love for him. I shan't be able to bear it otherwise.*

"Smells delicious." John sat at the table, looking a bit awkward.

He belongs here, Hannah thought.

"Thank you for inviting me to sup with you."

"You're always welcome at our table. I never have liked your coming for a meal and then going off and eating it alone. There's no sense in that."

"S'pose you're right there."

"Mum made custard." Thomas glanced at a covered crock sitting on the cupboard.

Hannah settled in a chair across the table from John. She acted serene, but inside she wanted to scream. They were acting as if life were normal, that all was as it should be, but it wasn't and never would be. *He remains with me because he must. He'll never walk away from his duty to me. Only I can do that, by giving him permission to move on.* The idea of a permanent split cut into her heart.

John grasped Thomas's hand and then took Hannah's. "Shall

we thank the Lord for this meal and for the woman who cooked it?" He bowed his head.

Hannah heard none of his prayer, all she knew was the rough comfort of his hand. Oh, how she missed him. She could see a dark tunnel of loneliness—years to come without him. How could she endure it? *God, I don't have the strength.*

"Amen." John looked up and smiled at Hannah. Inside she ached. He belonged here, and yet he didn't.

She picked up John's plate and served him two slices of beef and a pile of cabbage. Thomas held up his plate. Hannah dished his meal, then took one slice of beef and a small amount of cabbage for herself. She sought a safe topic for discussion. "Have there been any more sheep killed?"

"No. I figure we took care of the problem." He winked at Thomas. "Did a fine job, eh?"

Thomas leaned his arms on the table, fork in one hand and knife in the other. "Yer a fine shot. Don't figure we'll have any more trouble."

"Hopefully not. We'll have to keep a watch, though." John took a bite of cabbage and chewed. "Delicious, Hannah." Picking up his knife, he sliced off a bite of beef. "Heard of a man not far from here who has a couple of dogs guarding his sheep."

"Dogs?" Hannah offered a bowl of rolls, and John took two.

"Called a Kuvasz."

"A what?" Thomas grabbed a roll and bit into it.

"Kuvasz. They're from Belgium. They're guard dogs, not herding dogs like Jackson. He's got three, two males and a female. The female's ready to whelp any day. I was thinking it would be a fine idea to get one of the pups. After what happened, it might be wise to have a dog guarding the flocks."

"How do you train it?" Hannah cut into her meat.

"You don't, really. If I'm understanding things correctly, they simply know what to do—guard. They live with the sheep, just like one of them."

"Can they stand up to a dingo?"

"They're brave and big—over a hundred pounds."

"Wow!" Thomas's eyes looked bright. "That's a lot bigger than Jackson."

"Are they tame? What if one were to attack Thomas? Or turn on the sheep?"

"No worries. They're loyal and easy tempered, but protective."

"And they're not sheepdogs?" Hannah dabbed at her mouth with her napkin, wondering just how she was going to bring up the subject that truly needed to be discussed.

"They can do a bit of herding when needed, but generally they're not inclined."

"That's why we have Jackson," Thomas said with a grin.

"Having a guard dog out among the sheep would give me peace of mind. I figured if one worked out that maybe we'd get another."

"I suppose it wouldn't hurt," Hannah said, considering how long it would take a puppy to grow up enough to be a guard dog and thinking it strange to be speaking as if their lives would continue on just as they had.

"When can we get one?" Thomas asked.

"The pups aren't born yet, but they're due any day."

Thomas grinned. "I'd like to have a dog like that. Could he be my friend too?"

"Of course, but you won't be spending hours with the sheep."

Thomas pushed his nearly empty plate away and rested his chin on his hands. "How 'bout we do some fishing after dinner?"

"There's milking that needs done, then we can go." John pushed away from the table and leaned back in his chair. "Me, Quincy, and Mr. Connor are planning a boar hunt, two weeks hence." He looked at Thomas with approval. "I'd say you're old enough to join us."

Hannah felt a rush of concern. "Boar hunting is for men. He's only eleven."

"One day he'll be a man and will need to know how to safely hunt the beasts."

"One day he will be a man, but right now he's a boy." Hannah set her fork on her plate. "I don't want him going."

"Oh, Mum, I'll be safe enough with Dad." Thomas looked to his father. "Won't I."

"I'll make sure he stays with me. He'll never be out of my sight. And of course he'll not handle a musket. I'd just like him to experience a hunt."

"It's dangerous." Hannah studied Thomas. He so wanted to be like his father. She looked at John and suddenly realized the reason for the invitation. He was afraid he'd not have another chance to take Thomas! The thought tore at her. Working to keep her voice steady, she said, "All right. But I expect you to bring home some meat then, eh?" She smiled at her son.

"Right we will!" Thomas nearly jumped out of his chair.

"Thomas, calm yourself."

The rest of the meal passed quietly, with Thomas and John discussing fishing and the upcoming hunt. When they finished eating, Hannah cleared away the dishes. "Would you like your custard now?"

"I'm afraid I've overeaten." John scooted his chair back. "How 'bout after the milking and after we've caught ourselves a fish or two, eh?" His hazel eyes rested on Hannah.

A shiver ran through her and she felt passion ignite between them. "I'll have your dessert ready for you when you return."

Hannah sat on the veranda and watched while John and Thomas swaggered up the path from the river, fishing poles resting on their shoulders. She smiled. The two of them were good together. She stood. "Did you catch anything?"

"Only a couple of small ones, barely a mouthful." Thomas shrugged. "We'll do better tomorrow."

John clapped him on the back. "That we will."

Thomas hurried up the porch steps. "Can we have our custard now?"

"Well, I don't know . . . you did come back empty-handed."

"Mum!"

Hannah laughed. "Come in. I've been waiting for you."

John and Thomas took their places at the table while Hannah dished out three servings of the sweet dessert. "Here you are, then." She set a bowl in front of each, accidentally brushing her hand against John's as he reached for his bowl. A jolt of energy passed between them. Hannah pulled back her hand as if she'd been burned. Still feeling his touch, she retrieved her helping of custard and then sat at the table.

As the three ate, the room turned quiet. While preparing the evening meal, Hannah had felt almost as if life had been set right. If only it were possible to go on as if nothing had happened. She found it curious that Margaret hadn't pushed herself on John. Or maybe she had and Hannah was unaware that she had.

Thomas quickly devoured his custard, scraped up the last remnants, and licked his spoon clean. He stifled a yawn.

"It's time for you to be in bed," Hannah said.

"Do I have to? I'm not tired, not a bit."

"You're not, eh?" John grinned. "Looks to me like you're ready to fall asleep right where you sit." He stood. "I'll take you up."

Hannah dropped a kiss on Thomas's cheek and watched while John and the boy climbed the steps to the loft. They were as close as any father and son. Her heart warmed at the thought.

She cleared the bowls from the table and washed them. With things tidy, she went to her chair in front of the hearth and picked up her sewing basket and a pair of socks that needed mending.

A few moments later, John descended the ladder. "He's nearly asleep already."

"He had a busy day." Hannah put her sewing aside, wishing she could invite John to stay.

He stood at the bottom of the steps. "I guess I ought to get off to bed myself. Tomorrow holds enough work for two days." He moved to the door and opened it.

Hannah crossed to John, intending to close the door behind him.

He turned to her. "Good meal, Hannah. Thank you." His voice sounded unsettled and his eyes searched hers.

Hannah recognized the look of desire and felt her own passion flare. She didn't want him to go. "I'll see you tomorrow, then."

"Right." John bent and dropped a kiss on her cheek. Without intent, his lips found hers, barely caressing at first, then pressing gently and demanding nothing. When Hannah responded, his lips became possessive.

Hannah's responsiveness and emotions merged with his. She couldn't think. All she knew is that she couldn't say good night to John at the door. She needed him.

He pushed the door closed, lifted her into his arms, and moved to the bedroom. Hannah clung to him, beyond thought.

He set her gently on the bed and dropped down beside her. "I love you," he whispered, covering her mouth with his.

Hannah lay in the crook of John's arm, feeling as if she were wrapped within a haven of love. He kissed her forehead and caressed her hair. "I love you. I can't stop."

She snuggled closer. "I love you too."

Quietness covered them in a mantle of peace. Minutes passed, and Hannah slowly emerged from the warm cocoon. She didn't want to surface, to face the real world, and tried to remain, but something dragged her toward the truth. *What have I done? I've lain with a man who isn't my husband.*

"I want to move back in," John said. "We belong together."

Reality hit Hannah like a fist. She pushed herself upright, pulling the sheet about her. "No!" Clinging to the sheet, she left the bed. "We can't." She stepped back. "What have we done?" She picked up her clothing and started to dress.

"We've done nothing wrong. You're my wife. I'm your husband."

"No . . . John, you're not." The truth engulfed Hannah. "I'm not . . . I'm not your wife. Margaret is." She pressed a hand to her mouth. "I have to leave. I can't stay here. We can't live this close anymore."

"Hannah." John pulled on his trousers and moved toward her. "I want us to be together. We belong together."

Buttoning the top of her dress, she moved toward the front door. "I have to go."

He gaped at her. "In the middle of the night?"

"We knew this time was coming. I should have left the day we talked to Reverend Taylor. This is my fault."

"Nothing is your fault. We've done no wrong here."

"That's not true and you know it." Hannah hurried to the door and opened it.

"Hannah. No. If anyone leaves it will be me. I built this house for you."

"John, this is your farm. Not mine."

He stared at her, his eyes filled with disbelief. "No. I'll go. I can stay with David and Lydia. They've room."

"And what will become of this place?"

"I'll work here every day and then stay with David and Lydia at night."

Hannah fumbled through her mind. Could it work?

He moved toward her. "Please, Hannah, let's not do this."

Her hands clutching the collar of her dress, Hannah said, "John, you have a wife . . . and it's not me. It's Margaret." She opened the door wider. "Leave now."

Thomas appeared on the top steps. "What's wrong?" His eyes moved from his mother to his father.

"Nothing, Son. Go back to bed." John moved to Hannah. "Can't we talk about this more civilly in the light of day?"

Hannah closed her eyes. "I can't have you here. Either you go or I do."

John dropped his arms to his sides. "All right."

Thomas climbed down the steps and followed his father onto the porch. "Where are you going?"

"To town."

"No! You can't! You said we were going fishing tomorrow."

John rested a hand on Thomas's shoulder. "We can still fish."

"What about the boar hunt?"

"We'll go." John knelt in front of his son. "I'm still your father." He glanced at Hannah. "I'll never stop being your father . . . no matter what." He pulled the boy into his arms and held him tightly. Then, smoothing the crying lad's hair, he stood.

Hannah could barely look at him, but she needed to be strong, and so she met his steady gaze. Inwardly she winced at the hurt and loss she saw in his eyes, but she managed to hold his stare without flinching.

"I'll be at David and Lydia's." He moved down the steps and walked toward the barn.

6

Hannah smoothed the quilt and fluffed the pillows. She stared at the bed, feeling empty inside. When she'd married John, she'd never imagined he'd be torn from her, not like this.

Death would be better. Hannah quickly stifled the thought, ashamed she'd entertained it for even a moment. She wanted John to live, in fact she wanted him to have a joyous life, but the idea of his being with someone else was almost more than she could bear.

She picked up his pillow and squeezed it against her chest; she could still smell his scent. *Oh, Lord, how will I survive without him?*

He'd been staying with David and Lydia, and each day he made the trip from town to the station. Hannah found herself waiting for his arrival. Even though they spoke rarely and their occasional conversations were stilted, his presence on the station made her feel less alone. Margaret was never mentioned, and Hannah didn't know if John was spending time with her or not. Lydia hadn't said a thing about his first wife, and Hannah couldn't bring herself to ask.

Lord, give me the strength to release him . . . if that be your will. He deserves happiness. Bless him in all ways, and if Margaret is to be part of his life, then I pray they will find contentment together.

Hannah fumbled through the prayer and wiped away tears. Above all, she desired God's will, no matter how great the pain. Her mind wandered to the description of Jesus' prayer in the Garden of Gethsemane. In anguish he'd laid down his life, relinquishing his will to God. He was her example.

But I'm not Christ. I'm not strong. Hannah returned the pillow to its place, wishing her mum were still alive. She needed her now.

Her mind played over tender memories and dreams she and John had once shared. Now she needed dreams of her own, but when she tried to envision life without John, it was as if she'd gone blind—she could see nothing, only an endless black void.

The ache inside resonated, building until it felt as if it would engulf her. What would become of her and Thomas?

She tried to turn her thoughts away from despair and to think only on what the Lord had done for her. Her mind carried her to the story of Ruth and Naomi. Naomi had lost her husband and her two sons. She'd become bitter, and yet she saw God as almighty and her reverence for him never faded. *If only I could have such faith.*

Hannah looked about the room, and her gaze came to rest on the armoire. John's things were gone. Her gaze moved to the bureau. His drawers were empty. It wasn't right that he'd gone and she'd stayed. The farm belonged to him.

Hannah knew she would leave . . . eventually, but to where? The only place she knew was the Athertons'. Certainly they'd take her in, but she hated to place a burden on them. They'd already done so much for her. *Perhaps they need a housemaid.*

68

"Mum! Mum!" Thomas shouted from outside. His footsteps thumped up the front stairs and across the porch; the door swung open. "The pigs are out! They're in the potatoes!"

Hannah rushed to the door and looked out at the garden patch. The sow and her half-grown piglets were knee-deep in the soil, tearing into the winter crop. "Dear Lord!" She grabbed the broom off the porch and hurried down the steps. "Get a bucket of grain! Quickly now!"

While Thomas sprinted toward the barn, she ran to the garden, hollering and swinging the broom. The piglets squealed and darted away from her, but soon found new ground for foraging. A young boar seemed the most intent on getting his share. The sow lifted her head and stared at Hannah, a potato vine hanging from her mouth. She didn't seem to be the least disturbed and returned to her feast.

Hannah rammed the broom into the ground. What was she to do? The sow burrowed her nose into the soil and pulled up a cluster of young potatoes. "Let go of that!" Hannah shouted, trudging through the patch. She waved the broom at the huge pig, who simply snorted and moved a few steps away while munching on her prize. The piglets, their tails wagging, followed her. The boar kept munching and stared at Hannah. He'd been known to have a foul temper, and Hannah hated the thought of going up against him, young as he was.

Carrying a bucket, Thomas raced toward his mum. "Here's the grain." He handed her the pail.

"Find a stick while I see if I can tempt them." She moved toward the closest piglet, shaking the container and talking sweetly. "Come on now. Wouldn't you like some grain? It's much better than potatoes." The piglet pranced away. Hannah scooped out a handful and held it toward the animal. "Give it a try, eh." He paid no mind and instead snuffled the ground searching for more tender vines and young potatoes.

Hannah straightened, discouraged. How was she going to get the beasts back into the pen? She studied the sow. If she could get her interested in the grain, the rest would follow. "Eh, mama, I've got a tasty tidbit for you." She moved slowly, holding out a handful. "Just have a taste, now. I know you like it."

Thomas moved to the other side of the sow, holding his stick toward the bulky animal.

"Wait there." Hannah gingerly stepped closer to the pig, hand extended. Her dirty snout wriggling back and forth, she sniffed the air. She peered at Hannah through small eyes, then took a step toward her.

"That's right. Come on." Hannah moved backward. The sow followed, but then an uprooted batch of potatoes distracted her. She pulled them into her mouth and happily chomped on them.

If Hannah didn't do something quickly, her entire winter crop was in jeopardy. "Oh please, do come," she said, shaking the bucket. The sow grunted but didn't look up from her garden-fresh meal.

Hannah wanted to bash her with the broom, but instead she straightened and looked about, hoping to find someone who might be of help. John hadn't shown up yet, and Quincy had ridden out early. She wanted to sit down right where she was and cry. Why did life have to be so difficult? She gazed up at a blue sky splotched with dollops of white. "Lord, I need help," she prayed, and then decided a different tactic was needed.

"Thomas, did you notice if the gate was open to the pen?"

"No."

"Well, go and have a look. If it's not, make sure to open it.

70

And check the rest of the pen to make sure there's no way for these beasts to escape once we get them inside. When you come back, bring a sturdier branch. We'll have to force them."

"The boar's already bad tempered," Thomas said.

"I know. He may think he's a threat, but he's only half grown and no match for the two of us." She managed to send Thomas a smile, then turned back and glared at the animals who were destroying her garden. "Hurry, Thomas. Go." The lad raced to the pigpen while Hannah stood guard over a portion of the garden that hadn't yet been touched.

After managing makeshift repairs on the pen and making a quick search for a sturdier branch, Thomas hurried back with a stick in each hand. "The gate was closed, but part of the fence had been knocked down. I blocked it off, though, good enough to hold em 'til Dad can fix it."

"Good." Hannah studied the animals. They stood in a close bunch. "I'm afraid we'll have to whack them solidly to make them move. You stand in the back, and I'll take care of the sow. If I can get her moving, her piglets will follow."

Thomas immediately moved toward the swine. "Get out of 'ere. Now, I say." His voice was as big as he could make it. He struck one piglet soundly on the hindquarters. With a squeal, it trotted away.

Hannah moved up behind the sow and tapped her, but the animal barely looked up. "All right, then." She hauled back on the broom and swung it down hard across the animal's rump. With a squall, the sow lumbered off. Now all the pigs were agitated and moving.

"Get around on the other side of them. Don't let them get by you."

Thomas quickly moved to the outer edge of the mob, holding both branches out away from his body to steer them. The young boar charged toward him.

"Thomas, watch out for him."

He smacked the small pig across its side. Instead of producing obedience from the animal, it turned on Thomas. With a fierce grunt, he rushed him and bit into his calf.

Thomas didn't call out or even act as if he'd been hurt. Instead, he yelled, "Get on with ye! Go on!" He hit the animal across the back and then the side of its face, forcing him to turn away. The boar trotted toward its siblings.

"Are you all right?"

"I'm fine. It was just a nip." He smiled as he followed the sow and her litter away from the garden.

Once they were clear of the potato patch, the pigs seemed more than happy to trot back to their pen. Hannah and Thomas herded them through the opening and pushed the gate closed. Leaning on it, Hannah glared at the animals. "We should butcher the lot of you." As if understanding her intent, the young boar looked at her and squealed his displeasure. Hannah moved to the broken section of fencing and checked Thomas's temporary repair, adding one extra board for bracing. "I suppose that will do for now."

With a shake of her head, she started back toward the house, Thomas beside her. Stopping at the garden plot, they studied the carnage. A good deal of the crop had been lost.

"They did a job on it, eh," Thomas said.

"That they did. But we'll manage." Hannah rested a hand on his shoulder. "You did fine."

He swiped blond hair off his forehead and grinned. "It was a bit of excitement, wasn't it?"

"It was, indeed." She moved toward the house. "We'd best have a look at your leg."

When they reached the porch, Hannah dipped a cup of water from a barrel and sat beside Thomas on the top step. They both drank from the cup, and then she went back and refilled it, handing it to Thomas before going inside for soap, a washcloth, and bandages.

When she returned, she sat beside him. "Let me see how bad it is."

"Ah, it's all right."

"That may be, but we don't need it getting festered. Give me your leg."

Thomas pulled up his torn trouser and peered at the bleeding wound, then rested the leg on Hannah's lap.

She examined the gash. "Does it hurt?"

"Not much."

"It's not too bad. If that little rogue had been much bigger, he could have given you a serious bite." After dipping the cloth into the water, she soaped it and gently cleaned the wound. "I'll have to get this dirt off. It might hurt a bit."

"It won't hurt me." Thomas winced as Hannah probed. "I say he needs to be the first one butchered."

"And he shall be. We've no need of another boar." She looked at Thomas. "I'm sorry about this. It shouldn't have happened."

"It's all right. Just wish Dad were 'ere." Silence settled between the two. "Don't ye think he ought to move back?"

Heaviness pressed down on Hannah. Thomas was too young to understand. "It's not a good idea right now." Her voice trembled.

Thomas rested a hand on his mother's arm. "It'll be all right, Mum. Dad'll make it right."

If only he could. Hannah wound a bandage around the gash.

"I hate Margaret." Thomas scowled and crossed his arms over his chest.

"You don't even know her."

"Don't have to. She's not decent. Can't be. If she were, she wouldn't do this to us."

Hannah had wondered about that, but she dare not voice her qualms. It would only make Thomas's doubts stronger. "I understand why you're angry, but what if she sees us as the ones who've hurt her?" Hannah tied off the bandage. "After all, she was married to your father before he met me."

"But that was when he lived in London . . . and he didn't know ye then. If he would 'ave, he would've married ye instead of her."

Hannah smoothed the bandage. "Better?"

Thomas nodded and stood. "I'll talk to him, make him understand." He threw an arm over Hannah's shoulders. "He'll come back. I know he will. He loves us."

"Of course he does, very much. But this isn't about how much your father loves us."

Hannah wasn't ready to talk with Thomas about any of this, especially not about their eventual move. But she couldn't put it off any longer. "Thomas, your father can't stay here while I'm living in the house. It's not respectable."

"But he's yer husband."

"You've got to get that idea out of your head. We're not married." The statement felt like a punch to her stomach. *We're not married. We never were.*

"It'll work out . . . somehow," Thomas insisted.

"Things will work out, but not likely the way we want them to."

"Why not? Can't God make it happen?"

"God's ways are not always our ways, Son." She took his hand. "We'll have to move on . . ."

"Ye mean leave 'ere?"

"Yes. The farm belongs to your father."

Shock registered on Thomas's face. "Where would we go?"

"I don't know for certain. Maybe the Athertons' to begin with. They might have a position for me there."

"But what 'bout Dad? We can't leave him."

The idea of Thomas staying behind hurt deeply, as if a barb were piercing Hannah's heart. *I must let him choose.* "Of course you can stay here with your father if you like. You don't have to come with me."

"No. It's not right." He moved down the first step. "I won't leave and neither will ye." He stomped down the stairway. "The two of ye'll be together again. I know it."

Hannah had no energy left to convince him of the truth, so she let his statement stand. The day would come when she could no longer avoid the inevitable, but not today.

Dust kicked into the air, and Hannah saw a rider coming. It was John. He cantered up the drive, stopping in front of the house. "You look done in. Is everything all right?"

"Ye should 'ave been 'ere," Thomas said, accusation in his voice.

"Why? What's happened?" He dismounted, keeping hold of the reins.

"The pigs . . . they broke out of the pen." Hannah moved the soap into her other hand. "Thomas and I managed to get them back inside."

John half grinned. "Don't suppose that was much fun."

"No, indeed, it wasn't." Hannah stood, her irritation growing. "And while they were out having a bit of fun, they managed to devour a good deal of my potatoes. And the boar bit Thomas."

Concern replaced John's smile. "Are you all right, Son?"

"Fine." Thomas shoved his hands into his pockets and stamped the foot of his uninjured leg down on the porch step. "He didn't hurt me much." Defiantly, he stared at his father. "We're not leaving, are we?"

"Leaving? How do you mean?"

"Mum said we'll have to move. That this place is yers."

John's expression turned glum. "This is your home just as much as mine. Nothing can change that." He moved to Thomas and laid an arm over the lad's shoulders. "You never have to leave."

Furious, Hannah walked into the house. She knew differently. John was simply putting off the inevitable and misleading the boy. They would have to go.

John followed her indoors. "Hannah, I'll never make you leave. I promise."

"Don't make promises you can't keep."

"I mean it, Hannah. This will always be your home."

And what of your wife? What happens when she wants to move in? Hannah didn't have the energy to thrash any of it out. "Will you be here for dinner?"

"No. That's why I was late. Seems Murphy Connor's set to go boar hunting today. I came to get Thomas and Quincy."

"Oh. I haven't prepared anything for you."

"No need. Murphy's wife has it all taken care of."

Hannah felt the wrenching pain of the loss. She was no longer in possession of her wifely responsibilities, no longer John's partner.

76

"I'll take care of that pen and then we'll be off. We should be back day after tomorrow, unless we do well and get our boars right off."

"I'll get Thomas's things." She tried to keep her voice light.

John moved toward the door. "I'll tell him."

"Plan on dinner when you get back. I'll have something hot for you and Thomas when you return. You'll be hungry for sure."

John glanced at Hannah and rubbed his day's growth of beard. "That would be fine . . . except . . . I'll have to get back into town . . ." He seemed at a loss for words.

"Do you have something else planned?"

"I just promised to have dinner . . . with a friend."

Hannah knew. "You mean with Margaret."

John looked at the toes of his boots and then at Hannah. "I'll see you in two days. We'll be back in the afternoon, most likely." He walked out and down the steps.

Hannah's heart felt as if it had been crushed beneath her ribs, and she wondered if she'd ever breathe again.

7

Oblivious to the chill air and misting rain, John pulled his horse to a stop in front of Margaret's cabin. He leaned forward slightly in the saddle and studied the small cottage. A planter box crowded with colorful flowers that spilled over the rim rested beneath the front window. And on either side there were two wooden rockers resting on a cleanly swept porch. A disquieting image of him and Margaret sitting there together nudged him. It was Hannah he longed to spend tranquil moments with.

He dismounted and tied his horse to a post at the front of the porch. The smell of pork wafted from indoors as he moved toward the front steps. It reminded him of earlier days with Margaret. Pork was a favored dish, and the cook had prepared it often.

Unexpectedly the door opened. Margaret crossed her arms, a smile playing at her lips, and leaned against the doorjamb. Her dark eyes were alight with mischief. She wore a simple, pale green frock cut low across the bodice. It fit snugly at the waist before falling freely to the floor. John was careful to keep his eyes on her face.

"You've been standing out here for some time." She raised an eyebrow. "Perhaps you ought to come in. It would be more seemly if we sat at the table for our meal."

John swiped his hat off his head, embarrassed at being caught hanging back. "Of course. Just taking a moment for reflection."

Margaret's expression turned serious. "I don't mean to tease. I know this isn't easy . . . for either of us. I was just thinking that a bit of levity might ease the tension." She stepped back and opened the door wider. "Please, come in."

With his hat tucked beneath his arm, John walked up the steps and moved indoors. His eyes swept over the tidy, well-furnished room. "It would seem you've done well in my absence."

"I've managed. But not without cost." Sadness touched her eyes. "Last year my parents died, within days of each other."

"I'm sorry to hear that. They were fine people."

"Thank you. They were." She blinked back what looked to be tears. "It was the fever. But in God's mercy they went quickly."

John nodded, rooted in place.

Margaret closed the door behind him. "Your hat?"

He handed it to her, and she set it on a shelf beside the door.

"They were gone so quickly, we were all taken by surprise." Margaret helped him remove his coat.

She felt too close, the contact too familiar. John tried to keep from touching her.

Margaret hung his coat on a rack. "My brothers were kindly disposed toward me and included me in the family inheritance. It's enough to see me by." She moved to a small kitchen. "Dinner will be a few minutes longer. Might I get you a beverage?"

79

"Water will suit me fine." Unable to recall a time when he'd felt more awkward, John moved to a mahogany side chair and sat. His eyes went to a large Bible lying on an occasional table.

Margaret moved to it and rested a hand on the well-worn leather cover. "This was my mother's. I find comfort in it."

John didn't recall Margaret being especially religious, but he said, "Of course."

"I have wine if you'd prefer that. I understand it was grown locally."

"No. Water's fine. Thank you." John needed a clear head.

Margaret filled a glass with water. "It's fresh. I had the barrel filled this morning." She walked to John, her movements graceful and unhurried. She handed him the glass.

"Thank you." He took a long drink, wetting his dry mouth.

Margaret crossed to the hearth and knelt, lifting the lid of a pan. "Good. The rolls are nearly ready." She glanced over her shoulder at John.

She'd worn her auburn hair partially down, and hints of red gleamed in the lantern light. John tried not to notice.

"Could you help me with this pan? It's a bit heavy. The roast is overly large. I must say I was a bit surprised by the butcher's generosity."

"Most chaps in this town have healthy appetites. They work hard. I figure the wives . . ." The word "wife" rang through John's mind. Margaret was his wife. "The wives feed them well." He had to reach around Margaret to lift the pot. He could smell the subtle scent of roses and remembered it had been one of her favorite perfume fragrances. Disconcerted, he quickly straightened and stepped away. "Where would you like it?"

"On the table, please." She lifted a baking kettle out of the hearth and carried it to the table. "Our first meal together since . . . well, since you were arrested." She managed a tremulous smile. "It's an answer to prayer. I've made some of your favorites—pork, turnips, and carrots, plus fresh rolls. And I baked an apple cake for dessert."

Against his will, John's mind turned to Hannah. Her apple cake was the best he'd tasted. He doubted Margaret's would compare.

She perched on a settee.

John threw one leg over the other and tried to appear composed. He couldn't think of anything to talk about.

"I'm so pleased you accepted my invitation. I was afraid you might not."

What should he say? He couldn't tell her he was here out of duty. "I suppose it's inevitable . . . our spending time together."

She clasped her hands in her lap, appearing nearly as nervous as he. "I do hope you feel more than a sense of inevitability. We had a life together once. And it makes sense that we do again, don't you agree?" When John didn't answer right away, she added, "Surely you haven't forgotten how it was with us."

"No. I've not forgotten." John's mind carried him back to their early years—theirs had been a passionate marriage—in the beginning. "I'm just not accustomed to anyone but . . . Hannah."

"Of course." Margaret glanced at her hands. "She does understand, doesn't she?"

"Understand?"

"That you and I are married and that she is . . ." Margaret

hesitated, seeming to search for the right word. "Well, that you and she are no longer together."

"She knows," John said flatly, thinking how unfair life could be. "It will take time . . . for us all."

"Of course." She moved to the hearth and lifted the lid of the baking pan that held the rolls. "Ah, finally." Using a towel, she grasped the handle and carried it to the table. Standing beside her chair, she said, "Dinner is ready."

John moved to Margaret and pulled her chair out, then helped her scoot closer to the table.

"Thank you," she said, touching his hand.

Feeling as if he'd been burned, John forced himself not to jerk his hand away and then took his place. It felt peculiar to sit across the dinner table from Margaret as if it were a natural thing to do.

She sliced into the pork. As the juices spilled into the pan, the aroma of roasting meat intensified. She placed three wedges on his plate, added turnips, carrots, and two rolls, then set the meal in front of John. Handing him a crock with butter in it, she said, "It's fresh. A woman at the boardinghouse was kind enough to give me some. Perhaps I'll soon have a cow of my own for milk and butter." Her tone hinted at some unspoken desire.

John took a scoop and spread it over a roll. "It looks delicious. Thank you for going to the trouble."

"It's no trouble, not for you."

"I rarely recall you cooking when we lived in London."

"I learned . . . out of necessity. But I rather like it." She served herself.

John waited. "It's a grand meal."

"We've yet to taste it and so we can only guess as to its grandness." Margaret took two rolls and set them on her plate. "I still have a weakness for breads," she said apologetically. "I shan't be able to tie my stays if I continue to overindulge."

John thought the subject of her underclothes a bit too intimate, and yet what wife felt constrained to keep such topics from her husband?

She placed her napkin on her lap and looked at John. "Would you be so kind as to say a blessing over the food?"

John felt momentary confusion. Had she changed so much? None of this felt right. Still, he bowed his head. *Lord, what should I pray?* Silence hovered over the room.

"Heavenly Father, thy Word says life will be filled with the unexpected. Margaret and I are facing such a time, but I trust thee and know thy will shall be revealed in due time." Hannah's face flashed through his mind. Oh, how he missed her. "I ask thy blessing on this food and upon Margaret for her efforts in preparing this fine meal . . . Amen."

He looked up to see her staring at him, humor in her eyes. "Do you find our circumstances amusing?" he asked.

"Not at all."

"By the look on your face, it would seem you do."

"I can't know what look you see, but I assure you that all I feel at this moment is gratitude for being blessed with a husband as honorable as you."

"Oh." John knew he ought to say something more but couldn't find an appropriate response, so instead he picked up his fork and knife and cut off a bite of roast. He chewed. The meat was tender and savory. "It would seem you've become a first-rate cook. This is quite good."

"I'm glad it pleases you. I must confess to being nervous. I wanted our first meal to be special, and you've always had refined tastes."

John set his fork and knife on the plate. "A taste that is refined no longer. I spent too many months in the belly of a ship and in prison, hoping for just enough to stave off hunger."

"I can't imagine how horrible it was for you. It must have been dreadful."

"It was." John's mind carried him back to the putrid hold with its nightmares. The fear, the smells, and the hopelessness swept over him. And then he remembered Hannah and how she had brightened his days—just thinking about her had made life bearable. His gaze settled on Margaret. All those months, he'd hated her; she'd tormented his thoughts.

Picking up his knife and fork, John cut into a turnip and acted as if all was well, when in fact, he felt that he belonged at the farm with Hannah and Thomas. Sitting here at Margaret's table made him feel unfaithful to Hannah.

He stabbed the turnip with the fork. "Margaret, I don't know what you are hoping for or what you expect—"

"I'm expecting to share a pleasant meal with my husband." Her gaze caressed his face. She reached across the table and took his hand. "I know this can't be easy for you . . . or for Hannah. But it's time we set things right. It will be difficult, especially after what Henry did, but I believe we can begin again."

John stared at her hand. How should he respond? He didn't want to repair the marriage. He wanted Hannah. "I'm not sure what we ought to be doing," he finally said, letting out a long sigh.

Margaret smiled, her eyes alight with devilishness. "I remember a time when you knew exactly what to do." She pressed her lips to the palm of his hand.

John felt old passions flair. He had loved her, once. Was it possible to reclaim that love? Hannah's gentle smile and warm brown eyes cut through the thought. He took back his hand. "We can't create love."

"Of course not, but it was ours once."

"That was a long time ago."

Margaret's eyes welled up. "All the more reason to give ourselves time to rediscover it." She pushed her plate aside and rested her arms on the table. "I'd hoped being here together would spark some of the old feelings." Her expression hardened. "It seems you've set me aside."

"Margaret . . ." John stopped to collect his thoughts. He didn't want to misspeak. "I remember when we first met—our love, indeed, was fervent. But in time, that changed. I don't recall you having any passionate loyalty or love for me—I remember you going into the city too often, where you spent time with your friends. And I remember your extravagant expenditures in the London shops. I'm not familiar with this new domesticity. And . . . if I'm to be honest . . . it's a change I don't completely trust." He met her gaze, hoping to see what really lay behind Margaret's dark eyes. "Have you someone else? And if so, would you be agreeable to . . . divorce? That way you'd be free to marry anyone of your choice. You're a handsome woman. I'm sure there is a goodly number of gents hoping for your attention."

"Divorce?" She pressed a hand to her throat. "How can you ask that, after what I've told you? I don't want anyone else—only you. There never has been anyone but you." Tears spilled onto her cheeks. "How can you hand me off so easily?" She stood. "This is impossible."

"Margaret, please." John pushed to his feet. "I don't want to hurt you, but these matters must be discussed. The idea of divorce is no reflection upon you. I just needed to make sure you weren't hoping for your freedom."

"If that's what you wish for us, then so be it." She sniffled and tried to quiet a quivering chin. "However, I doubt the governor would grant a divorce in any case."

Flustered, John didn't know what to say. "I'm sorry. It's not my intention to cause you grief." He took a handkerchief from his pocket and offered it to her.

Taking the handkerchief, Margaret patted her eyes and face. "When I thought I'd lost you, all I could think about was how to find you again. I wanted to be with you."

"As you've seen, life in Parramatta is nothing like London. There are no fine shops or restaurants, no debutante balls or visiting royalty."

"I don't want any of those things. I just want you. Why can't you believe me?"

"It's not easily done. I believed something else for so long."

"That's not my fault." She blew softly into the handkerchief. "We must find a way."

John nodded. He didn't want to hurt her more. And if what she said was true, he would do the right thing.

Margaret glanced at his plate. "Have you finished?"

John looked at his partially eaten meal. He wasn't hungry but didn't want to risk offending Margaret further. "This is too delicious to let even one bite go to waste." He returned to his place at the table.

Margaret managed a smile and sat back down.

John cut off a bite of carrot and put it in his mouth. "This is quite good."

"Thank you. I believe it's the art of patience that makes the difference." She took a sip of wine. "You sure you wouldn't like a bit of wine? It's not the finest, but it is tasty."

"I suppose a bit wouldn't hurt."

Margaret fetched another glass, filled it, and handed it to him. She set the bottle on the table. "I understand you have a farm not far from here."

"Yes. It's small but growing."

She smiled. "I can barely imagine you a farmer."

"It's not farming exactly, although we do have a garden and other stock. Raising sheep is something altogether different from farming."

Margaret sipped her wine. The red of it nearly matched the color of her lips, reminding John of the passionate moments they'd once shared.

"What plans do you have for the estate?"

"It's not an estate by any measure, but I'll continue to increase the flock, which will mean more wool to sell. I've also been making tools for chaps 'round about, but I'll do less of that. I suppose I'll keep after it for a while, though."

⬛

After they'd finished their meal, Margaret cleared away the dishes. "Would you like your cake now?"

John rested a hand on his abdomen. "I'm so full I can barely eat another bite, but how can I refuse? It's one of my favorites."

She sliced two pieces of the heavy dessert and placed them in bowls. Setting one in front of John and another in her place at the table, she crossed to a cabinet and took out a pitcher. "Would you like cream?"

"That's the way I like it best."

"I remember." Margaret lifted one eyebrow as if sharing a secret. "There are many things I remember about you."

Her statement was innocent enough, but it implied intimacy. John was unnerved and wished she would leave the past alone, at least for now.

Margaret poured cream over both servings and then sat.

John cut into the cake with his spoon and took a bite. The flavor of apples and cinnamon was tasty, but he felt satisfaction that it wasn't as good as Hannah's. Questions whirled through his mind and were joined by a jumble of mixed emotions. Although he remembered how things had once been between himself and Margaret, he hadn't forgotten how ugly it could be as well. And he knew he'd never escape memories of Hannah.

"I'm still puzzled at why you've come to New South Wales at this late date, especially when you believed me to be in prison."

"I explained that to you. I didn't have the funds to come sooner, not until my parents' death. And it didn't matter to me if you were in gaol."

"And what would you have done if I was still a prisoner? I was given a life sentence."

"Just being close to you would be enough. And I knew that prisoners are sometimes given pardons."

John nodded slightly. "Try to understand, Margaret, I'm not even certain of who you are." She started to speak, but John held up a hand. "Hear me out."

Margaret waited.

"For so long I thought you'd betrayed me, you and Henry. I hated you. And I do have a wife, legal or not, whom I love." He could see the statement wounded her, but he continued, "You must give me time."

"I'll try, but I've yearned for the life we once had. I want to be at your side, sharing in the work at the farm—"

"You hate country living. You always have."

"You forget I was raised on a farm. I want only to take my place as your helpmate. And if that means living far from London or any city for that matter, here in New South Wales, then that is where I belong." She moved her bowl aside and leaned closer to John. "Do you still believe I did those horrible things?"

"It's not so much what I believe but that I still feel the betrayal. My head understands, but my heart has not yet caught up to my mind."

She dabbed at her lips with her napkin. "We should be together on the farm."

John knew she spoke the truth but couldn't imagine sending Hannah and Thomas away. *Lord, I don't understand. It's all such a mess. How can this be happening? Hannah's a fine woman, undeserving of this. How can I leave her? How can you expect it?*

"You seem far away." Margaret studied John's face, then captured both of his hands in hers. "I want to be us again. The way we were."

"It's not possible. We aren't the same people. And there's Hannah, plus I have a son, Thomas." He pulled his hands free and stood, moving to the window.

"I know your feelings for Hannah are deep, but she's not your wife. I am."

John couldn't think. He had no answers.

"If you like, Thomas can live with us."

Bleakness, like a black cloud, bore down on John and sucked the air from his lungs. "He belongs with his mother." John was angry now and whirled around to face her. "And where would you have me send them?"

Margaret took a step back. "I don't mean to be disrespectful or hard of heart, but Hannah must make a new life for herself. You're not responsible for her."

"Not responsible?" His anger billowed. "I'm to blame for her present situation. She's my wife! And Thomas is my son!" He balled his hands into fists. "I'm responsible for the whole lot of you. You, because you're my wife, Hannah because she was my wife, and Thomas because he has no one else . . . and because I love him." He moved toward the door and grabbed his coat off the rack. "Do you think I ought to abandon everyone for you?"

"Of course not. I didn't mean to sound disrespectful, I'm just trying to be practical." She stepped closer to him. "There is no easy answer, John. You must make a decision—now or later—but either way it will have to be made."

He knew that to be true, but each time his mind took him to that reality he felt as if he would be swept into a black pit—an empty place that would take his life from him.

His eyes found Margaret's imploring ones. *She's my wife.*

He pushed his arms into the coat sleeves. "No matter what you say, the farm is no place for you."

"Of course it is. You'll be there." She stepped toward John, but didn't touch him. "It will be difficult in the beginning, but we'll prosper. I believe in you. You've always been a fine businessman. It will be a good place for us, especially as our family grows."

Children. The thought took him by surprise. He'd forgotten about children. He'd told Hannah he trusted God for them, but he was no longer certain. They'd been married nearly two years. Shouldn't Hannah have conceived by now? He stared at Margaret. Although they'd not had any children while in

London, she'd promised him that one day they'd have a family. He loved Thomas and had thought the lad was enough for him . . . but a child he'd fathered himself was appealing. She could offer him something Hannah couldn't—offspring of his own.

8

"Shouldn't be long now," John said, watching a laboring ewe. "She's been at it awhile."

Thomas leaned against the gate. "Will she be all right?"

"I figure so. Just have to watch her." John rested his hand on Thomas's blond head. The ewe strained through a contraction. "We'll soon have another lamb to care for."

Two tiny feet appeared and the ewe pushed, producing front legs and finally expelling a soggy lump of wool. The newborn lay on the hay-covered floor, wet and helpless. The mother immediately set to licking it. The lamb didn't stir. John stepped in closer to have a look.

Its breaths were shallow. "You need a bit of help, eh." Using a rough cloth, John rubbed the animal all over. It remained quiet and unresponsive.

"What's wrong with him?" Thomas's voice was strident.

John swung the lamb up onto its feet, stopping abruptly to increase the flow of air to its lungs. The animal's breathing increased markedly, and the newborn shook himself from head to toe. "Ah, that seems to have done it."

He moved the lamb closer to its mother. Although tottering,

it came fully awake and made an effort to suckle. John stepped back and watched, arms folded over his chest.

Quincy shook his head. "New lambs seem set on dying the moment they're born."

"Is it gonna be all right?" Thomas asked.

"I'd say so." John draped an arm over Thomas's shoulders and looked over the lambing pens. "The Lord has blessed us. We'll have a good number to add to the flock."

Folding his arms on top of the gate, Thomas rested his chin in the bend of his elbows and studied the lamb. "He's eating well now."

"That he is." Exhaustion had set into John's very bones. Lambing had started in earnest two days earlier, and he'd spent nearly every hour since in the lambing shed. He didn't mind the weariness, though. Each new lamb meant more prosperity for the farm. He smiled at Quincy. "We've had twenty born since last night. 'Course that includes four sets of twins."

"It's a good lot, all right." Quincy lifted his hat and then resettled it over his short-cropped hair.

Thomas stepped closer to the ewe and her baby, watching as the little one ate, its tail flicking back and forth. The ewe worked to clean every inch of him.

"Can I have one of me own?" Thomas asked.

"And what would ye do with it?"

"Why . . . I'd feed it and pet it, and take it for walks."

John grinned. "I know it sounds like fun, but it's a lot of work. Do you think you're old enough for such a responsibility?"

"I'm eleven, nearly a man."

John couldn't keep from smiling. *Nearly a man. You might think so, but you've a ways to go.* "Fair enough," he said. "But you wouldn't want to separate a lamb from its mother."

"No. I guess not." Thomas frowned. "What 'bout if we lose a ewe? Could I care for its lamb, then?" He rested his hand on the back of the tiny sheep.

"And if we lose others? Are you prepared to care for them as well?"

Thomas thought for a moment. "I suppose. Do ye think there will be many lost?"

"I pray not."

Thomas pulled himself to his full height. "I can do it."

"All right, then. I'll put you in charge of the ones without mums."

Thomas smiled, his blue eyes coming to life. "I'll do a fine job. I know what it feels like to lose yer mum." Sorrow stole the light from his eyes.

John felt a pang of sadness. Thomas did know. He'd not only lost his mother but his sister and father as well. He gently squeezed the boy's shoulder.

Thomas squatted beside the ewe and its baby, watching closely. "This one's real hungry." The lamb butted its mother's udder, hoping for more milk. "He's going to be a strong one."

John chuckled. "Could be. He started out a bit slow, but looks like he's making a go of it." He glanced around the lambing shed. "Any more nearing their time?"

"I don't think there are any coming in the next hour," Quincy said. "Ye look done in. Why don't ye get some sleep? I'll watch over them." Using his thumb to push up his hat, he scratched his scalp. "With Thomas here to help, we'll be fine."

"I could do with a bit of sleep. But there's a lot else that needs to be done."

"What good will ye be if ye give way?"

John looked at the house. *How fine my bed would feel.* It

had been a good six weeks since he'd moved to town. But since lambing had begun, he'd been allowed to spend most nights in the barn. As he'd settle down to sleep at the end of each day, his mind went to Hannah. He missed her presence beside him. *If only things could be as they were.*

He trudged to the water barrel, dipped out a ladleful, and drank it down. Filling the dipper again, he sipped from it, then poured some into his palm and scrubbed his face. It refreshed him a bit. After hanging the ladle back in its place, he turned to the house, hoping to catch a glimpse of Hannah. She didn't appear.

"Mum made lemonade. Would ye like some? I'll get it for ye. Maybe we could rest on the porch for a bit, eh?"

"Don't know if that's such a good idea."

Thomas scowled. "Yer not even trying to make things better. Ye ought to talk to her. She's alone a lot. And she does most of the work on her own."

"I'm here nearly every day . . . I do my best."

"Ye left her . . . and me."

"It's not what I wanted." John reached for Thomas, pulling him to within arm's length before the lad balked. "I'm here now."

Thomas kicked at the ground, then looked at his father. "It's not enough." He glanced at the lamb, which had settled beside its mother. Thomas looked back at his father with an accusing gaze. "She made the lemonade for ye."

"I doubt that. You can drink enough for two people." John's attempt at levity fell flat.

"She made a whole pitcher full. More than me and her can drink." He crossed his arms over his chest and looked his father in the eyes. "Talk to her."

95

John's insides tightened. That's what he wanted—time with her, laughter, love, and real conversations the way it used to be.

Working to keep the emotion from his voice, John said, "Your mother's made it clear I'm to keep my distance. And she's right." John hated the reality of the statement, but he knew it to be true. With him and Margaret seeing each other and working toward reconciliation, it wasn't respectable to visit with Hannah even in an innocent way. And if he had any chance of putting his first marriage back together, he couldn't cozy up with her. "It's not proper for your mum and me to spend time together, Thomas. We're not together anymore."

"Ye could be." Thomas stomped off. He stopped and glared over his shoulder. "Ye could be . . . if ye wanted to," he shouted and ran toward the river. He pumped his arms up and down as he sprinted away.

The familiar ache settled around John's heart as he watched the boy go. If only he could make Thomas understand. *How can I do that? I don't even understand. This isn't right, none of it is.* He felt pressure on his shoulder and the squeeze of Quincy's hand.

"He'll be fine. Give him time."

John blew out a heavy breath and turned back to the shed. "I better have a look at some of those ewes." Frustration cut through him like a cold winter wind as he walked to the next pen.

Dishrag in hand, Hannah stepped onto the porch and watched Thomas run toward the river. She knew how much he liked working with his father and how excited he'd been about helping with the lambing. She'd expected him to spend every possible moment in the lambing shed.

He loves the river as well, she reasoned, but detected an intensity in his stride that alerted her to trouble. *I wonder if he and his father had words.* Thomas had made it clear that he loathed the present arrangement between his parents. *Lord, help him to understand that we've no choice. And give him peace in the midst of this storm.* Hannah wished the same for herself. She felt as if she'd been caught up in a maelstrom.

She returned to the kitchen and stared at the pitcher of lemonade on the counter. Thomas had convinced her to make enough for the both of them plus John and Quincy. She couldn't lie to herself; she'd hoped John might share some with her and Thomas. She removed the towel draped over the top of the pitcher and poured herself a glass.

After replacing the towel, she returned to the veranda and set the glass on a side table. A breeze blew up from the river, making the cool air feel almost cold. Pulling her shawl more tightly about her shoulders, she sat and closed her eyes, enjoying the fragrance of eucalyptus driven on the wind. She felt almost at peace.

The sound of a buggy carried up from the roadway, and she looked to see who was passing by, or perchance visiting. She hoped Lydia had come to call. It had been too long. Hannah stood and watched to see if the traveler turned onto their drive.

A buggy headed toward the house. Lydia wasn't driving. It was Margaret! A tremor shot through Hannah. *Why is she here?*

She sat down, not wanting to appear distressed and hoping

the shadows might hide her. Perhaps Margaret would go directly to the lambing shed and she'd not have to speak to her.

Instead, the buggy headed straight for the house. Hannah's heart raced and she fought to slow her rapid breathing. *What can she want with me?* When the buggy stopped in front of the porch, Hannah was forced to stand out of politeness. She clasped her hands tightly in front of her.

Margaret wore a painted cotton gown with blue flowers on a white background. It was stylishly snug through the torso, emphasizing her tiny waist. She had thrown a dark blue shawl over her shoulders and looked as if she were going to tea at the home of a gentlewoman. *She'll not find nobility here. This is a simple farm, and if she plans to visit the lambing shed, she'll have difficulty keeping that fine skirt out of the muck. It would serve her right.*

Knowing her thoughts were spiteful, Hannah couldn't help herself. No matter how much she told herself Margaret had every right to be with John, her presence here in New South Wales had cut off Hannah's life with the only man she'd ever loved. *There will never be anyone else for me.*

Margaret tied off the reins and set the brake. Peering from beneath a broad-brimmed bonnet, she carefully stepped from the buggy. Auburn tresses fell from beneath the hat and onto her shoulders. Hannah couldn't help but admire the color and sheen of her hair. Self-consciously she tucked up loose curls. She'd always considered her hair to be one of her flaws; it was too dark and too fine.

"Good day," Margaret said, in a friendly tone.

"Good day." *Or it was until you arrived.* "Is there anything I can do for you?" She moved to the railing.

"I was hoping I might have a word with John. And I've

brought him something to eat. He's been working so hard, I thought he was in need of a good meal."

He's fine. If he needs something, I can provide it, Hannah thought, but said, "Of course. I'm sure he's hungry by now." She glanced at the partially clouded sky. "It's nearly midday." She felt plain and disheveled in comparison to Margaret. "He's at the lambing shed. Just up there." She pointed toward the small barn.

Margaret remained where she was. "He's been spending a great deal of time here recently."

"He has no choice. Lambs are fragile creatures, they need extra care. If not for John's diligence, we'd lose a good deal of them." Hannah realized she'd used the term "we" and corrected it, saying, "I mean John would."

"Of course." Margaret looked as if she were about to return to the buggy, then stopped and instead walked to the bottom of the steps. "Might I have a word with you?"

Hannah moved back, wishing for a way to avoid having a conversation with this woman. *Don't be a coward. No matter what she's got to say, stand up to it. Certainly it can't be worse than what's happened already.* Her mind carried her grudgingly onward. *And she deserves respect, she's John's wife.*

"May I get you some refreshment? I made lemonade just this morning."

"That sounds lovely. Thank you." Margaret climbed the steps.

"I'll be just a moment." Hannah moved inside, finding it ironic that the lemonade she'd hoped to share with John would be drunk by his wife instead. Hands trembling, she poured the tangy drink into a glass, spilling some of it. She wiped up the mess, her mind awhirl with questions about why Margaret would want to talk to her.

When she returned to the porch, Margaret sat in one of the spindle-backed chairs. Handing her the glass, Hannah took a chair apposite her.

"Thank you." Margaret tasted the lemonade. "This is quite good. You must give me your recipe. I'm sure John is partial to it. On more than one occasion he's mentioned what a fine cook you are."

Rather than being flattered, Hannah felt as if John had breached a line of privacy between them. She didn't want Margaret to know anything about her life with John. "It's quite simple. I can write it down for you."

"That's very kind of you." Margaret took another drink and gazed at the lambing shed. "It seems a nasty business, sheep and lambs. I don't quite understand why anyone would raise animals that are born so frail that they need constant attention."

"John is counting on a growing market for the wool. They've begun shipments to Europe, and he's certain the demand will increase. And John likes the work." Knowing that she understood something about John that Margaret didn't made Hannah feel steadier.

"He did say something about that. But I was hoping we might raise beef or grow wheat. I understand there's more money in those markets."

"That may be, but John's always been intent on improving and increasing the flocks."

"Yes, he told me."

Hannah thought she detected irritation in Margaret's voice.

She was silent for a long moment, then said, "Well then . . . there are some things we ought to talk about."

Her voice was kindly, but Hannah couldn't imagine that Margaret had anything to say to her that would be a kindness.

Margaret set her gaze on Hannah. "Whether John raises sheep or cattle isn't the issue."

"I suppose you're right, except, of course, John's happiness is of consequence."

"I don't wish to be harsh, but his happiness no longer concerns you. You're not his wife. I apologize for being so blunt, but I think it's time we faced the truth. I know that what I have to say will cause you pain, but it must be said." She set her glass on the side table.

Hannah held her breath—waiting.

"John and I have made great strides toward restoring our marriage. And I believe it will only be a matter of weeks before we are fully man and wife again. I've waited for so long." She glanced at her hands, then back at Hannah. "I don't wish to hurt you, but we must do the right thing, for John's sake. You may doubt my love, but I assure you it is deep and genuine. A finer man cannot be found."

A roaring sound filled Hannah's ears, and she was having difficulty catching her breath. She knew how fine a man he was.

"I think it's time I took my rightful place here—on the farm." Margaret's expression was assertive but not combative. "John will let you stay as long as you wish. He's a noble man and would never ask you to leave."

Hannah knew that to be true. But she'd not wanted to confront the inevitable. Plainly, there was no way to avoid it any longer.

"I wouldn't presume to tell you when you should go, but I do think it is time that you thought about it."

"You're absolutely right, of course. In fact, I've been making plans . . . to leave."

Margaret's full lips turned up in a tight smile. She stood. "I knew you were a reasonable person. John wouldn't settle for less." She moved toward the steps. "I'm sorry that things have turned out like this. I empathize with your situation." Keeping a hand on the railing, she gracefully made her way down the steps. "Thank you for your understanding." She walked to the buggy, climbed in, and then with a slight nod, she drove toward the lambing shed.

Her heart throbbing, Hannah stared after her. *I'm sure the Athertons will let me stay with them, for now. Perhaps they need a domestic.*

She caught sight of Thomas dashing toward the house. How could she tell him? He loved this place. *Perhaps he should stay with John.* The thought only intensified Hannah's heartache, but Thomas should be allowed the decision. It wouldn't be right to force him to leave.

As he charged toward the porch, Hannah put on a smile.

Thomas stormed up the steps. "What did she want?"

9

Lightheaded and feeling queasy, Hannah lowered herself into a porch chair. *I pray I'm not coming down with something.*

Thomas tromped up the steps. "Why is she here?"

"She brought lunch for your father." Hannah's voice wavered as nausea swept over her.

"Ye all right? Did she do something?"

"I'm fine. And of course she didn't do anything." Hannah used her handkerchief to pat away perspiration on her face. "I'm just a bit under the weather."

"Ye look sickly. Should I get Dad?"

"No." Hannah straightened. "It's nothing."

Thomas lingered. "Would ye like some of that lemonade ye made? I can get it."

"I've already got some. But thank you."

Thomas watched her and after a few moments said, "Yer not drinking it."

"My stomach's a bit unsettled just now."

"Shall I get ye some water, then?"

"That would be fine. Thank you." Hannah didn't want water. She wanted to know how to tell Thomas they had to move.

He dipped a ladle into the barrel. "I heard that the Connors have a stomach ailment. Maybe that's what's wrong." He offered Hannah a drink.

"Perhaps." Hannah took a sip, then handed the dipper back to Thomas.

"Ye should come and see the new lambs. There's lots of them. When they're first born, they're all wet and dirty, but in no time at all they're fine looking."

He took her hand as if to pull her out of the chair. "One came just a few minutes ago." He tugged gently. "Come on, Mum. We'll have a look together, eh? Maybe walking 'bout will make ye feel better."

"Not just yet, Thomas."

He glanced at the lambing shed. John was helping Margaret out of the buggy. "Is it because of her?"

"No," Hannah said, but if the truth be told, the idea of visiting the lambing shed with John and Margaret was too much right now. "I need to talk with you about something."

"'Bout what?"

Hannah's nausea intensified and she wondered if she were going to be sick. She felt faint, her skin clammy. She closed her eyes.

"Mum?" When Hannah didn't answer, Thomas said, "Maybe ye ought to go to yer bed for a while. I'll see to things."

Thomas's compassion touched Hannah. She smiled at him. "You're a kind lad, but I just need a moment."

He sat on the top step and picked at a callous on his palm.

Hannah turned her mind to the cool breeze and the freshness of the air and waited. Gradually the churning in her stomach eased. "I'm better now. Can you come up here and sit by me? I've something I need to talk to you about."

Thomas pushed to his feet and moved to Hannah, standing in front of her. She took his hands and turned them palm up. They bore signs of hard work. "I was thinking I might go to work for the Athertons. Gwen said they need a housemaid."

Thomas stared at her for a long moment, then his eyes flashed with anger and he yanked his hands free. "She told ye to move, didn't she?" He glared in the direction of the lambing shed. "Dad said we could stay."

"Your father's been very generous. He's a good man. But it's time for us to leave. Margaret is his wife and she should live here."

Thomas turned and faced the river, crossing his arms over his chest. "This is our place, not hers."

"It is yours, but not mine. Margaret is your father's wife, and for that reason she belongs here, not me. It pains me to think of leaving, but we can make a new start. It will be like an adventure." Hannah pushed out of the chair and the world spun. She grabbed hold of the porch railing. *Oh, what is wrong with me?*

This wasn't the first time Hannah had been sick. For several days, now, she'd had bouts of nausea and dizziness. Her menses were late, and she'd wondered if she might possibly be in a family way. Common sense told her it wasn't possible—there had only been that one time. The idea of a baby created a mix of joy and sorrow.

Was it possible that after all this time she and John were to have a child? She laid a hand on her abdomen. It's what they'd wanted, prayed for, but now . . . it seemed cruel.

The dizziness passed and Hannah loosened her hold on the railing. She focused on Thomas. "You can stay here with your father, if you like."

105

Thomas frowned. "I can't stay without ye." He glanced at the buggy parked at the shed. "I won't live with her."

"I must leave, Thomas." Hannah's heart felt heavy. "I'll talk to the Athertons. When I used to work for them, I was grateful for my little house and good honest labor. It's quite nice there."

Thomas returned to his perch on the top step. Bracing his elbows on his thighs, he rested his face in his hands. "It's not fair, none of it."

"I know it feels that way now, but the Lord has a plan for us. You'll see."

Thomas looked up at her, his eyes hard. "I like the way things were . . . before her."

Hannah sat beside him and slipped an arm over his shoulders, pulling him close. "I liked it too. But sometimes life doesn't behave the way we expect. Even when things don't seem right, sometimes they are. We'll just have to see what God has in mind for us, eh?"

Thomas managed a grudging nod.

⚬⚬⚬

With the last of their things packed into the wagon, Hannah stood in the doorway of the house. She remembered how excited she'd been when John had built their first cabin. They'd spent their early days and nights without a roof, sleeping beneath a dark sky with stars winking at them. Tears were so close they burned, yet she managed to hold them back.

John stepped up behind her. "You don't have to go."

Hannah turned and looked at him. She loved his strong angular face, the flecks of gold in his eyes, and the way his dark hair sometimes fell onto his forehead, as it was now. She fought the impulse to sweep it back.

"Where do you expect me to stay? Here with Margaret?" She moved to the steps. "We've both known that my living here was only temporary, that one day Margaret would take her rightful place." A cavernous aching spread through Hannah. It was so deep and wide she wondered if it might completely overtake her.

"I've always admired your noble character, your strength. But not even you can take care of two wives. And if you try, it will be unfair to both of us." She gripped the railing. "It's better this way."

Taking the steps, she fought familiar wooziness. "It's time we were on our way." She glanced back at him. "You can see Thomas as often as you like. And he can stay here with you anytime." She looked at Thomas, who stood stoically beside the wagon. "He'll need some time, though."

John took a step toward her. "I hate this. I don't want this."

"Nor I." Hannah took a strengthening breath. "It can't be changed."

"I understand that in my head, but it gives me no ease for my heartache, Hannah."

He said her name with such tenderness Hannah felt her will waver. She moved quickly down the steps and away from him. As she walked toward the wagon, it felt as if her life were ebbing away.

Quincy waited on the seat, reins in hand. Thomas climbed into the back and sat with his legs dangling. Hannah climbed up onto the seat and settled beside Quincy, modestly tucking in her skirts. John moved to Thomas. "Son—"

"I'm not yer son." Thomas put his palms down on either side

of him and pressed against the wooden bed of the wagon. He stared at the ground.

"You know I don't want you to go."

"Ye've done a poor job of keeping us here, then." His tone was heavy with disdain.

"Thomas, you'll not speak to your father in such a manner," Hannah said.

Thomas pursed his lips and glowered.

"No matter what you might think, I love you . . . and your mother." Thomas didn't look at him. John remained a few moments longer, then moved to the front of the wagon on Hannah's side. "I'm sorry."

"It's not your fault. It's no one's fault." She glanced at Thomas. "And he knows it too." Hannah held back tears. She needed to be on her way and put this moment behind her. "Wait a few days and then come and see him," she whispered, then turned to Quincy. "We should go now."

Quincy tipped his head to John and then slapped the reins and guided the horses toward the road.

Hannah kept her eyes on the river. She wanted one last glimpse of the house and of John, but she knew what she would see and couldn't bear even a glance.

Perry and Gwen met the wagon as it rolled up the Atherton drive. "Hello there," Perry called to her. "Fine to see ye."

"Wish it was under different circumstances," Gwen added.

Hannah accepted a hand down from Perry.

Thomas leapt off the back, then stood with his hands in his pockets. "Are we going to live in the main house?"

"No. We'll be staying in one of the cabins."

"I'll show you which one is yours," Perry said, slinging an arm over the lad's shoulders. "Hey, Quincy, follow us." He set off with Thomas beside him and Quincy driving the wagon behind.

Gwen hooked an arm through Hannah's "The cabin's a nice one. Ye'll like it just fine. It's only two away from ours."

"Good." Hannah pressed a hand over Gwen's. "I'll like being neighbors again."

"Me too." Gwen pulled her closer. "So sorry things turned out badly. I can't imagine how ye must be feeling."

Hannah reached for strength. "It's not what I'd expected when I married John, but Thomas and I can begin again. We'll be fine."

Even as she said the words, hurt gnawed at Hannah's insides. She needed to think more optimistically, needed to remind herself of God's goodness. While on the prison ship and in the months following, she prayed only for good health and enough food. God had given her so much more—a son and now possibly a baby . . . John's child.

"Hannah." Catharine Atherton moved slowly down the steps and crossed the yard. When she reached Hannah, she pulled her into a long and sturdy embrace, as if she hoped to hug away the young woman's sorrow. "It will be all right, dear. I promise you it will be." She continued to hold her. "The Lord sees this. He's standing with you."

"I know." Hannah took a step back and smiled at Catharine. She could feel the older woman's love, and it warmed the cold place inside her. "It's grand to see you. I feel as if I've been greeted by my mother."

Catharine's eyes glinted with tears as she took Hannah's hand.

"Come along, then. While the men unload your things, you and I shall have some tea."

❦

The days settled into a pattern of work and rest. Thomas reluctantly spent the morning doing schoolwork and chores, but the afternoons were his. Most often he could be found at the river fishing or at Perry's side, learning all he could about making tools. Hannah found it ironic that now he'd taken an interest in John's trade when he no longer lived with his father.

She worked wherever she was needed, helping with household tasks and even assisting Mrs. Goudy in the kitchen from time to time. And she'd once again taken up sewing gowns for female prisoners. But no matter how busy she was, the ache of loss held her fast. Still, she managed to find contentment and even moments of happiness. And as the certainty of her baby's life grew, she experienced flashes of joy.

The entire household welcomed Hannah and Thomas. Even Dalton Keen, the houseman, made sure Hannah felt comfortable, making time for conversation and seeing that her needs were attended to. Gwen teased Hannah, saying Dalton must fancy her. Hannah knew it was nonsense. She couldn't imagine Dalton being interested in anyone in that way. He was far too reserved and much too practical for something as unreasonable as love. And besides, Hannah always thought he and Mrs. Goudy would make a fine pair.

Two weeks passed, and Hannah found herself looking for John, expecting him to come for a visit, to spend an afternoon with Thomas. It was time. She was almost certain Thomas would take kindly to seeing him.

When he didn't come the first week, she told herself John must be busy, but she'd heard Margaret had moved into the house and wondered if that was why he'd stayed away. After the second week, she'd started to wonder if he'd put both her and Thomas out of his life, although she couldn't imagine him setting Thomas aside in such a fashion. However, she'd seen the kind of influence a woman could have over a man. Perhaps Margaret had convinced him they needed to begin again without any prior encumbrances.

When Lydia told her that John had continued to sleep in the barn, Hannah knew she ought to hope for good things between him and Margaret, and yet she couldn't keep from feeling a measure of satisfaction and hope. Perhaps he would come to see Thomas soon.

Needing to know more about John, she sought out Perry one afternoon. She stepped into the shop. Thomas stood at the workbench and watched closely while Perry created a tack claw.

"Thomas, it's time for lunch." Hannah approached the two of them.

"Now?"

"Yes. Now."

"Can I come back after?"

"No. You didn't do your studies this morning. And I'll not have you growing up uneducated and illiterate."

"I won't. I already know how to read quite well."

"True." Hannah smiled. "But you'll still do your schoolwork." She rested a hand on his back. "I made you a sandwich and there's cake too, sent over by Mrs. Goudy."

"Ye don't want to miss out on her cake. She makes the best." Perry grinned.

"All right, then," Thomas said. "Can I come back tomorrow?"

"Is he being a bother to you?" Hannah asked Perry.

"Not at all. He's a fine lad. And a good helper."

Hannah gazed at Thomas, trying to look stern, but she couldn't suppress a smile. "You can come tomorrow, but not until you've finished your work."

"I'll be here by noon," he said and ran out of the shop.

Hannah watched him go, thankful for time alone with Perry. She stood and watched quietly, hoping he might say something about John. When he didn't, she asked as casually as possible, "Have you heard anything of John? Is he well?"

"Haven't seen him in some days." Perry's voice sounded sharp. He gave Hannah a questioning look. "Don't know how ye do it. Ye seem at peace with all this."

"I daresay, I'm not happy about it at all. But God has blessed me with good friends. And he sustains me and offers me peace."

Perry nodded. "I could do with a bit of yer peace. I'd like to box John's ears, letting ye go like that."

"He didn't let me go. I chose to leave. It was the only way. Please don't be hard on him. None of this is his fault. He had no recourse. An honorable man does the right thing even when it's painful."

"Well, he ought to at least take heed to his son."

"I'm sure he has good cause for his delay. He'll come soon." Hannah turned her attention to Perry's work. "I pray he finds happiness with Margaret." The words were out without thought, and Hannah was shocked to realize she meant them.

"Ye've more mercy than me. I thought he'd figure a way to divorce her."

"Do you think that would be honorable? Could you let go of Gwen so easily?"

"It's not the same thing. I love her. There's no finer wife."

"It is the same—marriage is marriage. Most people don't have the kind of love you have with Gwen or that John and I had. And remember, John once loved Margaret. Perhaps they'll rediscover it. But whether they do or not, John is a good man and will do the honorable thing."

"I know you're right. He's a fine chap. I ought to go and see him. Figure he could use a friend 'bout now."

"I'm sure he could." Hannah moved toward the door. "It would be good of you to speak to him. But I do hope he finds his way here, soon. Thomas hasn't said anything to me, but I know he's waiting for him."

She stepped out of the door and headed for the cabin. There was something she needed to take care of. It was time to speak with the reverend to make certain her marriage had been dissolved.

Hannah seated herself on the reverend's settee and clasped her hands in her lap. She'd sat in this same spot when she and John had come, hoping for a way to save their marriage. Now she was here to make certain it was ended.

"Can I get you some refreshment?" the reverend asked, brushing a thin strand of gray hair off his forehead.

"No, thank you. I'm fine."

The reverend was a small man, and when he settled into his chair, the cushion barely gave way. He sat back and threw one leg over the other. "What can I do for you, Hannah?"

The ticking of a clock sounded loud in the quiet room. Now that she was here, she wasn't sure just what to say. Doing her best to focus on what was at hand, she said, "As you know, John and I are no longer living together. I'm working at the Athertons'. John is at the farm and Margaret's moved into the house."

The reverend nodded sympathetically. "I heard. I've missed seeing him on Sundays but can appreciate his discomfort and yours. I hope he hasn't forsaken his faith."

"Oh no. He never would."

The reverend smiled. "I thought not."

Hannah had noticed John's absences. Each Sunday she looked for him, longing to see him, if only from a distance.

She turned her mind back to the present. "I was thinking it might be necessary to file for a dissolution to our marriage. John and Margaret belong together, and I don't wish to be a hindrance to their reconciliation." Hannah tried to keep her tone practical, hoping it would soften the harsh realities.

"I understand your concern. But I doubt you need to do anything. Your marriage vows were invalid." He pressed the palms of his hands together and leaned forward. "But just to make certain, I'll check with the governor and file any necessary papers."

"Thank you."

"Is there anything else I can do for you and for Thomas? This must be a trying time for you both."

"It is. But we're well. The Athertons are kind and we've good friends there. Thomas and Perry Littrell have become quite good chums. And given time, I'm sure John and Thomas will again share the bond of father and son."

"I'm glad to hear that." The reverend sat back. "And you, Hannah, what can I do for you?"

The tenderness in the minister's voice touched a place in Hannah's heart that she'd managed to hold in check . . . until that moment. Tears washed into her eyes. Barely able to speak, she said, "Pray for me . . . and for John. I'm sure he feels as displaced as I." She wondered if she dare tell him about the baby. She'd missed two menses and was certain now that she carried John's child.

"Might I ask that you . . . also pray . . . for the child I carry, Reverend?"

10

While listening to the sounds of a cool September rain, Hannah used a feather duster to reach the top of the parlor draperies. She liked the rain; it reminded her of London.

With the valance dust free, she stopped and gazed through the misted window at the sodden outdoors. A longing for home welled up inside, taking Hannah by surprise. It had been a long while since England felt like home. The idea of returning tempted her.

Hannah knew it was heaviness of heart that had set her off balance. She dismissed the appeal, reminding herself of London's deplorable conditions. Parramatta was home now.

Still, memories of her mother's seamstress shop, the coziness of their cottage, and the warmth of her mum's devotion tugged at her. They had spent many cheery evenings together tucked snugly inside their little house.

The hours spent side by side working on women's gowns had always given Hannah a feeling of contentment. She missed the days of creating fine dresses. Although she enjoyed making clothes for the women locked in New South Wale's prisons, it wasn't the same as working alongside her mother and creating gowns for the upper class. They'd worked with the finest fabrics, and Caroline Talbot's skills had been renowned in London.

Hannah returned to her dusting, but her mind moved to John. She couldn't keep from thinking about him and the life they once had. They'd also spent quiet evenings together. Sometimes they would both read or he'd work on some tool or other while she sewed.

John. A familiar throb of pain tightened in her chest and moved into her throat as Hannah held back tears. *Stop that now. It will do no good to think about him. He's nearly as far from me as Mum is. And there's nothing to be done about it.* She dusted more vigorously.

John had gone on with his life. She must do the same.

Someone cleared their throat, startling Hannah. She whirled about and found Dalton standing just inside the parlor doorway. "You've caught me woolgathering," she said, feeling a flush of embarrassment.

"We all do that from time to time." He made an attempt at a smile and moved to the window and looked out. "The world's turned a bit soggy."

"I like the rain. It makes everything smell good. And with any luck, it will turn the grasses green again."

"Not likely, not this time of year." Dalton stood there like a slender tree, still in the wind. He looked as if he would say more.

"Is there something I can do for you?" Hannah finally asked.

He clasped his hands behind his back and again cleared his throat. "I would like to have a word with you."

Hannah waited, but instead of speaking, Dalton looked from her to the window and then back at her.

"Is something wrong?"

"No. Not at all." He compressed his lips, dimpling his hollow cheeks. "But there is something that has been troubling me, and I've been trying to decide whether I ought to mention it or not. I've decided you should know."

"What is it?"

"It has to do with the other Mrs. Bradshaw."

Hannah's interest piqued. "Margaret?" *What can Dalton have to tell me about her?* "Is she unwell?"

"No. Not that I've heard, anyway."

Thinking Dalton's behavior a bit peculiar, Hannah waited for him to continue.

"There's been a bit of gossip about her." He moved to the hearth and then turned to face Hannah. "Mind you, it's nothing more than a rumor . . . but . . . it might be of some importance."

She wished he'd simply say whatever was on his mind. She prompted him with a "Yes?"

The solemn houseman leveled pale blue eyes on Hannah. "It seems there's some speculation . . . there's word that she may not be telling the entire truth about why she is in Parramatta."

"What reason could there be, other than the one she stated?"

"I can't say, but—"

"She's John's wife. That's clear. What motive could she have had to travel all this distance, if not to reconcile? She wouldn't come without just cause." Hannah couldn't imagine any other purpose powerful enough to compel her to take such a long and dangerous journey.

"That's true. But I've heard she can be bad tempered when provoked."

"So can we all, given circumstances. There must be more than that to the rumors."

"It seems she was ill-tempered with a maid at the board-inghouse, on more than one occasion." Dalton's eyebrows steepled.

"Perhaps it is the maid who brought about the displeasure," Hannah said gently. "A flash of temper can be had by anyone when enduring poor service."

"I can't imagine you ever behaving in such a manner, even if provoked."

"I've been known to let my frustrations get the better of me." Hannah's mind flared with shame, remembering her lack of forbearance with Thomas when he'd first come to live with her and John.

She stared out the window at the falling rain. "A bit of a bad mood is hardly cause to mistrust a person. I should hope people would be more tolerant of *my* shortcomings. And there seems little cause for gossip over something this trivial."

"True enough." Dalton folded his long arms over his chest. "There have also been rumors of a gentleman caller. He's been seen in her company more than once."

Hannah remembered seeing her with a man months before when she'd been in town. Dalton was not given to gossip and rarely said much of anything. Why would he speak now?

"I appreciate your concern, but I'd hate to charge someone unfairly. Perhaps the man in question was a business acquaintance or someone else of no consequence. Have you heard anything substantial that would discredit Mrs. Bradshaw?"

Dalton didn't answer right away, then said, "No. I can't say that I have." He tapped the toe of a polished shoe against the wooden floor. "I just thought that perhaps . . . under the cir-

119

cumstances you ought to be aware. I know you'd not want John or your son exposed to deceit of any kind. And if it turned out that Mrs. Bradshaw were part of something fraudulent, is it possible that your marriage might be restored?"

And then Hannah understood Dalton. He wanted happiness for her. His kindness warmed her heart. "Thank you for caring. I do appreciate your thoughtfulness. But I've given up on the life I once had, and I've turned my eyes to the future. Looking for treachery where there is none and hoping for personal opportunities is immoral. And I won't do it. I shan't do anything to jeopardize John's happiness."

Hannah gripped the feather duster more tightly. "If you come to me with proof of wrongdoing that shows me Margaret is unfit to be his wife, I shall do my utmost to help him. But that is not the case at present. And therefore, since she is his wife, she should be treated with the utmost respect and decency."

"You're right, of course." Dalton's tone was contrite.

Hannah offered him a smile. "I do thank you for caring, Dalton."

With a nod, he turned and walked away, leaving Hannah to ponder whether there was any basis for the rumors. *How deplorable that would be. Poor John, if such were true.* Although Hannah understood the proclivity of people to enjoy a tasty rumor, she knew she'd not discard the information and would be attentive to any unusual behavior.

With the dusting completed, Hannah walked toward her cottage. It was time she fixed lunch for her and Thomas. The rain had stopped, leaving the world looking as if it had been washed clean. Hannah took a deep breath, delighting in the fragrance of damp earth and fresh air.

Although she'd tried to rid her mind of Dalton's veiled accusations, they remained with her. If the rumors were true, would that change the situation between her and John, or had they already journeyed too far from one another?

A carriage moved up the drive and stopped in front of the house. A woman Hannah had never seen before stepped out and walked to the veranda steps and up to the front door. She was dressed simply, but she carried herself with distinction.

It's none of my concern, Hannah thought, stepping around a puddle and continuing to the cottage, hoping Thomas would be there. When he wasn't, she set off for the tool shop, the most likely place to find him. *I'll have to speak to him; he's not making time for his studies.*

When Hannah stepped into the shop, Perry stood at a workbench, his attention on a tool of some sort. Thomas wasn't about. "Perry, have you seen Thomas?"

He looked up. "He was 'ere a bit earlier, but I haven't seen him in some time. Most likely when the rain stopped, he went down to the river to do some fishing. Ye know how he likes that."

"Oh yes, I do." She moved toward the door. "If you see him, please tell him I'm waiting lunch for him."

"I surely will."

Hannah stepped outside and started for the river when she saw that the visitor was heading to her cottage. *What could she want with me?* Hoping to greet the woman at the door, Hannah hurried her steps.

"Good day. May I be of help?" she asked when she'd nearly reached her caller.

The woman stopped and waited for Hannah. She was small and frail-looking.

"Good day." She straightened her bonnet. "I'm Lucinda Davies." She set eyes the color of a pale blue sky on Hannah, eyes the same color as Thomas's.

The name Davies struck Hannah like a blow. Thomas didn't have any family. She barely managed to ask, "How can I help you?"

"I'm Charles Davies' sister, Thomas's aunt. It's my understanding that he lives here with you."

"He does, indeed." Like an evil mist, dread enveloped Hannah.

Lucinda's expression was one of apprehension as she said, "I've come for him."

"Come for him? How do you mean?"

"I've traveled all the way from England to bring him home with me."

"I understood he had no living relatives."

"I can assure you that I am alive, and so is his grandfather."

Hannah's legs went weak. "He has a grandfather? I don't understand—"

"My brother was my father's only son. When we received word of his death, my dad wanted to come, but his health has not been good. So he sent me to bring Thomas home."

Hannah couldn't think. How would she manage without Thomas? "He's been living with my husband and me."

"I was told that you and your husband are no longer . . . sharing your lives as husband and wife."

"That's true." Hannah glanced down at her hands. "But Thomas sees his father . . . I mean, John often." She knew it wasn't exactly true but was certain that in time he and Thomas would return to their previous comfortable rapport.

"It would be unseemly for a child to remain in your care

under these circumstances. We've a fine farm in Cambridge." She stared at Hannah. "I've papers if you need proof."

"Do you have them with you?"

"I do."

"Yes, then. I would like to see them." Fear and grief enveloped Hannah as she watched Lucinda take folded papers out of her reticule.

Hands trembling, she read through the document. It was true. Thomas belonged to his family in Cambridge. She had no legal right to him. Hannah grabbed hold of the porch railing to steady herself and returned the papers. "How do I know these are authentic?"

Shock registered on Lucinda's face. "I can't believe you would doubt me. I would not have taken that horrid voyage from London all the way to this godforsaken place for a child of no significance." She closed her eyes and took in a breath, then continued more kindly. "I know this must be distressing to you, but it's best that Thomas be with his family. And he'll inherit a fine farm one day. I promise to remain with him until he's grown. He won't be motherless. I've lived my life on the farm and don't plan to marry. I'll be happy to take the boy in hand." She offered a stiff smile.

This unexpected heartache took hold of Hannah. "Thomas is happy here." *Lord, there must be some way to persuade her.* "He has a fine life."

The woman glanced at the small cottage. "You've nothing of your own. You're a domestic. How can you offer him what he needs?"

Her words thrust the truth at Hannah. "I love him," she said, her voice barely more than a whisper. "He needs love more than anything."

"And he'll be loved . . . in England."

Hannah thought she heard compassion in Lucinda's voice. "Please let him stay. He's already lost so much."

"I know what he's lost. We loved his family too. This is best for him. My brother would have wanted his son to have a future."

Hannah searched her mind for something she could say, something that would convince Lucinda to leave Thomas with her. "He has a father," she blurted. "John is a fine father, a better man you will not find."

Lucinda's eyes turned hard. "Thomas's father is dead." She looked about. "Please, can you tell me where he is?"

"I'm not certain. I was just going to call him in to eat when you arrived."

"You don't know where he is? A boy unattended is one that's getting into mischief." She looked like a bristling hen. "I'll have my man find him."

Hannah recognized the inevitable. "No. It's better if I go." She closed the door. "He's most likely at the river." Stepping off the porch, she added, "Thomas loves to fish." Sorrow churned inside Hannah and she was unable to hold back tears. "I'll check the workroom first. That's closer."

With Lucinda following, Hannah walked toward the shop. She hoped Thomas wasn't there, although she knew his absence would be of no real help. At best, all she could do was delay the inevitable. She opened the door and peeked inside. Thomas stood beside Perry, watching him work.

Hannah looked at Lucinda. "Can you give us a moment? This will not be easy for him."

"Certainly. I'll wait here."

Hannah stepped inside the shop, closed the door, and walked

toward Thomas, feeling as if she were living in a nightmare. How would she tell him? Did he even remember his aunt Lucinda or his grandfather?

Perry looked up. "I told him to go on home, but he insisted ... Hannah? What is it?"

"I need to speak with Thomas."

"Is it John?"

"No." She placed a hand on Thomas's shoulder and knelt in front of the boy. "It seems you've an aunt Lucinda, your father's sister."

"Aunt Lucinda?" His eyes held a question, then brightened. "Oh right, I remember me dad telling me 'bout her. Don't recall meeting her, though."

Hannah gently grasped Thomas's arms. "She's come to see you—all the way from England."

"Is she going to live here too?"

"No." Hannah's throat felt as if it had closed. "She's come to ... to take you home with her."

Thomas's eyes widened. Hannah heard a gasp from Perry. The boy stepped back. "But I don't even know her."

"She knows you, and your grandfather's longing to see you. They've a lovely farm that will belong to you one day."

"I don't want a farm." He shoved his chin out. "This is me home. Didn't ye tell her?"

"I did. But she has legal papers."

"I won't go."

Hannah felt helpless. What was she to do? Settling hands on his shoulders, she said gently, "You have to go, Thomas."

"But yer me mum and what 'bout Dad?"

"We never legally adopted you. John simply brought you home and you became part of our family."

Tears washed into the boy's eyes. His chin quivered and he crossed his arms over his chest.

"If I could change it, you know I would."

He squared his jaw. "She can't make me go."

"It will be hard at first, but I'm sure you'll learn to love your family. And living in the countryside in England will be delightful. It's much cooler there than here, and green."

Thomas stared at her with unbelieving eyes.

"I'm sorry, but you must go."

"I won't! I'll run away." He charged out of the shop, leaving the door ajar.

Hannah started to go after him when Perry grabbed her arm. "Let him be. He needs time."

Hannah's heart felt as if it had been impaled. "I don't know that I can bear this. It's too much." Without waiting for a reply from Perry, she turned and walked out.

Lucinda stood just outside the door. "He ran that way," she said, pointing toward the river. "I'm truly sorry. I have no choice in this matter. It will be the best thing for him."

Hannah stopped and stared at the woman. At that moment, she hated her. Without comment, she ran after Thomas.

11

Hannah quaked inside. She could still feel Thomas's arms clutching her. She could hear his tearful determined voice demanding that he wouldn't go. She'd never imagined losing him. She must hurry. Perhaps John could make Thomas's aunt see reason.

"Let me go for ye," Perry said. "It's better me than a woman alone on the road. Ye never know what ye might come across."

"No." Hannah knew Perry's suggestion was sensible, but she couldn't wait here while he went. She had to do something. "I've already told Mrs. Atherton I'm leaving. Dalton is preparing the buggy."

"Let me go along, then."

"It's not necessary. I'm quite capable of looking after myself."

"I know that, but . . ." Perry folded his arms over his chest and shook his head. "Yer a stubborn woman."

"That I am."

"This is just too much, Hannah. At least let Perry go with ye," Gwen entreated.

Trying to maintain a calm exterior, Hannah said, "I'll be fine. I should be the one to go. This is about me and my son." She glanced at the carriage house. "I've got to be on my way. John needs to know what's happened. And the sooner the better."

Dalton drove the buggy around to Hannah's cabin and stopped. Hannah hurried to meet him. "It's kind of you to help."

"I'll be more than happy to drive you."

"Thank you, but I'd rather go unaccompanied." Hannah understood the good sense behind the offer, but she desperately wanted to be alone. She wished people would just let her be. Her emotions were a jumble, and she needed time by herself to sort them out and to weep. She doubted there was anything that could be done to bring Thomas home. She tried to stay focused on what was at hand, but the future stretched out before her—endless and empty without him. Tears stormed the back of her eyes. *Not now. Not yet.*

She tilted her chin up and, in the most practical tone she could muster, said, "I prefer to go alone." She'd not forgotten that Margaret now lived in John's house. It would be difficult to face her, and she'd rather manage that emotional obstacle on her own.

Dalton climbed down, his long legs carrying him easily to the ground. He faced Hannah. "Very well, then. But I'd feel better if—"

"I know you would. And I thank you for caring." Hannah moved past him to the buggy. "It's best this way. None of this is your concern anyway."

Dalton held his body stiffly and Gwen's eyes teared. Perry put an arm about his wife. "Not our concern? We've been friends a long while, Hannah. I've known ye since the prison ship. And Gwen and Dalton nearly as long. We're family."

Hannah realized her insensitive blunder. "Of course you're concerned. I'm sorry, I didn't mean any offense. I just didn't want to put this burden upon your shoulders. You've no need to carry it."

Gwen moved to Hannah and grasped her hand. "What hurts ye hurts us. And God's Word says we're to help carry one another's burdens. We want to help carry this one."

A wave of love rolled over Hannah. "I'm grateful for your kindness, but I've got to go alone."

"Why so?" Gwen asked, squeezing Hannah's hand. "Please let us help."

Hannah didn't know what to say. She hurt so deeply she wasn't able to share this burden just yet. She needed solitude. "I just can't share any of this right now. But I'm grateful for your love and your prayers." She looked at Perry and Dalton and then turned to the buggy. "I must be on my way."

Dalton gave Hannah a hand up and then stepped back.

She lifted the reins. "I'll be home as soon as I can. Please don't worry about me."

She glanced at Mrs. Atherton, who stood on the porch steps. Her face was lined with worry, and she held her hands clasped tightly in front of her. Hannah knew she was praying and would continue to do so until all was well. Looking at her friends, she said, "Pray for us. Pray Thomas can return to us."

"We will. Ye can count on it," Gwen said. She wiped tears from her eyes. "God won't let them take him, not now. He'll see to it that Thomas stays with ye. I'm sure of it."

With a nod to her friends, Hannah slapped the reins, and the horses trotted forward. She wanted to believe, but she wasn't at all certain God would do any such thing. She'd come to understand that his plans did not always agree with her own.

But the idea of Thomas traveling across oceans and living so far from Parramatta was too much for her. She pleaded with God. *Please don't send him away. I need him. I can't believe this is your will.*

Even as Hannah prayed, trying to believe, she feared England might truly be God's plan for Thomas. He'd adjust, and she and John would become a memory. He would have a fine family and a successful farm to claim as his own when he came of age. *Perhaps it's where he belongs.*

Lord, if it is your desire, then I pray you will mend the wound his going will leave in my heart. And if you mean for him to stay, I ask for your strength and your wisdom. Show me what to do.

As she headed for John's, the encounter with Lucinda wound through her mind again and again. Lucinda had tried to be civil, but she'd come prepared to fight, and in the end she'd had her way. *For now, just for now.*

In her mind, Hannah scanned the papers again. They'd seemed legitimate. How could she make certain they were? And what if Lucinda and Thomas sailed away before she and John could find out?

She whipped the reins, hurrying the team along. Gazing through a blur of tears, she trusted the horses to keep to the road. The air was warm and carried the heady scent of wattle mixed with the sweet fragrance of boronia. Normally she would have enjoyed the fragrance, but today it felt suffocating.

Thomas. Oh, Thomas. Her heart constricted and she returned to prayer, beseeching the Lord for clear thinking. She couldn't envision life without the boy. He'd come to her and John hurting and angry. Deeply wounded by the world's injustice and the loss of his family, he'd been determined not to love them. And Hannah's own defiance was as strong as his.

The two had seemed impossibly incompatible, but God had been gracious and patient. Over time they became a family. He couldn't have brought them together to separate them again, could he?

Why would you take him from me now? Is this a part of the penalty for my sin? If I could bring back the child I prayed away, I would. Hannah remembered the awful night she'd lost the baby. It had been created in an act of violence and then shamefully disposed of. She'd never forget the sound of the slop bucket lid that had hidden it while being carried to its grave. *I know you've forgiven me, so why? Why, Lord? Please put a stop to this. It's too much.*

Hopelessness pressed itself down on Hannah. Would the consequences of a desperate prayer whispered long ago never end? Fear erupted in her, rising until it felt as if it would choke off her life.

She lifted the reins and slapped them across the horses' backsides. "Faster, now," she called. She needed John. He'd know what to do.

Barely slowing as she turned the team onto his drive, she headed toward the house. Margaret stood on the porch, a cup in her hand. In spite of the warm weather, she was dressed in a heavy taffeta gown. Hannah thought her foolish, but knew in time she'd relinquish her elegant dresses for something more sensible.

Margaret set her cup on a side table and walked down the steps, where she waited for Hannah. She smiled and, using a handkerchief, patted at the sheen on her face. "Good day. What can I do for you?" She studied Hannah. "Has something happened? You look troubled."

One of the geldings tossed its head and blew a blast of air

from his nose. "I must speak to John straightaway." She didn't want to tell Margaret what had happened. It was a private ordeal. "Can you tell me where I might find him?"

"That all depends on why you need to speak to him." She leaned against the railing. "Hannah, you must come to accept things as they are. Theatrics will not get you back into John's good graces."

Closing her eyes, Hannah pushed down an angry retort and then refocused on the woman. "I'm aware of that, but it is urgent that I speak to him."

Margaret moved toward the carriage. "He's quite busy. The end of lambing, you know. He can't take any chances of losing lambs, with the market as it is."

"He'll want to speak to me about this matter." Hannah could barely contain her growing frustration. "Is he in the lambing shed?"

Margaret stared at her, eyes cool. "No. He's not. And he's not available for visitors. He's working in the far pastures, making certain there are no ewes who have yet to lamb. I can tell him you stopped by when he returns for dinner."

"I see." Hannah didn't know what else to say. She must speak to him. She looked about, trying to come up with an answer. *I'll have to go after Thomas myself. Perhaps I can convince Lucinda to stay until I can have her papers verified.*

"All right, then. Tell him to contact me. It's of utmost importance. I'll be in Sydney Town at the boardinghouse."

"It might be better if you explained the matter to me and then I'd be better able to inform him."

Hannah knew it was a reasonable request, but she couldn't bring herself to speak of it, not to Margaret. "No. It's best if I tell him myself."

"Of course. I'll let him know when he returns." Margaret moved back up the steps.

Disheartened, Hannah grabbed the reins tightly and started to turn the buggy toward the road. John stepped out of the shadows of a nearby shed. *John!*

Throttled by anger, Hannah glared at Margaret. "It seems you're mistaken. He is here."

"I do apologize. I had no idea. He must have come back while I was working inside."

Hannah lifted the reins, clicked her tongue, and turned the horses toward John. She glanced back at the house, where Margaret stood on the bottom step. *Perhaps she's not to be trusted.*

That was something to consider at another time. Right now Thomas was all that mattered. She urged the horses forward.

Grabbing the harness, John looked up at Hannah, concern lining his face. "What is it? I can see something's wrong. Is it Thomas? What's happened to him?"

Overcome with emotion, she longed to throw herself into John's strong protective arms and sob out the story. Of course, such an idea was unseemly, and she maintained a false sense of calm as she stepped down from the buggy. She was not unaware of his steady grip on her hand. "Thank you." She suddenly felt uncertain of how to tell him. "I am here about Thomas."

"Is he sick?"

"No."

"Injured?"

"No." Hannah took a steadying breath. "It seems Thomas has a family in England, his aunt Lucinda Davies and his grand-father Davies."

"He never mentioned anyone."

"He told me he remembers his father talking about an aunt, but it seems he knows very little about her or his grandfather. It would seem his father and mother rarely had contact with the family."

"What does that have to do with Thomas now?"

"Lucinda came to the Athertons' today . . ." Hannah paused, wishing there were an easy way to tell John the awful news. "She wants to take him back to England with her."

"Take him back?"

"She seems well intentioned. Her father, Thomas's grandfather, has a farm there and wants to see that Thomas inherits it when he dies."

"Are there no other living relatives, no uncles or . . . ?" He held out his hands palms up, looking vulnerable.

"Lucinda said Thomas's father was her only sibling. And now she and her father and Thomas are all that's left."

"Where is she?"

"She and Thomas set out for Sydney Town more than an hour ago." Again, Hannah feared the unimaginable. She'd been so distraught she'd failed to ask when the ship sailed. If the ship left before Lucinda could be stopped, she'd never see Thomas again. Fear pulsed through her and she barely managed to keep her tears in check.

"She showed me legal papers signed by the court, but how can we be certain they're legitimate?"

"I can have the governor confirm or disavow them."

"I'm afraid their ship will leave before we can do anything." Hannah felt the tattered seams holding her together begin to come apart.

John grasped her arms and squeezed gently. "Don't worry.

I'll see that he's brought home. I'm sure the governor can do something. Thomas belongs with us."

"What can be done if his family has legal claim?" Hannah could no longer hold back the tears. "I can't bear to lose him." The scene when Lucinda took him flashed through her mind. "He was so distraught, begging me to allow him to stay. I had to force him to go."

"I'll bring him back. Trust me."

Before Hannah knew what was happening, John pulled her to him. She couldn't resist the consolation and pressed her face against his shirt. The smell of him and the strength of his arms comforted her. She longed to cling to him and never let go.

Getting a hold of her emotions, she disengaged herself and took a step away from John, wiping at her tears. "I'll go with you."

"I'd like that, but I can ride faster alone. If I can overtake their carriage, perhaps we can stop this thing."

"What will you do? Lucinda seemed quite set on carrying out her duty. What can you say to convince her otherwise?"

"I don't know. But I do know that Thomas can't leave New South Wales. I'll do whatever I must. There has to be a way."

Inside Hannah screamed at the loss but managed to extend an outward composure. She looked at the house. Margaret was watching.

"You go home. When I've got him, I'll bring him straight to the Athertons'."

Hannah nodded, daring to believe John. A flicker of hope burned inside her as she watched him stride to the barn and disappear inside. She climbed into the buggy and waited. She wouldn't leave until he did.

John appeared a few minutes later, his horse saddled and

ready. He offered a smile. "Remember, God sees us and he knows Thomas belongs here in New South Wales."

"I pray you're right."

"I am." He climbed onto the horse, rode up to the buggy, and then reached out and placed a hand on Hannah's cheek. "Take heart. I'll bring him home. I promise."

He rode to the porch, talked with Margaret for a moment, and then headed off at a full gallop. Hannah could still feel the warmth of his hand against her skin. She covered the place with her own and watched until all she could see was the dust raised by his horse. *Lord, carry him safely. And I beg you to bring back my son.*

12

Guilt held a tight grip on John as he headed toward Sydney Town. Leaning forward in his saddle, he urged his horse onward, faster and faster. He had to find Thomas. The road flashed beneath rider and animal.

I should have gone to see him. I should have made the time.

Self-recrimination served no good purpose now. He needed to focus on finding his son, needed to focus on the road, focus on a way to get him back.

He'll be fine. He's a strong lad, he told himself, pushing the horse harder. *I've got to catch them.* But he wondered what would happen when he did overtake them. How would he persuade Lucinda to relinquish the boy?

His horse in a lather, its sides heaving, John knew he'd have to slow his pace soon or he'd kill the animal. Still, he kept moving. He must convince Lucinda to let Thomas stay. *He's not meant to live in England. When I explain to her, she'll see reason.*

Even as the thoughts rolled through his mind, John had little hope. If the woman who had taken Thomas was truly his aunt, she had rights to him. And according to Hannah, Lucinda was not predisposed to accommodate Thomas's New South Wales family.

To the west, dark clouds billowed and piled into great dark mounds. A wall of rain moved toward him. John slowed and took a coat out of his saddle pack and pushed his arms into the sleeves. He moved his hat forward, tipped his head down, and continued on.

The rain started in big droplets, splattering the brim of his hat and the shoulders of his coat. Dry ground quickly turned wet. When the wall of moisture reached John, he peered through a wet haze. The horse trudged forward, splashing through fresh mud and water that flowed into ruts, creating small rivers. Rain dripped from his hat.

Wretched miles passed, but John never came upon a carriage. *They had too great a lead,* he conceded. When his horse slipped and nearly went down, he stopped beneath the broad mantle of an acacia. Dusk had already reached the nearby valleys and crept toward the road and the river.

Miserable and wet, John sheltered beneath the tree until the rain stopped. Darkness was fast approaching, and John decided it would be too dangerous to continue. He'd stay put for the night and set out early in the morning.

He led his horse to the river to drink, then tethered him. "Sorry I rode you so hard," he said, giving the animal a pat. The evening haze crept over the hillsides and up the river as John removed the saddle and blanket. He set them in the driest spot he could find, beneath the sprawling branches of the acacia, then gathered a handful of dry grass from the base of the tree and with great effort managed to bring a fledgling fire to life. He added dry bits of bark and tinder and finally pushed back the darkness and warmed his sodden body.

Miserable and cold, he sat on the ground and rested his back against his saddle and drank from a flask, wishing he'd thought to bring food. His empty stomach grumbled. He stared at the fire for a long while, then lay down and tried to sleep. A breeze stirred the trees, and birds fluttered within the branches, their calls quiet and throaty as they settled for the night.

John's mind returned to Hannah and Thomas. They'd all been through so much. *Lord, why this? Haven't we had trials enough?* He stared at blue and orange flames licking at the wood. *What purpose can there be in this? Certainly Thomas belongs here. Hannah needs him.*

He turned onto his back and gazed at the dark sky, wishing God would speak to him. The only sounds he heard were the chirp of frogs, the quiet flow of the river, and the pop of burning wood. Where was God?

Frustration and fear were a blight. Unable to lie still a moment longer, John pushed to his feet. Shoving his hands into his pockets, he stared into the fire, then paced back and forth in front of it. What if he couldn't convince Lucinda to leave Thomas? What if he never saw the boy again? He looked up at the sky where clouds had parted, revealing a glimmer of light from a full moon. "And what if I never stop loving Hannah?"

Suddenly angry and overwhelmed by the weight of his life, he shouted, "I can't do this! I can't! Don't ask any more of me!"

He squatted right where he stood, covered his head with his arms, and sobbed. Why would God require so much from him? Why?

Spent and knowing sleep would not come, John decided to move on. His horse had rested; the clouds cleared, revealing a round, yellow moon to light his way. After putting out the fire, he saddled his horse, climbed onto his back, and set off toward Sydney Town.

The moon illuminated fields and rolling hills, but they were mostly in shadow and looked ominous. From time to time he'd see lantern light from inside a barn or a house. There was an occasional mournful howl of a dingo and the flutter of creatures in the darkness.

The eerie cry of a curlew cut through the night—*wer-loo, wer-loo.* The hair on the back of John's neck prickled, and he thought it an absurd response to a gangly, harmless bird. The familiar thump of a kangaroo on the road ahead caused his horse to balk. The gelding tossed his head and wouldn't move. "Get on with you. There's nothing to fear from a roo." He kicked the horse's sides, and the animal pranced forward.

He gazed into the darkness, barely able to make out vague shapes of trees and other vegetation. The sharp snap of a breaking branch fractured the hush. Continuing on probably hadn't been a good idea. John stared at the shadows, wondering what had made the sound. He hoped it was nothing of consequence. He rested a hand on his pistol. Aborigines and escaped prisoners were known to travel during the night so as not to be seen.

When the lights of Sydney Town finally winked at John from the distance, he felt relief and a renewed urge to find Thomas. The search would have to wait until morning, however. To look would be of little use at this hour. And he could do with a bit of sleep. *Most likely she's got him at the boardinghouse. I'll go over first thing.*

John led his horse into the livery. "I've need of a stall," he told a boy sitting on a hay-strewn floor dozing with his back pressed against the wall.

The lad jumped to his feet, looking bleary-eyed. "That one there's empty," he said, pointing at a stall just beyond the door.

"Thank you." John led the horse into the enclosure and re-

140

moved the saddle, blanket, and bridle, then fed him a handful of grain. Running his hand along the animal's side, he said, "Thank you for carrying me so faithfully." With a pat, he walked out and asked the boy, "Can you see to it that he gets a drink?"

"I can do that all right."

"And feed him in the morning?"

"Yes, sir."

"Thank you. I'll pay you tomorrow before I leave." John walked out and headed down the street toward the hotel. Stepping into the lobby, he wondered if Lucinda Davies was anywhere about. He walked to the front desk. "I'll need a bed for the night."

"What's left of it," the clerk said tersely. "Sign the register." His eyelids drooping, he turned the ledger so it faced John and handed him a quill.

John glanced down the list of names but didn't see a Lucinda Davies. *As I thought, she's at the boardinghouse. Or she might have used a different name.* He leaned on the counter. "Can you tell me if a woman and a boy checked in earlier?"

"Not that I know. Never saw no one like that. Why you looking for them?"

John sought a suitable answer. "I'm supposed to meet them here. I'm certain they'll arrive tomorrow. Must have been held up by something or other." He signed the registry, accepted his key and a candle, then walked up a dimly lit stairway and down the corridor to his room.

Opening the door, John set the candle on a bureau and dropped onto the bed, exhausted. He closed his eyes and his mind immediately went to Thomas. The lad must be frightened and longing for home. *Lord, how am I going to convince Lucinda to let him stay? Tell me what to say.*

Knowing he'd need his wits when he met with Lucinda, he blew out the candle, pulled a blanket up to his chest, and rolled onto his side, hoping for sleep. Even at this late hour, sounds of revelry from a pub drifted up the street. John turned onto his back and stared at the ceiling. Quiet is what he needed, not just in the world but in his soul.

He threw off the blanket and moved to the window. His eyes went to the harbor where a ship lay at anchor. Light from port windows shimmered in the darkness, reflecting off flat waters. Was this the ship, the one that threatened to carry Thomas across the sea? The thought skewered his insides.

He stared at it, and memories of his own passage rushed at him—a dark hold teeming with noxious smells, death, and despair. He scrubbed his face with his hands, trying to rid himself of the images; he had a new life now.

Back then he'd not been able to imagine that goodness waited for him. Yet, he now had a family and a fine farm. He'd make a name for himself and Hannah . . . "Hannah." For a moment he'd forgotten she'd been lost to him. As if he'd only just realized the terrible truth, sorrow swelled and threatened to bury John in misery. He looked at a cloudless sky. The moon disappeared beyond the horizon and stars flickered. *If only it were Hannah and me.* He squeezed his eyes shut. *Lord, I've tried to love Margaret. But I don't. I can't create something that doesn't exist.*

John knew he was pitying himself and tried to stand against it. *Marriage isn't just about love. It's about commitment and creating something for the future. Margaret and I can do that together.*

He returned to his bed, stretching out on his back, hands clasped over his stomach. In the morning he'd rescue Thomas and take him home.

A tiny thought crept into the back of his mind. *Margaret and I can have others.* Loathing himself for allowing such an idea even a moment of consideration, he said, "Thomas can't be replaced."

But you'd best make peace with the possibility of his going.

John knew life didn't always give a man what he desired, but Scripture reassured him that all things had a purpose. It was time that he accepted his new life—time to fully commit to Margaret.

He pulled the blanket over him and fell into a fitful sleep.

<hr />

He woke to the gray light of morning and was immediately fully alert. He threw off the blanket and moved to the pitcher and bowl on the bureau. Pouring water into the bowl, he splashed his face and patted it dry with a rough towel, then stared at himself in a distorted mirror. "You must find a way to convince her."

He dressed and headed for the boardinghouse. A buxom woman with blue eyes and graying brown hair met him at the door. "It's a bit early to be looking for a room, but I've got one if ye have a need."

"Actually, I'm looking for someone. I believe they're staying here."

The woman's expression turned suspicious. "And might I ask your intentions?"

"My son is with a woman called Lucinda Davies. Her intention is to take him out of the country."

"That sounds like real trouble."

"That it is. She's not asked my permission or proven to me that she has legal claim to him."

The woman's eyes widened and she lifted a brow. "What rights can she have if he's your son?"

"I adopted him," John admitted reluctantly.

"I see." She glanced up the staircase. "You can wait in the parlor. I'll tell her you're here."

"Thank you." He watched as the woman climbed the stairs. She made a small "oof" sound with each step, her extra weight adding a burden to the climb.

John moved to the parlor, remembering that this was the place he'd met with Margaret when she'd first come to Sydney Town. At the time he'd been distracted and hadn't really looked at the room. It was tidy and simply furnished. A fire burned low in the hearth, and a woven rug hugged a scarred wooden floor. A harpsichord sat in one corner. John wondered if anyone ever played it.

He crossed to the window and stared out at the street. In the soft light of morning, all seemed serene. He walked to the doorway, his footsteps echoing against the wooden planking, and looked up at the empty staircase. With a sigh, he returned to his post at the window. A dray lumbered past.

John's muscles felt tight, and he rolled his shoulders, hoping to loosen them and gentle his nerves. What should he say to Miss Davies? After much thought, he was still uncertain how to approach her.

The rustle of skirts preceded her. John turned as a small, plain-looking woman walked through the door. Her light brown hair was disheveled and her eyes were red-rimmed and puffy.

"Are you John Bradshaw?" she asked.

"That I am."

"Good. I'm glad you're here."

John was taken aback at the greeting. He'd expected they'd be at odds. "My wife . . . I mean, Hannah said you're Thomas's aunt and that you intend to take him with you when you return to England."

"That's true." She moved to the divan and sat. "I have every right to take him. He is my nephew. My father and I are his only blood relatives." She clasped and unclasped her hands and gazed at the window. Her voice barely more than a whisper, she said, "There's been a bit of a trouble."

"Trouble?"

"Yes. He's gone." Anxious eyes met John's. "When I arose this morning, his bed was empty. I can't find him." Her voice sounded strident.

"You've no idea where he is?"

Her eyes glistened with tears. "I can only speculate. My best guess would be that he's making his way back to Parramatta."

"When did you last see him?"

"I slept little during the night. I checked him at 3:00 a.m. He seemed to be sleeping." She stood and walked to the hearth. "The ship will be leaving tomorrow with the tide, and I haven't the least idea of how to find him. I've booked passage for us both."

John didn't know what to say. He hoped Thomas was far from Sydney Town, yet he knew a lad traveling the road alone could be in danger.

Using a handkerchief, Lucinda dabbed at her tears. "I shouldn't have come. I've made a mess of things. My father insisted Thomas return to England."

"Perhaps if I spoke to him."

"That's impossible."

"But why not?"

145

"He's in England."

"He sent a woman alone?"

"No. Of course not. I have an escort—Garrett Bradley. He works for my father." Her eyes glinted with defiance. "However, if I'd have chosen to travel on my own, I would have done so. I'm quite capable. Since my brother left, it's just been me and my father. The management of the farm has been my responsibility."

Her tone softer, she continued, "Father would have come, but his health is not good." She tucked her handkerchief into a pocket of her dress and tipped up her chin. "I've not seen my brother in many years, but I know he was a good man. He didn't deserve to be transported. He was hardworking and honest. Difficulty with a debt was his undoing."

"He had a fine reputation."

"My father's never gotten over his arrest or his death. Having Thomas with him will ease his suffering."

John felt sorry for the woman, but knew he had to think about Thomas. "That may be, but your father's at the end of his life. Thomas is only just beginning his. He has a fine life here. And you must consider that, if his father wanted him to live in England, he would have returned after serving his time."

Indecision flickered in Lucinda's eyes.

"It seems clear to me that Thomas has no desire to live in England. Otherwise he wouldn't have run off."

"I must admit that after spending time with the lad, I've come to understand how much he loves you and your wife. He doesn't want to leave." A button on her cuff had come undone, and she pushed it back into place. "If it were up to me, I'd not be here at all." She met John's gaze. "Please believe me when I say that I have no wish to cause you or Thomas harm. I find him to be a bright and upstanding lad."

She held her hands primly in front of her and glanced toward the window. "Something terrible could happen to him here. This is a wild place."

"I'd say there are more dangers to consider traveling across the seas than he'll find here."

Lucinda's expression registered her agreement. "Can you find him?"

"And bring him back here to you?" John shook his head. "He's a strong-willed lad. If you try to force him, he'll only run again."

Lucinda closed her eyes and tipped her face toward the ceiling as if saying a silent prayer. When John had first seen her, she seemed frail, but now he could feel her strength of will.

"I know that." She dropped her arms to her sides. "All right, then. I'll see to it that the papers are transferred, allowing you legal rights to adopt him. My father will have to accept it."

"Thank you." John was surprised she'd surrendered so easily and wondered if she could be trusted. He was uncertain of just what to do. Should he go after Thomas or make sure Lucinda took care of the legal matters as she'd said she would? "You'll go to the governor's office today?"

"Yes, of course."

"And leave the papers with the solicitor?"

"I pledge that I will."

John studied her, trying to discern if she were telling the truth or not. He had little choice but to trust her. He needed to find Thomas. At any rate, the boy wouldn't be going to England. "All right, then. I'd better get after Thomas and find him."

She reached out a hand toward John. "From time to time will you send word to me of his well-being? And if ever he desires to travel to England, please tell him he is welcome to visit our farm."

"Of course."

She moved to a desk, sat down, and took out pen and ink. "I'll leave my address with you." She wrote the information on the paper, blew on the ink, and handed it to John, her eyes shimmering with tears. "Remind him of his aunt Lucinda and his grandfather Davies."

"I will." John glanced at the address, then folded the paper and shoved it into his jacket pocket. Graditude filled him. "You can't know how much this means to me and to Hannah. Thank you. God's good will to you."

"And to you," she said.

With a tip of his hat, he hurried to the door. He needed to find his son.

John hurried from business to business, asking if anyone had seen Thomas. With each answer of no, he became more concerned. Had the lad left town before dawn? He'd be in danger on the highway at night.

He set out on the road to Parramatta, praying that Thomas was safe and simply in a hurry to get home. Each time he met someone on the road, he asked if they'd seen a boy, but no one had. John began to wonder if Thomas might have decided to hide out somewhere for a time. Still, he moved on, stopping occasionally along the river to see if the lad might be hiding in the rushes along the banks. He found nothing, not a sign of him.

When night fell, John stopped. He couldn't take a chance of missing him in the dark. He watered and tethered his horse and settled down beside a small fire to a meal of bread and dried beef he'd procured from an inn. He stared into the flames, wondering just where Thomas could be and if he might have missed him. He wished there were some way to continue his search.

The hoot of an owl and the chirping of frogs filled the emptiness. Clouds closed out the moon and a cold mist reached a hand over the territory. John bundled inside his coat and moved closer to the fire. He stared into the darkness, imagining how cold and frightened Thomas must be.

The snap of a branch disrupted the chorus of night sounds. Frogs turned silent. John sat upright, trying to see into the blackness. "Is someone there?" He grabbed his pistol and pushed to his feet. Something moved in the bushes. "Who's there?" He held up the pistol. "I'll not hesitate to use my weapon."

"It's me."

"Thomas?"

The bushes trembled and then parted. Thomas stepped into the light of the fire. He stared at John, his gaze bold. "I'll not go back. Ye can't make me. And if ye try, I'll run away again."

John smiled at the boy's boldness and pushed his pistol into its holster. "Come here, lad. You nearly scared the life out of me."

Hesitantly, Thomas moved toward him. "I mean it, I'll not go back."

"You don't have to. Your aunt has agreed to let you stay."

"Truly?"

"As long as you like."

A smile broke out on Thomas's face.

John held out his arms and the lad ran into them.

Thomas hugged John tightly. "I'm glad ye came for me."

"Did you think I wouldn't?"

"I didn't know. You've not come to see me or Mum since we left the farm."

"I know. I'm sorry. I meant to, but there's been so much work to be done." John held him more securely. "From now on we'll see each other often."

Thomas tightened his hold on his father.

Finally, John held the boy away from him. He tried to look stern. "You shouldn't have run off the way you did."

"I'm sorry, but I just couldn't get on that boat. I couldn't leave ye . . . or Mum."

"I know." John embraced him again. "Your aunt Lucinda cares about you. We have reason to thank her. I'd say a letter is in order, just as soon as you get home."

Thomas moved toward the fire. "She was kind to me. Told me all 'bout me grandfather. Maybe one day I'll get to meet him, eh?"

"Perhaps." John took off his coat. "You look cold and your cheeks feel like ice." He draped the coat about the boy's shoulders.

The two settled on the ground, huddling together for warmth. Thomas ate some of the bread and dried beef, then drank half a container of water. John pulled Thomas into a sideways hug. "Your mother will be glad to see you."

"I feared I'd lost ye both."

"How'd you find me?" John asked.

"Didn't really. Ye rode past and I've been following." Thomas grinned, then his expression turned serious. "I was afraid ye'd take me back, so I stayed hidden."

"Well, you have no worries there. You'll always be mine and Hannah's . . . and Margaret's."

Thomas's lips tightened into a line. "So yer to make a go of it with her, then?"

"Yes. She's my wife. Do you understand?"

He shrugged. "Don't know for sure. Maybe. But I wish things were the way they used to be."

"Margaret's a fine woman. And she cares about you. Give her a chance and you might grow to love her."

"I'll do me best, but . . . well, I can't see my lovin' her. Anyways, not like Mum."

John understood all too well. He cared about Margaret, but his heart still belonged to Hannah.

13

Hannah smoothed a crease in Thomas's collar. "Did you pack your bag?"

"Yes, Mum."

Although Thomas had spent only two nights with his aunt, it had felt like a lifetime. This visit with his father would be a full week, and Hannah knew she'd miss him terribly.

"Ye look worried, Mum."

"Do I? I'm not. It's just that I'll miss you."

"I won't be gone that long."

Hannah brushed back his thick blond hair. "I know. Don't worry about me. I'll be fine." She held him at arm's length and studied him. "You're getting so grown up."

Thomas smiled and threw back his shoulders. "Dad said I can help with the shearing."

"He has quite a few sheep. He'll need help." She tipped his face up so his eyes met hers. "But you're not old enough to do any shearing. I don't want you handling the shears."

Thomas's eyes momentarily turned defiant, then cooled. "All right. Anyway, there's going to be help this year."

"I heard that." Hannah straightened. "Your dad will be here any moment. You're sure you have everything?"

"Yes, Mum."

Thomas glanced out the window. "'Course there's Percy and the Connors are gonna be there and me friend Douglas. And there'll be food, lots of it. Dad said Margaret's been cooking all week."

"I heard she's a fine cook." Hannah felt a pang of resentment. She and John had planned for this day when the farm had prospered enough to need help with shearing and she'd be cooking for everyone and lending a hand.

Still watching out the window, Thomas said, "Margaret's not as good a cook as ye are, though."

Hannah smiled, warmed by his loyalty.

The sound of an approaching wagon announced John's arrival. Hannah tousled Thomas's blond mop. "You're in need of a haircut." She took his hat down from the shelf. "This will keep the sun off your face."

"Thanks, Mum." Thomas pushed it down on his head and opened the door.

"Now, mind your manners." She kissed his cheek. "And have a fine time, eh?"

"I will." He stepped onto the porch.

John pulled the wagon to a stop in front of the cabin. Hannah's stomach dropped at the sight of Margaret sitting beside him. Hannah hadn't expected her, but of course she'd want to accompany John whenever possible. Life on the farm could be lonely.

"Good day." John climbed down.

Thomas ran to his father and flung his arms about his waist. "I've been waiting."

"Hello there." He laughed and scooped Thomas up, even as big as he was. "Sorry for being late." John smiled at the lad and set him back on the ground. "You're not a bit eager, are you?" he teased.

"Just want to get going. I figure there's lots to do."

"True. I've plenty of work for you."

"I'm ready." Thomas climbed into the back of the wagon and stood behind the seat. "Hello, Margaret," he said politely.

She smiled at him. "Grand to see you, Thomas."

Hat in his hands, John walked to the porch steps. "It's a fine day."

Hannah glanced at the blue sky. "A good one for shearing." She looked into his hazel eyes and immediately old feelings surfaced. She turned her attention to the wagon. "It seems your dream has come true."

"I've a lot to thank God for."

Hannah thought she heard sorrow in his voice. She glanced at him. "We both do," she said, knowing they were each thinking of the dreams they'd shared together.

"I've still a lot of work to do, it never ends. But the sheep are healthy, and we've had no trouble with dingoes."

"Good."

He acted as if he had something more to say.

Finally, John tucked his hat under one arm and put a foot on the bottom step. "Margaret was hoping to have a word with you," he said quietly. "Would you mind?"

Hannah glanced at the woman, wondering what more she could possibly have to say. The last time the two had spoken, Margaret had made it clear Hannah no longer belonged at the farm. The memory stung. "Of course I'll speak to her."

"Good then. I'll visit with Perry whilst you two chat." He

resettled his hat on his head and walked to the wagon, giving Margaret a hand down.

Hannah tried not to watch when Margaret stepped close to John and gazed up at him with admiration. "I won't be long," she said, her voice gentle.

Thomas had jumped down from the back of the wagon and stood beside his father. The sight of the three together was unnerving. "I'll be back shortly," John said and walked toward the shop, Thomas at his side. Hannah felt like an outsider.

She rested a hand on her stomach, feeling the small swell where her child grew inside her. *We'll have each other.* One day she'd have to tell John about the baby. Its presence would complicate things.

Hannah had considered moving away and saying nothing at all to John about the child, but that would be unfair to everyone, especially to the baby who would grow up not knowing its father. She'd know the proper time and would tell him then.

Margaret walked toward her. She was dressed in a lightweight summer frock and had pinned up only some of her hair, allowing the rest to fall in rich auburn waves down her back. She moved with ease and confidence, holding her reticule close to her abdomen as if it contained something of importance.

"Good morning," Hannah said, managing to smile.

"It is a fine morning indeed, even with the heat."

"November's always quite warm," Hannah said. *I suppose I'll have to invite her in,* she thought, balking at the idea. "Please, come in. Would you like tea?"

"I would. I'm thirsty after that drive." She followed Hannah inside. "It's dreadfully hot."

Taking down two of her best cups and saucers, Hannah filled

them with tea left from the morning's breakfast. It felt strange to have Margaret in her home and acting as if they were friends. *Why shouldn't we be? She seems a fine lady, refined.* Hannah felt plain in comparison, especially now that she'd taken to wearing shifts to conceal her condition.

Margaret sat demurely in a chair at Hannah's small table. She kept her hands in front of her, resting them on her reticule. "This is quite nice. Small, but charming."

"Thank you." Hannah placed the cups and saucers on a tray along with spoons and a bowl of sugar. It was the last of the sugar, but Hannah didn't want Margaret thinking she was impoverished. "Thomas and I are content here."

"I'm pleased to hear that."

Hannah set the tray on the table and sat down. She handed Margaret a cup and saucer. "There's sugar if you like."

"I prefer mine with a bit of milk, if you have it."

"Oh. I'm sorry, but I've none in the house right now." Hannah felt a flush of embarrassment.

"Not to worry. This is fine." Margaret sipped. "It's very good, not at all bitter."

Hannah took a drink. She'd have preferred sugar, but it was a luxury she could do without. She didn't want to take advantage of Mrs. Goudy's generosity.

A fearsome silence hung between the two women. Hannah had no idea what to say. If she allowed herself to dwell on all that had transpired since Margaret had come to New South Wales, anger would consume her. If not for Margaret, she and John would still be sharing their lives. Why was she here in her house? What more could she possibly want?

"I daresay, I don't know how I'll tolerate the heat. England is much cooler. And the bugs here are dreadful."

156

"You'll become accustomed. But December and January will most likely be worse."

"That's not reassuring." Margaret set her cup in its saucer. "I suppose you're curious about why I'm here."

"Yes, I am."

"It's my hope that we can mend any hard feelings between us. I've never been comfortable with contentiousness. I've always been one to seek out the good in others and to achieve harmony, if possible. And I'm concerned about Thomas. It's especially important for him that we have a good rapport. He's such a bright lad and will surely feel any strain that might exist between us."

"Of course you're right. But I assure you, I've accepted my new life and I'm quite all right, not the least bit troubled." Hannah wasn't about to let Margaret know her true feelings.

"I thought that you might feel wronged. And if that's true, I understand completely. If the circumstances were reversed, I would certainly be distraught."

Hannah didn't speak but waited to hear what else Margaret had to say.

"I'd like us to be friends. I admire you greatly for your stalwart support of John through all this. And I can see you've a kind spirit. No woman should have to experience what you have, and yet you've managed to do so with grace."

Hannah was taken aback. She hadn't expected kindness from Margaret. Also, she knew that inside she was none of the things Margaret had said. Self-reproach nagged at her.

"Thank you for your thoughtfulness, and I quite agree we should maintain a good rapport. It will make life more pleasant for all of us." Even though she spoke calmly and with grace, Hannah felt a tumult inside. She didn't want to be friends with this woman.

"You can't imagine how relieved I am to hear you say that." Margaret smiled. "I want to give you something to show my high regard for you." Margaret opened her reticule and took out a small gift box. She handed it to Hannah.

"That's very kind of you, but not necessary."

"It pleases me to give it to you."

Hannah looked at the floral decoupage box. "It's lovely." She opened it and inside lay a delicate sachet. "How charming." She lifted out the cloth packet, smelling its delicate sweet bouquet and wondering if this were a ploy of some kind.

Margaret smiled. "I picked the most fragrant flowers I could find and dried them myself."

"Thank you." Hannah settled the sachet in its box. She felt a flush of shame. Did she no longer trust anyone? She'd allowed the cruel rumors to tarnish her thinking. "I do hope we can be friends."

Margaret's dark eyes warmed. "I look forward to more visits, then." She stood. "Now I'd best be on my way. I'm sure John is anxious to get home. There's much to be done."

Hannah followed her to the door. "Margaret . . . I'm glad you came."

"Me too." She strolled toward the wagon, where John and Thomas already waited.

What an odd turn of events, Hannah thought, glancing at the box in her hand, now more convinced than ever that Margaret was a decent person. *She'll be good for John and for Thomas.* John assisted Margaret into the wagon, and against her will, a painful stab of loss pierced Hannah. Although she was convinced she could accept the change and Margaret, she also understood that she'd never stop loving John.

John clipped away the last of the wool from a distressed ewe and then set her free to scramble toward an outside pen. He straightened, pressing a hand against his aching lower back, and wiped sweat from his brow. "I could use a drink."

"I'll get ye some," Thomas said, hurrying to a water barrel and scooping out a dipperful. He splashed water as he rushed back to his dad. Handing the ladle to John, he asked, "Can I have a hand at shearing?"

John downed the water and looked at the enthusiastic eleven-year-old. "You think you're strong enough?"

"I am."

John smiled. "I think you need a few years' growth yet."

"I'm strong for me age. Ye said so yerself."

"True, and you are, but this work is for men. And I'll not have you handling clippers." He held up the ones he'd been using. "Your mother'd never forgive me if I sent you home minus a finger. Besides, I need your help with the wool. It takes a good eye to clear it of dirt and bugs."

The light dimmed in Thomas's blue eyes. "Next year, then?"

"We'll see." John clapped him on the back.

Thomas gathered up the wool at John's feet and carried it to the sorting table.

Quincy joined him. "Nasty work, eh."

"That it is." Thomas looked through the white thicket of wool, picking out most of the filth.

"I'd say it's time for a rest and some food." Quincy glanced at John. "Yer dad looks done in."

"You're right there," John said. "I could do with a break."

Margaret stepped into the shed. "I've got lunch set out. You best come and eat before the flies get to it." She wrinkled up her nose. "It stinks to the rafters in here."

"What else would you expect with a barnful of sheep?" John grinned.

Margaret moved to him. "You're working too hard. You should rest."

She put an arm about his waist, and John fought the impulse to pull away. He wasn't used to the familiarity. *She's your wife, man. And she needs more from you, more than you've offered her.* He gave her a quick sideways hug. "You'd better keep your distance. I'm filthy."

Margaret eyed him. "You are at that." She stepped back and turned to watch some of the helpers. They were grubby and sweating, each with a bawling ewe pinned against them or against the floor and their clippers steadily cutting away heavy wool coats. "This is too much," Margaret said. "The noise and smell . . . how does one manage?"

"I rather like it," Thomas said, standing beside his father.

John rested a hand on Thomas's head. "It gets in your blood."

"Well, it's not in mine, not yet." Margaret's voice sounded shrill. She looked as if she were trying to calm herself and then said more cordially, "You and the others should eat. I'd hate for my hard work to go to waste."

"I'll be there directly." John wondered if Hannah would have complained or been put off by the smell and grime. He knew the answer. She'd be grateful for it. She'd see the reward of hard work and do everything she could to help.

"Come on, then." Margaret strode out of the shed, swatting at flies buzzing about her head. "Oh, these bugs are merciless."

She glanced back at John. "If we were in England, I wouldn't have had to cover all the food."

"We'll be there straightaway." John was unable to keep the irritation out of his voice. Margaret's eyes registered her hurt. "I'll tell the shearers," he said more kindly.

"Thank you." Margaret headed for the house.

"My stomach told me it was time to eat hours ago," Quincy said with a grin. He called to the others, "Lunch! Soon's ye finish the sheep ye've got, come and get something to eat." He started for the door. "Mrs. Bradshaw's a fine cook."

One by one, the men finished. Each stopped at the water barrel to quench their thirst before heading to the house. Some splashed their faces and rinsed grime from their arms and hands.

His celebratory mood gone, John watched. He grabbed up armloads of wool and set them on the table.

Thomas stuck his head in the door. "Dad, come on."

"I'll just do this first."

Thomas stared at him. "Everything all right?"

"Fine. You go ahead. There's one last ewe in this batch. I'll finish her up and then I'll be in."

"All right." Thomas turned reluctantly and walked toward the house.

John moved to the pen. The ewe stood with her face to a corner as if she were hoping to be overlooked. Afraid he'd have to chase her down, John headed toward her. She remained still, and he was able to grab her. "Come on, then. Your turn."

He hefted the sheep and carried her to the shearing floor. Bracing her against his leg, he started clipping away wool. Bleating, she struggled to get free, but he held her firmly. Finally she settled down and allowed herself to be shorn.

John's mind was elsewhere—with Hannah. This was their dream, not his and Margaret's. Hannah would have worked alongside him, and she'd not have fussed about the inconveniences. In the past, she'd cleaned and skirted the wool, saying it was better than having to sleep on it the way she'd done at the Female Factory.

He turned the ewe onto her other side and clipped away the rest of her fleece. She was quiet now. He finished as quickly as possible and carried her to the chute to join the rest of the naked mob.

He picked up the wool and hauled it to the table and started cleaning it. Feeling as if he were being watched, he turned to see Quincy standing just inside the door studying him.

His expression was serious. "You'd better come get something to eat before it's gone. Those men are hungry, and they'll not think to leave anything for ye." He grinned.

"I'm coming," John said with a sigh.

"What's wrong, eh? This is a good day, one ye've been working toward a long while." He looked at the bundles of wool. "Ye'll make a fine profit. The quality's good, and so are the prices." He leaned against the doorjamb, arms folded over his chest. "I remember when ye first moved onto the place; ye had a mere fifty acres and a shack." He chuckled. "A real land baron ye were then."

"I remember."

"Ye've a fine farm here, John. One might even call it an estate, eh?" A smile played at Quincy's lips. "Figure it's time I had a better house."

"You deserve one. I'll see to it that you get it. As soon as I get paid for this latest batch of wool, we'll start work on a new place for you."

"Suits me fine."

John smiled, but he couldn't rid himself of the heaviness of heart. He lifted his hat and swiped back his hair. "It's not the way I imagined it." He pushed his hat back on his head and squatted with his back pressed against the barn wall.

Quincy hunkered down beside him. "What's wrong, eh?"

John didn't know whether to say anything or not. What good would it do? But Hannah's presence was almost palpable. He longed for her. "Hannah's supposed to be here. I started this with her; it was supposed to me and her, not . . ."

"Not Margaret?" Quincy glanced at the men sitting in the shade eating their midday meal. "She made a fine lunch for all of us."

"Yeah. I know; she's trying." John shrugged.

"So it's not what ye planned, it's still good. Ye've a fine place and a beautiful woman who loves ye. I'd say ye ought to be grateful for what ye've been given. A woman like her would never give me a second look."

John blew out a breath and smiled. "I know a few gals 'round who'd like you to come calling."

"That so?" Quincy grinned. "I don't mind calling, just don't want them to follow me home."

"There's a lot to be said for having a woman beside you, makes life more agreeable. But it's got to be the right woman."

"Who's to say Margaret's not?" Quincy picked up a piece of straw and rolled it between his fingers. "When ye lived in London, she's the one ye picked. If ye'd not been arrested and never met Hannah, ye'd be right pleased to have her . . . wouldn't ye?"

The question hung in the air. In the beginning he'd loved her, then he'd grown used to her. And after a time, they chose different paths. She was enticed by merrymaking and shopping and everything else that London offered. He'd wanted to explore the world and eventually settle down to a quiet life.

"What I wanted then is of no consequence. I have to live with what's happened, even if it means accepting less than I'd hoped for."

14

Catharine walked alongside Hannah, her limp more pronounced than usual. Offering an arm to her friend and employer, Hannah said, "I can get you a remedy from Doctor Gelson while I'm in Parramatta."

"Thank you dear, but he left a powder for me when he visited last." With a shake of her head, she added, "Sadly, there are days it seems to do little good." She turned her attention to Dalton and the buggy. "I think it would be wise if Dalton drove you into town. I'm always a bit nervous when any of you gals go off on your own."

"Parramatta's not far and I've heard no reports of aboriginal trouble nor of prison escapes." Hannah knew having an escort would be wise, but today she wanted to be alone, to travel the road with her thoughts and no one else's.

"And with the quinsy going around—perhaps you should wait. There have been at least three cases so far, two in Parramatta and another at the Female Factory. You can buy fabric when we're sure it's safe to be in town." She turned concerned eyes on Hannah. "You've been a bit under the weather recently and may be vulnerable."

"I'm perfectly healthy," Hannah said, knowing Catharine was referring to the queasiness and vomiting she'd experienced early in her pregnancy. That had passed and she now felt quite robust. "Whatever it was, I've had no recent trouble. You worry too much." She offered a reassuring smile.

"I care about you." Catharine patted Hannah's hand.

"It warms my heart to know that, but if I were to stay home every time some malady or other was going around, I'd never leave my house."

Catharine gave her a dour look. "You know well enough that quinsy is not just a 'malady,' it can be dreadful and deadly." She pressed a hand to the base of her throat. "I've known entire families who have succumbed to it."

"Yes, but that can be said of many diseases." Hannah kissed Catharine's cheek. "I'm glad for your concern, but try not to worry. I'll be careful and do only what I must, then come straight home after seeing Lydia." She set a hand on the wheel of the buggy. "It will be pure pleasure to shop for fabric. My head is already awhirl with design ideas for dresses. I can scarcely wait to begin sewing for the ladies at the Factory. I remember how receiving a new dress lifted my spirits. We had so little."

"I wish I could do more to help those poor women."

"When you visited the prison, it felt as if an angel had come to us. And not just because of the dresses, but because you looked kindly upon us. Most didn't care a whit about us or the conditions. Sadly, there are still few who give the unfortunate souls in the prisons any thought."

Catharine gave Hannah's arm a gentle squeeze. "Thank you, dear."

Hannah climbed into the buggy. "I'd better be off or I'll have no time to visit with Lydia."

"Be watchful," Catharine warned.

"I shall." Hannah tightened the sash of her bonnet. "I'll be home by early afternoon." She slapped the reins, and the horses set off.

It felt good to be on her way somewhere, anywhere. The Athertons were kind and her cottage was more than adequate, but traveling, even if only to Parramatta, distracted Hannah from the shadow of sadness that had been with her these past months.

As the roadway disappeared beneath the wheels of the buggy, heat and biting flies besieged her. The peaceful, pleasurable trip she'd imagined wasn't to be. Instead, she swatted at flies and urged the horses to a faster pace, hoping to create a cooling breeze.

A barge loaded with crates and bags of grain moved upriver. Two men drove poles into the muddy river bottom and pushed it forward. The image carried Hannah back to her journey inland from Sydney Town. The Female Factory and its squalor had awaited her. She envisioned the poor souls imprisoned there now. Rosalyn's and Marjorie's tragic ends and Abigail's plain angular face came to mind. Abigail had always seemed resilient, but the last time Hannah had visited the Factory, she could see that years of deprivation had taken a toll on the sturdy woman.

Hannah put the image from her mind. This was to be a time of rest for her—to think on pleasantries. She let her eyes roam over the trees and bushes along the riverside. They were alive with squawking, trilling birds, each contending to have its voice heard. Hannah tried to count them but stopped at forty. There were too many, most dressed in bright feathers—reds, yellows, oranges, and myriad shades of blue. They lit up the foliage.

Hannah listened to the songs, thinking it must feel good to have something to sing about or to be free to let out whatever emotion you felt without thought or care to what someone might think. *It would be rather nice to be a bird.*

In spite of the heat and bugs, Hannah enjoyed her drive to Parramatta. Once there, it didn't take long to complete her errands. Her arms laden with bundles of cloth and a bag of thread and new needles, she walked toward the buggy, anxious to meet with Lydia.

Her empty stomach grumbled, and she hoped Lydia would be able to join her for lunch. She'd had no opportunity to send a message.

After placing her purchases in the buggy, she strolled down the street toward the apothecary. She felt a strange fluttering sensation in her abdomen and stopped. It came again. *What is it?* she wondered, then realized the cause. "The baby," she whispered, wonderment filling her. *My baby.*

"Mum, how grand to see ye!"

Hannah looked up to see Lottie running toward her. The little girl's red curls bounced as she ran.

She threw her arms about Hannah's waist and hugged her. "Oh, I've missed ye."

"Lottie. What a surprise." Hannah gazed at cheery brown eyes and a freckled face. She knelt in front of the little girl. "How about a proper hug, eh?" She opened her arms.

Lottie smiled and moved closer, wrapping her arms around Hannah's neck and holding her tightly. "I've not been in church and I've missed seeing all me friends."

"And why haven't you been there? Have you been on holiday?"

Lottie loosened her hold and stepped back, glancing at her mother, who walked toward them. "Mum's been sick and then Dad."

"Nothing serious I hope."

"Oh no. Everyone is well now. Good as gold is what Mum says." She smiled. "What are ye doing in town?"

"I had errands to run for Mrs. Atherton, and I hope to visit Lydia."

"Is Thomas with ye?"

"No. He decided to stay at the Athertons' and help Perry. He's learning toolmaking and he quite likes it."

"Oh. It would be nice to see him." Lottie sounded disappointed, then brightened. "Tell him hello from me, then."

"I will. Perhaps you and your mum can come for a visit soon."

"I'd like that." She looked at her mother as she approached.

"Good morning," Grace Parnell said. "How nice to see you out and about."

Feeling a momentary flair of irritation, Hannah wondered if her separation from John meant she was expected to remain in seclusion. Knowing Grace would never purposely insult anyone, she smiled and said, "Life goes on."

"You're quite right. It does." Grace glanced at Lottie. "Charles and I were sad to hear the news, though. You and Thomas have been in our prayers."

"Thank you. Your prayers are welcome." Hannah looked up the street toward the apothecary, anxious to move on. The subject of what had happened between her and John still brought spasms of pain. "Thomas and I are getting along quite well.

We feel at home at the Athertons'. And as I was telling Lottie, Thomas is learning toolmaking. Perry Littrell has taken him under his wing. Thomas is quite good and may well grow up to be a toolmaker like John."

"That's grand news. It's a good trade, indeed."

An uncomfortable silence settled between the women. Grace finally said, "Lottie and I will be taking our midday meal at the café. Would you care to join us?"

"I'd love to, but I already have plans to spend lunch with Lydia."

"Mum," Lottie said, "can we visit Hannah and Thomas soon?"

"Of course. I'll send a note to Catharine."

"I'll look forward to seeing you. And I'm sure Thomas will as well."

"Just as soon as possible, then." Grace caressed Lottie's curls. "I fear we may all be locked in our homes soon with this dreadful outbreak of quinsy."

"There's an outbreak? I heard there were only three cases and one of them is at the Female Factory."

"We can't be too careful." Grace looked up the street as if she might spot someone with the dread disease walking toward them. "I wasn't certain I should come into town at all, but some things must be done. I pray it doesn't become widespread."

"I'm sure Doctor Gelson has everything well in hand. He's a fine physician."

"He is, at that." Grace took Lottie's hand. "It was a pleasure to see you. Say hello to Catharine for me."

"I will." Hannah accepted a quick one-armed hug from Lottie. "I look forward to your visit."

"Me too." Lottie smiled. "I'll see ye at church this Sunday, eh?"

"See you then."

Lottie and her mum walked toward the café.

⚬

Hannah continued on to the apothecary. When she stepped inside, a pungent odor like the dampness of an English forest settled over her. With the smell came a childhood memory. She and her mother and father had gone on a picnic outside the city. She'd explored the shadowed woods and then lay down in cool fragrant grasses, staring up through the limbs of a monstrous tree. When she rolled to one side, a giant fungus that resembled a face of a troll she'd once seen drawn in a book was only inches from her. Startled, she'd shrieked and jumped to her feet. Her father had laughed and then shown her it was nothing more than a growth coming from the tree. She could still smell its sharp odor.

Lydia stepped into the room. "Hannah! How good to see ye." She pulled her friend into a tight hug, then releasing her, said, "I'd planned to come visit ye this afternoon. And here ye are." Her green eyes looked brighter than usual.

She closed the door behind Hannah. "Do ye have errands to do?"

"I've finished already. I found some beautiful fabric. Mrs. Atherton wants me to make gowns for the women at the Female Factory and some for the poor ladies in the Sydney Town prison."

"So she's still watching out for the women, then."

"She is."

171

Lydia smiled. "I remember well her kindness, the Lord bless her." Moving toward a door that led to her living quarters, she asked, "Can ye stay for tea?"

"I was hoping for more than that. Can you join me for lunch at the café? I've been putting a little aside from my wages just for a special occasion."

"Lunch out is a grand idea. I'll tell David. I'm sure he won't mind. I'll be right back." Lydia disappeared into the house.

Hannah roamed the small shop. David was committed to taking good care of the people in Parramatta, and so the small store contained most any kind of elixir or remedy one might need. An earthenware bowl sat on the counter, a pestle still lying in it. An herb of some sort had been ground up and waited to be bottled. Hannah bent over it and sniffed. The odor was sharp, making her nose sting. She straightened and pinched her nostrils closed.

The door to the house opened, and Lydia stepped out. Pinning her bonnet in place, she said, "Actually, I'm not allowed in the apothecary these days. David's concerned about my health."

"Your health?"

"It's the quinsy. He's worried an ill patient will come for medicine. He's nearly locked me in the house."

"Does he think it's a serious outbreak?"

"He's not greatly alarmed, but he's had several calls from people who are scared they have it and some who do. I doubt we have much to worry 'bout, though." She smiled and, placing a hand on Hannah's back, steered her toward the door. "I'm starved. And it will be good to get out of the house."

The two friends settled at a table in the corner of the café. Lottie waved at them when they walked in. She and her mother sat at a table near the front windows. "I've got to say hello," Lydia said and hurried across the room. Hannah followed.

"So how ye keeping, eh?" Lydia asked, giving Lottie a hug.

"We're fine now." She looked at her mum.

Grace nodded. "Charles and I were laid up with some sort of fever, but are quite well these days." She smiled. "You're looking fit."

"I am."

Grace glanced at Hannah. "So good to see you again."

"It would seem we've chosen similar paths today."

"Indeed."

"We'll let ye finish yer lunch," Lydia said. "Good day."

"I'll look for you on Sunday, then."

"Yes. We'll be there." Lydia circled Hannah's waist and they moved across the café to a table in the corner. "Lottie's looking lovely, isn't she?"

"Yes. Very."

"When we were on the ship, she was such a frail little thing."

"Those days were beastly, especially for the children." Hannah could still see Lottie, a resolute little waif. She'd needed a mum after losing hers, and Hannah had needed Lottie. The two had comforted and bolstered one another. "Her strength carried her through."

"That and yer mothering."

Mild melancholy touched Hannah. To this day, she missed being Lottie's mother. "God was good in giving her Grace. She's a fine mum."

"That she is." Lydia leaned her elbows on the table and rested her chin in her hands. "Ye look good, Hannah."

"Thank you. I'm well. Thomas and I are . . . comfortable." She studied her friend, thinking something was different about her. "You're looking especially pretty today. Have you changed something? Your hair or . . . I don't know just what it is, but you're quite beautiful."

"Beautiful? Me? I've never considered myself something to look at."

"You've always been lovely."

"What, me with my freckles and square hips?" She smiled and sat back, keeping her hands on the table in front of her. "Something is different, though." She waited for a moment, as if holding a secret. "I'm going to have a baby."

"Oh Lydia, how wonderful!" Hannah glanced at her friend's abdomen mostly hidden behind the table. "When?"

"Sometime in May, anyway that's what David thinks." She smiled brightly. "I can barely believe it. I'm going to be a mum." Her eyes dimmed slightly. "I wanted ye to be the first to know. I just wish ye had a little one of yer own."

"Don't worry about me. I'm thrilled for you." Hannah smiled. Should she tell Lydia about her own condition? She'd decided John should be the first to know, but Lydia might be of help. Hannah was uncertain of just how to tell him.

She clasped her hands in front of her on the table. "I have news, as well." She pressed her palms against the tabletop. "It would seem we have something in common."

Lydia studied her, a question in her eyes.

"I'm also in the family way," Hannah whispered.

Lydia's green eyes widened. "But how . . . ?"

"If you don't know the answer to that, then you're not as bright as I thought."

"Of course I know how . . . but . . ."

"Just before John moved out ... well, we ... we gave in to passion. That's why he moved to town. If we'd not been living so close, it wouldn't have happened. I told him I'd go to the Athertons', but he insisted on being the one to leave."

Lydia leaned across the table and quietly asked, "Does he know?"

"Not yet. I don't know how to tell him."

"Well, ye'll have to soon. Ye must be nearly five months gone."

"Four and a half, but I can barely tell."

Lydia smirked. "I wondered why ye'd taken to wearing those shifts."

Hannah glanced down at her plain dress. "In time, even this will not hide the truth."

"When do ye plan to tell him?"

"I don't know. What do I say? This complicates everything. I've actually considered moving away."

"Ye can't do that."

"I know. I can't take Thomas away from John."

"Of course not. But ye've no reason to fear telling John. He'll be a fine father, and when he hears the truth, he'll be delighted."

"Delighted? Lydia, have you forgotten we're not married. It will be a scandal."

"Well, ye were still married ... sort of ... when it happened."

"I'll be ruined."

"I doubt ye'll be ruined. I'd say people will be more likely to pity ye."

"I don't want that either." Hannah hadn't wanted to think about the ramifications, but soon she'd be forced to. "There's nothing to be done about it now. Unlike my first, I cherish this baby. And no matter the consequences I'm thankful for its life. I'll have a part of John with me."

Lydia reached across and rested a hand over Hannah's. "I'll do anything I can to help." She glanced about the nearly empty café. "And if anyone says an unkind word, I'll set them straight."

Hannah had to smile. She could imagine just how Lydia would stand up for her. A memory of Ruby flashed through her mind. Lydia was like her old chum. Hannah wondered how Ruby fared in London. She'd not thought of her in some time. "Thank you," she told Lydia. "I couldn't have a better friend."

Lydia took a deep breath, and the light seemed to fade from her eyes. "I'm hoping the baby will set well with David's parents. Perhaps they won't be so vexed over his marrying me."

"I should think they'd be thrilled to have a grandchild."

Lydia smiled. "I hope so."

A heavyset woman walked up to the table. In a bored tone she said, "We've vegetable soup, mutton, or roasted chicken. There are carrots and turnips along with bread."

"I'll have roasted chicken," Lydia said. "And some tea, please."

"And you?" the woman asked Hannah.

"Just a bit of soup, thank you."

"Anything to drink?"

"Tea will be fine."

With a nod, the woman walked away.

"Hannah, ye've got to eat better than that. Ye've a babe to think 'bout."

"I thought I was hungry when I came in, but my appetite's disappeared." Her mind was on John and the upcoming scandal she'd been trying not to think about. She'd experienced disgrace before, and although her friends had been loyal, it had been a painful ordeal. "I hope John will be happy. There will be those who'll be appalled. And they'll make no attempt to hide their feelings."

"Ye can't spend yer time worrying 'bout them. Those types are nothing but a lot of hot air. Ye've got to think 'bout that baby." She smiled. "We'll both have little ones to raise together. It will be grand."

Hannah loved Lydia's enthusiasm, and she felt her own spirits lift. "There's something else troubling me. I probably shouldn't even bring it up, but it's been nagging at me." She unfolded her napkin. "Some time ago, Dalton came to me. He'd heard rumors about Margaret. He was told she's not who she says she is, that she has a foul temper."

"I've never liked her, ye know that." Lydia shrugged. "But I can't say I've heard anything shocking 'bout her."

"Everyone can have a fit of temper now and again. She's been kind to Thomas and to me. In fact, she brought me a lovely gift box with a sachet in it."

"Really?"

"She said she hoped we could put aside our harsh feelings . . . for Thomas's sake."

Lydia cocked an eyebrow. "Must say, that surprises me."

"You've not heard anything I ought to be concerned about?"

"No. I've seen nothing, but she does unsettle me a bit. Of course I've cause. She took my closest friend's husband from her."

"John was married to Margaret first."

"True enough." Lydia thought for a minute. "I did see her with a man once."

"Do you know anything about him?"

"No. He came into town with her is all. It was months ago."

Hannah leaned back and folded her arms over her chest. "He could be most anyone—a business associate or even her brother—she has brothers."

"True enough."

"I'm not generally one to listen to gossip. But if you see or hear anything that doesn't seem quite right, will you tell me? I don't want to cause John or Margaret harm, but . . . well, I'd hate to see John hurt again."

"Of course I'd tell ye. From the moment she showed up in Sydney Town, I thought there was something unseemly going on."

15

Hannah gazed at a hazy blue sky, wishing that a cleansing rain would wash away the dust. Summer sun and heat had parched the land, leaving it dry and thirsty. Each breath of wind carried withered grass and soil skyward, casting a dirty veil over the heavens. Heat waves flickered like flames above brown fields, and the air smelled of burnt grass.

Turning to her task, Hannah walked to the clothesline, a basket of wet laundry braced against her hip. Fevered air pressed down on her and felt heavy in her lungs. *I don't recall November being this hot.*

She set the basket on the ground, and taking a handkerchief from her apron pocket, she patted the moisture on her face. Returning the cloth to her pocket, she lifted one of Mr. Atherton's shirts from the basket and clipped it to the line with a wooden clothespin.

The pounding of horse's hooves reverberated from the drive. Hannah turned to see a rider leaning over his horse and spurring it to a full run. *What kind of person would ride so hard in such heat?* She shaded her eyes, looking to see who would risk their mount's life. Dust billowed around the horse. The rider turned and headed toward the cottages. It was Quincy! Hannah felt a tremor of fear. He wouldn't jeopardize his horse's life without cause. Something was wrong.

Leaving the basket of clothes, she lifted her skirt and ran toward the cabins. Quincy had stopped at hers and was already on the porch. "Quincy!" she called.

He must not have heard because he knocked and then opened the door.

Sucking heated air into her lungs, Hannah ran to the porch and into the cabin. "What's wrong? What's happened?"

Quincy turned to her, his face red and dripping with sweat. "Praise be. Hannah." He dragged off his hat. "It's John. He's sick . . . bad sick. I went for Doctor Gelson, but he's not home. I didn't know who else to ask for help. I figured ye'd know best what to do."

Panic rising, Hannah pressed her fingertips to her temples to soothe the sudden pounding in her head. "How sick is he? What are his symptoms?"

"He's off his feet and heated up real bad. And fighting for breath." He glanced at the hat in his hands. "Could be quinsy."

"I pray not." Hannah moved to the door. "Where's Margaret?"

"She's gone—to Sydney Town—yesterday."

"I'll come. First let me speak to Mrs. Atherton." Hannah stepped onto the porch. "Can you see to the buggy? I'll be there momentarily."

"I'll get it ready for ye."

Quincy strode toward the barn, and Hannah hurried to the main house.

Catharine stood at the top of the veranda steps, her face pinched with concern. "What is it?"

"It's John. He's sick. Could be quinsy. Doctor Gelson's gone and Margaret's not home, so Quincy came for me. I have to go."

"Of course. But do be careful. We can't have you fall ill as well. Quinsy is a terrible disease." She pressed a hand to her throat as if she could feel the pain of the disease. "Perhaps someone else should go. If you were to get sick . . . well, what would become of Thomas?"

Catharine's statement felt like a hot prod being thrust into Hannah's gut. She'd not even thought of Thomas, nor her baby. She should have.

"I can't leave John to die." She glanced toward the carriage house, then back at Catharine. "If something should happen . . ." Hannah couldn't finish the request. It was too terrible to contemplate. "There's no one else. I must go."

Catharine nodded. "I'll have Mrs. Goudy pack some food and remedies for you."

"Thank you. Quincy's gone to get the buggy. I assumed . . . you wouldn't mind. I apologize if I've overstepped my place."

"Don't be silly. Of course you can use the buggy. And 'your place' is one of friendship." She took Hannah's hand. "Now then, you go and do what you must."

Hannah knew this could be bad—that she might not return. She hugged Catharine.

"Now then, take whatever you need. I'm sure Mrs. Goudy knows what's best for quinsy."

"Thank you." Hannah stopped and looked at Catharine. She might not see her again. "I love you. You're like a mum to me."

Catharine's eyes teared and she gave Hannah an extra squeeze.

With his horse tied behind the buggy, Quincy urged the team forward. Hannah asked, "How bad is he?"

"I don't know 'bout such things." He shook his head slightly. "I never seen him this sick, though. I'd say he's bad." He slapped the reins over the horse's hindquarters. "Ye know what to do for quinsy?"

"A little. I've never actually seen anyone who had it." Hannah clutched a bag in her lap. "Mrs. Goudy put together these remedies. They're supposed to help. She told me what to do."

John had a better chance of fighting off the suffocating disease than a child might, but Hannah understood that no matter whom the illness struck, it was always serious and took victims as it willed. In spite of the heat, she felt her skin prickle with fear. What if she were to get it? What of the baby? Was she being foolishly careless with her child's life, like she'd been with the first? *Lord, John needs me. I ask for your protection—for me and my little one. And I beseech you to lay your hand of healing upon John.*

The buggy bounced over a rut, nearly tossing Hannah off the seat. She grabbed for a handhold and did her best to turn her mind away from her fears. "Do you know when Margaret is supposed to return?"

"Nope. All I know is she had errands to see to in Sydney Town." He jutted out his jaw. "John was already sick when she left."

Hannah felt rising outrage. "How could she leave him when he's so ill?"

"John told her to go, said he'd be all right . . . said it was nothing but a bit of a sore throat."

"Even so, I would have stayed," Hannah said, unable to disguise her ire although she knew quinsy usually started out innocuously—presenting as a simple sore throat. "Did you speak to Lydia when you went for the doctor?"

"I did. Told me she'd give him the message when he returned. He's out at the Fairgates—both of their children are down sick."

"With quinsy?"

"That's what I heard."

"Oh, no." Hannah said a silent prayer for the children. How cruel sickness could be, especially for young ones like the Fairgate boys. The oldest was only three and the younger not yet a year. If they did have quinsy, they'd most likely die.

"I never thought much 'bout my name before. But quinsy and Quincy sounds an awful lot alike. After this, I might start using me middle name."

Hannah patted his arm. Under the circumstances, Quincy did seem a wretched name.

Quincy drove to the barn and stopped the buggy there.

"He's not in the house?"

"No. Even as sick as he is, he said it's not right for him to be living there."

Hannah didn't wait for Quincy to help her down but climbed from the buggy and hurried into the barn, making her way around a pile of hay with a pitchfork thrust into it. She moved to the small tack room and found John lying prostrate on a cot. He looked alarmingly sick, his skin pale and damp. With each breath, a whistling sound emanated from the back of his throat.

"Oh, John," Hannah said, going to him. He didn't respond. She knelt beside the bed and placed a hand on his brow. His skin was hot. "John. I'm here. I'll help you," she said softly, trying to keep the terror out of her voice.

John squinted up at her, his eyes more closed than open. His lips tightened into a grimace. "No. Go . . ." He struggled for breath. "Go away."

"I'll be going nowhere, except with you into the house." She stood and looked at Quincy, who stared at John from the doorway. "He needs a proper bed." She glanced about the tiny room. "This is no place for a sick man. Help me get him indoors."

"Right." Quincy moved quickly to the cot and hefted John, draping an arm around his shoulder. Hannah braced him on the other side. Together they half carried, half dragged him to the house and up the front steps. John tried to walk but couldn't muster enough strength.

"How'd he get so ill so quickly? I thought you said he had only a sore throat yesterday?"

"Like I said, he was sick when Margaret left and got worse as the day went on, but not so much that I was worried. When I came upon him this morning, I was truly shocked at his state."

Fury reached for Hannah. *Margaret shouldn't have gone.*

Once they made it up the stairs, Quincy held on to John while Hannah opened the door. With a grunt, Quincy picked him up and carried him to the bedroom. Hannah hurried ahead and pulled back the blankets. Fear swelled as she watched Quincy lower John to the bed. He reminded her of a rag doll she'd once had. "It's intolerably hot in here. Can you open the windows?"

"The flies are bad."

"Then they'll just have to be bad. He needs air." Hannah turned her attention to John while Quincy moved about the house, opening windows. She leaned over John, but he didn't open his eyes. Each breath sounded as if he were being strangled by unseen hands. A deluge of uncertainty threatened to overwhelm Hannah. Her mind flashed back to her mother. She'd been so ill. Hannah hadn't known what to do. And she didn't know now. *Lord, please bring David.*

Moving to the armoire, she rifled through the clothing, searching for something John could wear. She found a nightshirt and laid it out on the bed. "We'll have to get you out of these filthy clothes," she said, reaching to unbutton John's shirt.

He looked at her, suddenly seeming alert. "I can do it." He tried to sit up but only managed to make it halfway before stopping to rest against the headboard. His fingers fumbled to unbutton his shirt. He managed, but the effort took so much from him that he lay gasping.

"Let me help you." Hannah pulled him upright, allowing him to rest against her, and gently removed the garment. After laying him back down, she stripped off his trousers.

"I can't . . . breathe." John's voice sounded thick.

Trying to keep her tone light, Hannah said, "Of course you can. Otherwise you wouldn't be able to talk." She rested a hand on his bare chest, frightened at the heat she felt and the rapid thumping of his heart.

"I'll be back in a moment." She took the basin from the bureau and went to get water from the barrel on the front porch. She filled it halfway, then retrieved a washcloth from the kitchen. Returning to John, she sat on the edge of the bed and gently washed him, then helped him into his nightshirt.

John rested against her. "You shouldn't . . . be . . . here," he panted. "You could . . . get sick."

"No need to worry about me." While he leaned against her, Hannah managed to fluff his pillow and then lowered him to the bed. "I'd say you could do with some broth and a bit of milk. Mrs. Goudy said they might help."

"I can't . . . swa . . . llow."

"I'm sure you can get some down if you try," she said cheerfully, but inside she felt panic. He was deathly ill. Not since her time on the ship had she seen anyone this sick. Hannah stood and turned to find Quincy standing in the doorway. He stared at John, his expression morose. "Quincy, could you be so kind as to bring some milk from the springhouse?"

"Sure." He remained for a moment, his eyes on John. "Ye think he'll be all right?"

"Of course." Hannah's tone was confident. She didn't dare give in to her fears or negative thoughts.

Looking unconvinced, Quincy left. Hannah turned back to John. If it were possible, his breathing sounded more labored than before. She pulled him upright and pushed another pillow behind him, propping him up. It seemed to ease his breathing a bit.

Hannah stared at him. He was so focused on finding his next breath that he seemed unaware of anything else. The same alarm she'd felt when she'd watched her mother die crept inside Hannah. *Lord, please help him. Don't let him die.*

She forced herself to leave him and went to the kitchen. Mrs. Goudy had packed at least two dozen onions with instructions to roast them and then mash them into a poultice. Hannah set out several onions.

Quincy returned with the milk. "It's already been strained and is cool."

"Thank you. Can you build a fire for me?"

"I can, but what ye going to do with a fire in this heat?"

"Cook onions for a poultice."

Quincy's eyes went to the onions on the counter. "All right, then." He headed outside, seeming glad for something to do.

While Quincy roasted the onions, Hannah unsuccessfully tried to get John to drink some water, then took a glass of milk in for him. She set the glass on the bed stand and scooted a chair next to the bed. The strident sound coming from John's throat and his fierce fever terrified her. "John, have a go at this. It will help." She put a hand behind his head and held the glass to his lips.

He tried to drink, but mostly gagged and coughed. Almost none of it went down.

Quincy stepped into the room. "The onions are cooked." He stared at John, unable to disguise his fear.

"Thank you. Can you put them in the kitchen?"

"Right. I can do that." Quincy backed out of the room.

Hannah let John's head rest against the pillows and set the milk on the nightstand. "I'll just be in the kitchen if you need me." John didn't respond.

Hannah set to work crushing the onions. They were still hot. Both her eyes and fingers stung. She added the herbs Mrs. Goudy had sent along, then tied the mixture into a muslin bag. She returned to John. "Mrs. Goudy said this is just the thing."

John tried to lift his eyelids, but it was as if they were too heavy.

Hannah tied the compress about his neck.

"What . . . is . . . that?" He put a hand to the reeking bundle.

187

"An onion poultice. It will ease your breathing."

"It stinks . . ." John choked and started again. "Smells like . . . burned garbage."

"That it does." Hannah pressed her hand to the concoction. "But it will help."

The day passed, and although Hannah did everything she knew to do, John grew worse. She changed the poultice several times and tried to get John to drink a bit of milk, but he couldn't get it down. He managed to swallow a small amount of broth, but choked so badly Hannah feared he'd suffocate.

She moved a rocking chair into the room and sat reading and watching John. Often, she'd stop and pray. And when he thrashed about or complained that his head hurt, she'd gently rub his temples until he relaxed.

Late in the day, the sound of a carriage approaching carried hope. Perhaps it was David Gelson . . . or Margaret. The idea of Margaret's arrival wasn't comforting. Hannah didn't trust the woman to care for John.

She moved to the window and looked out. "David! Praise be!" She rushed outside and met him as he climbed down from his buggy. "I'm so glad you're here. Nothing I do is helping."

"I came as soon as I could." Looking weary and troubled, he grabbed a leather satchel and moved toward the house.

"David, you look done in. Are you all right?"

"Just tired. I could do with a bit of coffee, if you have some."

"I'll make it."

"No. Don't bother." He started up the steps. "Where is he?"

"The downstairs bedroom."

Hannah hurried to the bedroom with David following. John seemed to be unconscious. His chest heaved with the effort to breathe, and drool trickled from his mouth and onto his chin.

David gently wiped the spittle away and began his examination.

John roused. "David. Glad you're . . ." he stopped and tried to swallow, giving up on whatever it was he'd intended to say.

David listened to John's heart and lungs, then said, "Let me have a look at your throat. Open your mouth."

John did as he was told. Hannah hovered, afraid of what David would find.

Using a wooden tongue depressor, he examined John's throat. His brow furrowed. "You can close your mouth." He dropped the depressor into his bag. "You've got quinsy, all right." He straightened and folded his arms over his chest. "But you've a strong constitution, so I expect you'll soon be right as rain."

Although his words were confident, his eyes said something else. David reached into his bag and took out a vial of powder. "I'll need a glass of water."

Hannah filled a glass and gave it to David. "He can barely swallow. I don't know that you'll be able to get anything down him."

He stirred a teaspoon of the powder into the water. "Give it to him a bit at a time, then. It's a diaphoretic and will make him sweat. Sweating helps purge the infection." He inspected the onion poultice. "This is fine, but a muffler will serve well too. Just make sure it's as hot as he can bear."

He set the diaphoretic on the bed stand and closed his bag. "Make sure he continues to drink, keep him warm, and if you can get more broth or milk into him, that will help keep his strength up." He rested a hand on John's shoulder. "I'll be back tomorrow."

John didn't reply. He'd returned to oblivion.

David stood and moved to the door.

Hannah followed. "Will he be all right?"

"I'll not lie to you. He's got a bad case. I'd like to stay if I could, but there are others."

"How many?"

"I've about ten cases right now; it's spreading. Make sure you keep yourself rested and well fed. You'll be no good to John if you're sick as well."

Hannah took a quaking breath. "Is he going to die?"

David gently grasped Hannah's upper arm. "I don't know. He has an abscess over his throat that's blocking his airway. If his body can fight off the infection before the abscess cuts off his air, he'll make it. Otherwise . . ." He gave a slow shrug. "I'm sorry. I wish I could offer you more hope." He moved onto the veranda. "Lydia and I will be praying." His steps heavy, he walked to the buggy.

Hannah stared after him, tears blurring her vision. *Lord, I couldn't bear it. And Thomas . . . please remember Thomas. He loves his dad.* She closed the door, wiped at her tears, and returned to John's bedside.

Sometime during the night, Quincy came in and woke Hannah. She'd been sleeping in the chair. "Ye ought to go to bed. I'll sit with him."

Barely awake, Hannah peered up at Quincy in the dim lantern light.

"If ye get sick, ye'll be no good to him or to yer son."

Or my baby, she thought. "All right. I'll go up and sleep in Thomas's bed. Call me . . . if anything changes."

"I will."

Hannah pushed out of the chair, and with one last look at John, she left the room and climbed the ladder to the loft. When she lay down, her mind went to Margaret. Why hadn't she returned? Quincy said he'd sent word to the boardinghouse. Was it possible she was also sick?

16

Four agonizing days and nights passed, and Hannah remained at John's side. Margaret hadn't returned.

The morning of the fifth day, Hannah dozed in the rocker in John's room. With first light she roused and knew immediately that something was different. John's labored breathing had stopped. Fear, like a fire out of control, burned through her. She pushed out of the chair. *Lord, no. Please, no.*

Her eyes on John, she moved to the bed. In the half light of morning, she was unable to see him clearly. Was he breathing? Her hand quaking, she reached out and placed a palm on his chest. He was warm. Beneath her hand she felt the steady rhythm of his heart. *Praise you, Lord.* She leaned closer and could hear him breathing—unobstructed.

John opened his eyes and looked at Hannah.

She placed a hand to his cool brow. "You're better."

He nodded and croaked, "Water?"

Hannah quickly poured him a glass, helped him sit upright, and then held it to his lips. He managed to drink most of the contents.

"Tastes wonderful," he said, and lay back down.

Hannah stood looking at him, joy replacing trepidation. "You're going to be just fine."

"That I am," he said, his voice barely more than a whisper. He closed his eyes and fell into a restful sleep.

Hannah put an arm around John's shoulders and helped him sit up. "Are you sure you're ready for this? Your fever broke only this morning. I'd hate for you to overtax yourself."

"I can't bear this bed another minute." He eased his legs over the side, leaning heavily against Hannah. He grabbed hold of the headboard. "I'm a bit unsteady yet." He took several deep breaths. "Give me a moment, the room is spinning."

"You've been abed for five days with nothing to eat and barely enough to drink to keep a body alive. I can hardly believe you're even attempting to get out of bed."

"I'll just sit here a moment. Can I have more water? I've a thirst that can't be satisfied."

Hannah gave him a glass of water, and he drank it down.

Holding the empty glass, he said, "Oh, that tastes good."

Hannah set the glass on the bed stand. This was unbelievable. Only yesterday, she'd feared he would die. "I thank the Lord you've rallied, but you'd best be careful so not to relapse."

"I've things to do. And I'll never regain my strength if I stay in this bed."

"Do you think you can make it to the chair?"

He nodded and scooted to the edge of the mattress. As John pushed to his feet, Hannah braced him by pushing her shoulder under his arm. He wobbled, but managed to maintain his balance.

"Are you sure you're ready?"

With a nod, John rested his weight on Hannah and took a step. "I think the porch is a fine place to rest."

The porch? Inwardly Hannah chided John but knew better than to scold him. He wouldn't hear it anyway.

John looked at the window. "I want to smell fresh air—the heated fields and the gum trees."

"Are you certain you can make it? If you were to fall . . ."

"I'll not fall." He straightened slightly and took another step and then another. Sweat beaded up on his face.

By the time John reached the porch chair, he leaned heavily on Hannah and made a huffing sound with each breath. Hannah worried he'd done too much.

"Do you need a blanket?" She helped him sit.

"In this heat?" He smiled. "Now you're being silly." His gaze went to the field and then to the river. "I wondered if I'd ever see it again."

Hannah rested a hand on his shoulder, unable to speak, her words choked off by emotion. John grasped her hand. Although knowing it was inappropriate, Hannah let her hand remain in his. Just for the moment it would be all right; for the moment they need not ignore their love. They'd survived a tempest together. This was a time to rejoice together.

Finally, Hannah released his hand. "I'll see to your bedding. It badly needs changing."

John caught hold of her arm. "Wait."

His grip was surprisingly firm. Hannah felt her heart quicken. She moved so that she stood in front of him, but was unable to meet his eyes. "John, it's—"

"Hush." He pressed the back of her fingers to his lips.

Hannah didn't have the will to extract her hand.

194

"Dear Hannah, thank you. Without you, I would have died. You put your life in jeopardy for me."

She found the courage to look at him. His expression was tender, his eyes filled with love. For a moment she was swept away. *Please, don't look at me like that.*

As matter-of-factly as possible, she said, "Someone had to take care of you. Poor Quincy was beside himself. He had no idea what to do."

John grinned. "I much prefer your nursing over his."

Hannah smiled. "He's the one who went for the doctor . . . after Margaret left."

A question touched John's eyes. "And then he got you." He took her other hand and pulled her closer. "I'm convinced I would have died if you hadn't come."

"I did what I could, God did the rest. You should thank him for your life."

"And I do."

A buggy rolled up the drive. It was Lydia.

Hannah snatched her hand back and stepped away from John.

Lydia stopped in front of the porch and quickly climbed down from the buggy. "John? I declare, I can hardly believe what I'm seeing! David said you were terribly sick."

"I was, but this morning I woke up nearly feeling like a real person." John's voice trembled, and he sounded breathless, but he managed a smile.

"I convinced him to let me come for a visit as long as I stayed outdoors." She glanced at her abdomen and rested her hands there. "He wants me to be especially careful now, with a little one on the way."

"As you should be. To do otherwise would be a sin."

195

His statement assailed Hannah. She'd had those same thoughts before coming to care for John, but . . . *I had no choice.* Did God see it as a sin, or had it been an act of faithful obedience? She chose to believe the latter.

"Hannah, David told me you were here. How kind of you to help John."

"I did what anyone would have." The topic of her presence here made Hannah uncomfortable. It really wasn't her place. She glanced at John. Her time here had only strengthened her love for him. *Perhaps I should have asked someone else to stay with him. This was a mistake.* Now she'd have to return to the Athertons' and learn to live without him once more.

"I suppose I'll be returning to the Athertons' in a day or two. Of course if Margaret comes home, I won't be needed."

"Margaret?" Lydia huffed. "Where is she? Shouldn't she be here now, caring for her husband?" She leveled green eyes on John. "Why hasn't she returned from Sydney Town?"

John shook his head. "I can't be sure. I supposed she's unaware of my condition."

"Unaware?" Lydia folded her arms over her chest and tossed a glance at the road. "I think not. Word was sent. She knows full well you've been ill. What kind of wife deserts her husband when she's most needed?"

"Lydia," John's voice was sharp, "I'll not have you speak of her in such a tone."

"I don't mean to offend, but someone must speak their mind. It just as well be me."

Hannah was surprised at her friend's outburst. It was a bit much even for Lydia.

"I'm sure she has good reason for not returning," John said. "And has it occurred to you that she might also have fallen ill?

196

I've been more concerned than anything else. I've been hoping to hear of her situation."

Lydia's eyes remained heated. "I'd also be interested to know how she's passed the time these last days." Her lips tightened into a line. "I suppose it's possible she's ill. But then I'd expect we would have heard something."

"Perhaps," John said tersely.

Lydia leaned against the porch railing, her expression softening. "I don't mean to be harsh, but sometimes my ire gets up and . . . well, ye know I tend to speak my mind."

"I know." John managed a smile. "No harm done. But please give poor Margaret the benefit of the doubt."

Lydia held out a basket. "I brought soup, fresh bread, and peach jam. Thought ye might like some when ye were feeling better, which it seems ye are." She moved up the steps, setting the basket on the table.

"I appreciate your thoughtfulness." John lifted the cloth protecting the contents of the basket and peered inside. "Thank you. I'm hungry. And I think my throat will accommodate a meal." He smiled and sat back, looking weary and pallid.

"I'd invite you in," Hannah said, "but as you said, you don't dare, not yet. The house will need a good scrubbing."

John looked up at Hannah. "You go along and have a visit. It's time you did something other than look after me."

Lydia eyed John and then Hannah. A knowing smile played at her lips. Hannah didn't like it. She knew Lydia could see the love between them.

"John, would you like to eat first?" she asked.

"I can manage on my own, thank you. I think I'll try the bread and preserves."

"Well, let me get you a knife and spoon, then." Hannah quickly retrieved the items, and then she and Lydia started down the steps. "I'll be close if you need me." She turned and looked at him. She'd not let him out of her sight for days, and now it didn't feel right to leave him on his own. What if he were to relapse suddenly? "Are you sure there's nothing you need?"

"I'm fine right here in the shade where I can look out over the farm. It's good to be outdoors." He closed his eyes and took a deep breath. "It smells good too, like roasting chestnuts."

"That's the sun cooking the fields," Lydia teased. "Ye better be praying for rain."

"It will come. I have no doubt." Peace emanated from John.

Hannah understood. When death comes close, life is more precious. *And when love is lost, one holds it more dear.*

She moved down the steps and linked arms with Lydia. They strolled toward the river. "I'm glad you came. I've needed you."

"Ye look a bit done in. And John, I can see he's been through an ordeal."

Hannah took in an uneven breath. "For a time, I thought he would die." She glanced back at the house. "He's lost to me, but I'm grateful for his life."

Lydia placed a hand over Hannah's. "I can see that ye still love each other. My heart breaks for ye both." Her eyes turned hard and she squared her jaw. "Margaret doesn't deserve him."

"Maybe so, but that doesn't matter, not really. She's his wife."

"A loving wife would have been here to take care for her husband."

"We've no reason to doubt her love. There are a number of reasons that would explain her absence. We ought to be praying for her. Especially if she's ill. I've seen how dreadful this disease is." She shuddered. "It's horrid."

"I've word she's fine and in the company of a man named Weston Douglas."

"Who told you such a thing?"

"People come in and out of the store—they talk."

"I thought David had banned you from the apothecary and his office."

"That's true. But he hired a woman to oversee when he's gone. She's friendly with people and she hears a lot."

"It's just gossip and you shouldn't listen," Hannah said, although her own curiosity was piqued. Was there something behind the rumor?

Lydia steered Hannah toward a tree at the river bank. "Mrs. Stevens came in to get medicine for her husband's gout, and she said that a man who works for them had seen Margaret."

"And what does he know about her?" Hannah didn't know why she was defending the woman, except that she couldn't bear to discover that she was deceitful. John had suffered too much already. It could devastate him.

"Word gets out 'bout people. She's new here, and I'll admit a bit striking in appearance, and there's always talk 'bout a newcomer. Plus everyone knows what happened to ye and John because of her."

"I daresay, people are quick to gossip and such talk can't be trusted. Did this man see Margaret with this Mr. Douglas?"

"Indeed he did. And he said they seemed quite friendly toward each other."

Against her will, suspicion grew in Hannah. What if Margaret was unfaithful to John? But why would she do such a thing? John was noble and handsome, and he owned a fine piece of property. She turned to Lydia and challenged, "If Margaret doesn't love John, then why would she travel all the way from England? I'm sure there's been a misunderstanding."

"People don't always have reasons for the things they do, we've lived long enough to know that." Lydia's eyes glinted with mischief. "If she is up to no good, I'd like to see her get what's coming to her."

"Lydia. You've decided she's guilty of some sort of evil, when you've no idea if anything you've heard is true or not. If she was seen with a Mr. Douglas, there's no reason to assume she's done something wrong. He could be a business acquaintance."

Lydia threw her arms down, slapping the side of her skirt. "Why won't you believe any of this? I'd think you'd be glad for it. If she's straying, that would be grounds for divorce. And then you and John could—"

"No. I will not wish heartache on John so that I can be happy." Feeling abysmal, Hannah moved to a gum tree and leaned against its smooth bark. It felt cool in the heat. "He's suffered enough, as have I."

Lydia plucked a stem of dried grass and, standing beside Hannah, pressed her back to the tree. She stared at the slow-moving river. "I don't want John hurt, but I do want life to be fair to him and to you. And it's not been." She turned her green eyes on Hannah. "I've watched ye be strong and noble. And I've admired ye for being so, but that doesn't make any of this right. And what if Margaret is up to no good . . . if she escapes the consequences of her misdeeds, it will only cause more injury." She twirled the dry grass between her fingers. "And I've had some worries . . . that she might even wish some kind of harm toward John."

"What do you mean?"

"I don't know that she's done anything, but what if she's come for reasons we know nothing about?"

"Lydia, you can't throw out accusations with no basis."

Lydia was quiet for a long moment. "I just have a feeling is all." She shrugged. "I think she's wicked."

"Until there's proof of wrongdoing, it's falderal. And I won't bring more hardship to John or Margaret because of a feeling and a few gossips." Without looking at Lydia, she added, "I'm not unhappy. Thomas and I have a fine life."

"Yes. But one without John." Lydia stepped in front of Hannah. "I know you love him."

"I do. And I thank you for caring about me, but a vendetta will not help. To do evil for self-gain will only bring more heartache." Hannah looked back at the house. John's chin rested on his chest. He'd fallen asleep. "I'll always love John. And because I do, I'll not interfere." She gripped Lydia's forearms firmly. "Please, let this go."

Lydia frowned. "But what if this Mr. Douglas turns out to be someone suspicious, what then?"

"If such is the case, then I shall consider what to do."

"You should go to Sydney Town and find out more 'bout him."

Hannah blew out a breath of frustration. "And what am I looking for?"

"Just see who he is, why he's in Sydney Town. If he's a legitimate businessman . . . well, then perhaps Margaret has good cause to spend time with him."

A breeze cooled Hannah's hot skin and teased her hair. She studied Lydia. She'd always been a reasonable person, not given to flights of fancy. Perhaps her feelings now were valid. She turned her gaze to the river. If Lydia was right, John should know.

"All right. I'll go."

17

Hannah stood in the doorway of the Atherton study, trying to think of the best way to approach Catharine about making a trip into Sydney Town. She was embarrassed to even speak of her intentions, afraid she'd sound as if she were meddling and that she'd be seen as someone trying to fulfill personal desires. She wasn't even certain she trusted her motives. Was it possible she wanted to believe something was wrong because she longed for the life she'd once had with John?

Catharine looked up from her writing. "Oh Hannah, dear. How long have you been standing there?"

"Not long. I didn't want to intrude."

She set her pen aside. "Please, come in."

Still wondering how to explain what she wanted, Hannah approached Catharine. "You look busy. Perhaps I should come another time."

"No. I'm just writing a letter."

"Oh." Hannah glanced at the letter, knowing she was putting off her request.

"I'm writing to the governor, hoping to convince him to provide better care for prisoners. Those poor souls, they live in such appalling conditions. Sometimes I lie awake thinking about them. I do want to help."

"You already do so much. I've been a recipient, remember?"

"I do indeed."

"It's not just the food and clothes you provide, it's your tender way, the love you offer the women. When I think on it, I can feel it still."

Catharine's expression turned gentle. "Thank you." She pressed her hands on either side of the letter. "I've written to the governor three times, without success. I thought that if I pestered him enough, he might make some changes, especially in the food and by offering more physician care and bathing."

"Perhaps this letter will make a difference." Hannah remembered—filth, rats, inedible food, disease—conditions had been frightful, especially at the Female Factory. "I always believed gaols were for the wicked. But so many of those locked away are decent people who simply fell upon hard times or have been unjustly accused."

"Indeed. Your offense was not deserving of prison. Stealing a loaf of bread is hardly cause for fourteen years transportation."

"I was also accused of stealing a silver chalice."

"Unjustly accused. Judge Walker should have been placed in the stocks for what he did."

Hannah stifled a shudder at the thought of her former employer, but had to smile at the idea of the judge being constrained in the stocks. "I would like to have seen that," she said.

"Now then, what is it you needed, dear?"

She met Catharine's kind eyes, suddenly remembering why she'd come. "I have need of a few days leave, if it's not an imposition. Especially since I was with John for several days."

"No imposition. What is it that requires your attention? Is everything all right? You're not ill are you?"

"No. Nothing like that." Hannah searched her mind, wishing there were some way to explain a trip to Sydney Town that didn't include spying on Mr. Douglas. "I've no real need, mum."

"And you've no need to be so formal with me. We're friends, remember."

"Yes. I remember. It's just that since I've returned to your employ, it feels disrespectful to call you by your Christian name."

"It's not at all." She looked at Hannah with affection. "It would please me if you referred to me as Catharine." She slid the unfinished letter to the side and clasping her hands in front of her, she leaned on the desk. "Now then, how much time shall you need?"

"I'm not certain, perhaps three days, possibly four. Just enough to drive to Sydney Town, complete some business, and then a day's travel back."

Catharine studied Hannah as if waiting for further explanation.

"I have some things to attend to," Hannah said, knowing she ought to add more details. She stared at her feet before continuing. "There have been rumors . . . about Margaret. It's possible she may be here on false pretenses. Lydia has convinced me of the wisdom of looking into Margaret's circumstances."

Catharine's back straightened, making her taller in the chair. "What do you mean by false pretenses? Whatever reason can Margaret have other than the one stated?"

"It seems she's been seen in the company of a man, a Mr. Weston Douglas. And while John was abed, she spent several days in Sydney Town."

"And you see it as your responsibility to see what she's been doing?"

"Not exactly." Hannah could feel Catharine's disapproval. "I'd rather it wasn't me, but I suppose someone ought to see that she has John's best interests at heart."

"In light of the rumors, that may be, but I'm not at all certain it should be you."

"I care more about him than anyone."

"That's my concern. You care too dearly to be evenhanded. Your affection for him complicates the situation." Her kind expression deepened. "I worry about you. If you were to make an error in judgment, I know you'd take it to heart and carry the burden of guilt."

"All you say is true and so I will go with caution. If Lydia were to explore this further, her loyalty to me would cloud her vision—in fact, anyone who cares for me will be prejudiced. For that reason I'm the only one who can seek the truth with pure motives. I have John's best interests at heart, not my own."

Catharine met Hannah's gaze squarely. "Are you sure of that?"

Hannah was taken off guard by Catharine's directness. "I can't be completely certain, but I will do my best not to let my emotions tread upon the truth."

"I know you will do your best. But guard your heart, dear."

"I will," Hannah said, and added, "Lydia will be traveling with me."

Catharine gave a wry smile. "Beware. She has loyalties for you, as you said."

"Yes, but I have need of support. Her presence will bolster my courage. But I promise you, I'll not presume anything simply because Lydia has an opinion."

Catharine nodded. "I trust you. You're a wise young woman. And of course you have my permission to go. And please take the carriage. It's more comfortable than a wagon or buggy. And make certain Dalton goes with you. I'll not have you and Lydia traveling all that way unattended. There are dangers on the road—highwaymen and such. In light of the aboriginal raid that took place at the Johnsons' recently, I'd feel more at ease with him accompanying you."

"Of course," Hannah said, but couldn't imagine Dalton being of much help in the face of a skirmish. He was much too digni-fied. "I shan't be gone more than four days at most."

"Take whatever time you need." Catharine picked up her pen. "I'll keep you in my prayers. And I do hope you find the truth. It's time you left the past and moved forward with your life. Perhaps this will help."

"Thank you." Hannah turned and walked out of the study, feeling the sharpness of a reprimand, although she was certain Catharine meant no reproof. Still, Hannah knew it was time to leave John to his new life and to go on with her own.

I shouldn't be going to Sydney Town at all, she told herself, but she knew she would go because she must.

⊷⊶

"It was kind of Mrs. Atherton to let us use the carriage," Lydia said, leaning out the window and watching the river flow past.

A front wheel bounced through a rut, followed by the back, tossing the women off their seats. Lydia laughed and tidied her hat. "I say, the baby is getting a good jostling."

"Truly," Hannah said, protectively resting a hand on her abdomen. She hoped the rough roadway was in no way harmful to her child. "The road is deplorable. Perhaps we should have waited and taken the barge."

"We'd have had to wait another three days. What if that Mr. Douglas were to leave?"

"If so, then we most likely will have no reason to investigate him. If something were going on between him and Margaret, he'd no doubt stay in town."

"We shall know soon enough."

Hannah's mind turned to the possibilities. What if the rumors were true? What would she do then? She couldn't rein in hopeful thoughts of life on the farm—her, John, Thomas, and the baby.

"Hannah, where've ye gone to? Ye look as if yer a hundred miles away."

"I'm here, but wishing I weren't. I find this whole business deplorable. Sneaking about spying on someone feels criminal. And it's not right to go behind John's back. What if he finds out and believes I'm being vindictive?"

"He'll only hear of it if we discover something he ought to know. In that case, we'll tell him ourselves and he'll be thanking ye for looking out for him. I've no doubt he'd much rather be sharing his life with ye instead of her anyway."

"You don't know that. He once loved her very much. Perhaps he still does."

With disdain, Lydia puffed air through her lips. "I doubt that's the case. He's still in love with ye, Hannah. Ye know that.

He's got no reason to think yer being vindictive. In truth, ye've done yer best to be fair to Margaret. And honestly, it's getting a bit annoying. She doesn't deserve yer kindness."

"Until there's proof of wrongdoing, she deserves respect, especially mine. I know how difficult this has been, not just for me but for her as well."

Lydia shook her head. "There's wrongdoing here. I know it."

"Have you never been mistaken about someone?"

"No one is right all the time, but I've a feeling and I trust it." She looked at Hannah straight on. "And if I am right, then we have cause to worry 'bout John."

"I fear what it might do to him. He's suffered so much already."

Lydia cooled herself with a fan. "This heat is unbearable." Staring at a man leading a milk cow, she asked, "Did ye find out why Margaret was in Sydney Town when John was sick?"

"Thomas said she'd made purchases for him and for John and that she'd had a dress fitting."

"And that's all?" She stopped fanning herself.

"He mentioned something about a friend."

"A friend? Indeed. How convenient. And was that friend's name Douglas?"

"I don't know. He didn't say." Hannah shook her head. "You're being unfair."

"Perhaps. But I doubt that she'd spend time with a friend when her husband is deathly ill."

"She said she didn't know John was sick." Dust roiled up from under the carriage and in through the windows. Hannah covered her nose with a handkerchief.

With a cough, Lydia tipped her head against the back of

the seat, briskly fanning the air. "And what did ye tell Thomas 'bout our trip to Sydney Town?"

"Just that we planned to do some shopping. I'll have to see if I can find a little something for him while we're there."

When they approached Sydney Town, Hannah felt her tension grow. *What am I doing? This scheme is ridiculous. I ought to tell Dalton to turn the carriage about and return to the Athertons'.*

"Shall we stay at the hotel?" Lydia asked.

"That's fine." Hannah leaned out of the window and shouted up at Dalton. "We'll be staying at the hotel."

"Right," he called as he steered the team into town.

When they drove past the boardinghouse, Hannah studied the building. If Margaret had a gentleman friend, he'd mostly likely be there—the hotel was too expensive for long stays. She tried to remember what the man she'd seen with Margaret had looked like. It had been a long while. He wasn't very tall, not much taller than Margaret, and built rather stocky.

Dalton stopped the carriage in front of the hotel and disembarked. He opened the door and assisted the women. Sweat ran in rivulets down his face, then disappeared inside his shirt collar. He took the luggage from its rack and carried it indoors. "Mrs. Atherton said she'd cover the expenses."

"How kind of her," Lydia said. "But I'm quite capable of—"

Dalton stopped. "She wants to pay for your stay." Without another word, he stepped up to the registration desk.

"It's not necessary, really," Lydia told Hannah. "David and I are doing well."

209

"Of course, but it pleases Catharine." Hannah smiled. "And I suppose she wants to make certain you and the baby are comfortable. You're beginning to show, you know."

Lydia glanced at her slightly rounded abdomen, then looked at Hannah, a flush in her cheeks. "Ye can tell, really?"

Hannah nodded.

"I have gotten a bit thick 'round the middle." Her expression softened. "I don't mind, though. I just wish ye were free to share yer joy as well." She looked more closely at Hannah. "Those shifts ye've been wearing do nothing for ye."

"I'm dressed fine for a housemaid."

"I wish John knew. He'd be thrilled."

"At the proper time. Although I doubt the news will be well received." Hannah kept her voice low.

Lydia studied Hannah. "I can scarcely tell. If ye'd not told me, I'd have no idea."

"I'm thankful for that."

"When will ye speak to him? It will have to be soon. Ye can't keep it hidden forever."

Hannah knew that, but she wasn't ready for anyone to know, not just yet. "I'll tell him at the proper time." Hannah could barely abide the idea. Margaret would be livid and she had a right to be. John would be shocked, but after a bit of time he'd accept the news graciously. But others . . . well, there would be talk. She and John weren't married. People would count the months and know that they'd been reckless . . . after Margaret had arrived. Humiliation filled Hannah and she could feel her face burn with shame. Before, when her friends and most in the church had learned of her past, they'd been gracious, but would they be so willing again?

No matter. She pressed her hand against her abdomen. *I cherish you.*

Dalton moved to Hannah and Lydia, bags in hand. "You're all checked in. They've rooms for you on the second floor. Right this way." He walked toward the staircase, leading the way. He settled Lydia in her room first, then took Hannah's bag to hers. "I'll take the carriage to the livery and will return promptly. If you have need of anything, I'll be down the hall in room 210."

"Thank you, Dalton. You've been a great help." Suddenly overcome with gratitude at his presence, Hannah rested a hand on his arm. He glanced at it, clearly uncomfortable at the familiarity. "I just want you to know I appreciate your friendship." She removed her hand.

"And I value yours."

"Lydia and I will be having dinner in the dining room, if you'd like to join us."

"Thank you, but I've friends in town. And I've promised to sup with them."

"All right, then. I'll see you tomorrow. Lydia and I plan to inquire about Mr. Douglas first thing."

"I asked after him at the desk, but he's not registered here."

"Then he must be at the boardinghouse or has left town. I hope he's not in town and that this has all been a terrible mistake."

Dalton's gaze softened. "I do hope you're right, but I've a bad feeling."

"This time, I will be glad to find you mistaken. I'd like to return home with our minds at ease."

"We can hope, eh." With a nod, he left the room.

Hannah stood at the door for a moment, watching until Dalton turned down the hallway to the staircase. She hadn't been completely honest with Dalton. She was torn between wanting

John's happiness and wondering if reconciliation would come if the rumors were true.

Lydia opened her door and stepped into the hallway. "Ye ready for dinner or would ye rather inquire 'bout Mr. Douglas first?"

"I'm not hungry. Dalton said there's no one by the name of Douglas registered here."

"Shall we go to the boardinghouse, then?"

"I suppose that would be the best thing. Might as well do what we must." Butterflies took flight in Hannah's stomach.

Hoping to appear nonchalant, the two friends walked down the staircase, across the lobby, and out to the street. Hannah stopped on the sidewalk and took a deep breath. "I don't know that I can do this."

"Of course ye can. We've done lots worse things." She smiled at Hannah and linked arms with her. "This is nothing when ye think of all we've been through."

"I suppose you're right. I've nothing to fear." Inside, though, Hannah knew that what they discovered had the potential to change her life.

"Come on, then." Lydia led the way across the street. "We might as well do what we came here for."

When they reached the boardinghouse, Hannah let Lydia go in first. The smell of roasting meat and vegetables greeted them. There was no one at the front desk.

"I'd hate to intrude on the boarders' evening meal. Perhaps we should return later."

Lydia looked at Hannah, her hands on her hips. "Anyone managing a boardinghouse expects interruptions." She put a hand on Hannah's arm. "Don't be scared. If we find nothing, yer life remains just as it is. And if we do, it could give John back to ye. Ye've nothing to lose, Hannah."

"I know you're not callused, but haven't you thought what this can mean? It could cause great sorrow, especially to John." Hannah looked at the polished wood floor. "If we're wrong and John discovers what we've done, I'll know his contempt. I don't think I can bear that."

"Ye've got no choice except to find out."

"I do have a choice. I can turn around right now and go home."

Lydia stared at her. "And then where are ye?" She folded her arms over her chest. "Yer willing to leave John at the fate of a wicked woman? Can ye live with that?"

Hannah felt anger rise up inside her and she lashed out. "You have everything in life that you could want—a good man who loves you, a fine living, and a child on the way." Hannah suddenly realized she envied Lydia. "How can you know what I feel or need?" she asked, with less vigor.

Lydia's green eyes turned hard. "Have you such a short memory, Hannah? It's not been so long ago that I had nothing—lost me mum, me freedom, me life."

Remorse at her reckless words sucked the air from Hannah's lungs. "I'm sorry. I didn't mean anything by it." She grabbed hold of Lydia's hand. "I'm happy for you. Truly I am." She squeezed her friend's hand. "Please, forgive me. You're my dearest friend."

Lydia squeezed back. "I'm afraid we're both a bit tight, eh." She smiled.

"I suppose. And you're right, I have to find out."

The sounds of footsteps from the hallway quieted the two friends.

"Good evening to ye," said a heavyset woman with a big friendly face. "Are ye looking for the proprietor?"

"Yes, we are," Hannah said.

"That would be me, then." She smiled.

"We were . . ." She'd not thought about what to say. How could she inquire about a guest without raising suspicions. "Have you any rooms available or do you have a houseful of tenants just now?"

"I have rooms. It's been rather quiet the last few days. I've only one new boarder, well, two actually—a young man here on business and an elderly gent and his wife, and I've a man from London who's been here quite some time, several months in fact."

"Oh? I'm from London. Perhaps I know him."

"I doubt that. London's a big place. Name's Weston Douglas. He seems a fine gentleman."

The room whirled. Hannah grabbed the edge of the desk to steady herself and tried to concentrate on the woman's face. "The name is familiar. Is he a lawyer?"

"No, I don't believe so. He's a . . . well, I'm not certain exactly what he does. He has an office in town, but spends little time there. I think he's a merchant of some sort. Seems well off, though. Said he plans to return to London, but I don't know how his lady friend will like that. I suppose they may go together."

"Lady friend?" Lydia asked.

"Oh yes, what is her name?" The proprietor rested a finger against her chin. "Mary . . . no that's not right. It begins with an *M* I'm sure. Oh, yes. Margaret. She comes by now and again. I think I heard him say they plan to return to London together just as soon as they complete some business or other."

Hannah's heart galloped erratically. "Return? Did he say when?"

"I've said too much already." The woman clicked her tongue. "My mouth sometimes runs amuck. He usually spends dinner with us. You can ask him yerself."

"Thank you, but we've already registered at the hotel." Hannah backed toward the door. She needed to get out. How could this be true? Was the Margaret seeing Mr. Douglas the same one married to John? It was too much to be a coincidence.

"We'll let ye know tomorrow if we decide to make a change in our accomodations," Lydia said, taking Hannah by the elbow and escorting her out the door. Once on the sidewalk, she stopped. "Ye look like ye've seen a ghost."

"I feel worse."

"It's just as I said. She's up to something. I knew it. Going back to London, is she?"

"Why? Why would she do such a thing? Does she think John's going to leave his home here and return with her? And what about Mr. Douglas?" Hannah started walking, taking quick short steps. "Perhaps it's not the same woman."

"Hannah, for heaven's sake, you're not making sense. Of course it is. Who else could it be?" Lydia's stride outdistanced Hannah's. "We have to find out what she's up to."

18

"I knew it," Lydia said. "In my heart I knew. I thought maybe it was my loyalty to ye that made me dislike her, but I was right." She strode across the street.

"Lydia, we have only assumptions. We don't know anything for certain. What if Margaret had a reason to see Mr. Douglas, an acceptable reason?"

"And what might that be? What good motive could she have to sneak off to Sydney Town while her husband lies abed . . . near death."

"She did no sneaking, and John wasn't that terribly sick when she left." Inside Hannah felt as if two storms were battling. She didn't want to believe Margaret would do anything so dishonorable, and yet she knew that if it were so, she and John might possibly reunite. *Lord, forgive me for my selfishness.*

"John should know," Lydia said.

"Not yet. We need to make certain there *is* something amiss."

Lydia led the way into the dining room, where the smell of coffee and roasting pork welcomed them. "The only way to discover more is to spend time with Mr. Douglas."

Hannah followed her friend to a table and sat across from her. "And how shall we manage that without raising suspicions?"

"I don't know for certain, but our opportunities will be better if we stay at the boardinghouse." She leaned an elbow on the table and rested a cheek in her hand. "I wouldn't mind that. Whatever that woman was cooking smelled awfully good." She grinned.

"How can you jest at a time like this? John's life may well be torn asunder . . . again. He's taken Margaret in, he's trusted her." Hannah felt sick inside. "If our fears are true, he'll face more suffering and humiliation. I can barely stand the thought."

Lydia straightened. "What's wrong with ye? Yer making no sense. Don't ye want John back?" She leaned closer to Hannah, lowering her voice. "If this is true, ye can be together again. Ye know he loves ye. And this thing with Margaret may hurt him, but in time it will be forgotten. In the end ye'll both get what ye really want."

"I can't even allow myself to think of the possibility." Hannah clasped her hands on the table in front of her. Mrs. Atherton's warning rang through her mind, turning her cold with apprehension. Could she trust her motives? "If we're to find the truth, I can't permit my needs to even enter my mind. The idea of taking advantage of another person's tragedy for personal reward is repulsive."

"That's not what yer doing, Hannah. Yer setting a wrong to rights. If Margaret has done what we think she has, then it should be made right."

"Poor John. Hasn't he suffered enough?"

"Yes. He has and I'm not about to let this woman continue to misuse him."

"It's not up to you or to me."

"Then who?" Lydia sat back, crossed her arms over her chest, and blew out an exasperated breath. "Don't be foolish."

Hannah felt the sting of disapproval. "You believe me foolish?"

A bit of Lydia's bluster faded. "I didn't mean for it to come out that way. Of course yer not, but in this . . . I just think ye ought to be strong enough to dig out the truth."

"Even if it's not pleasing to God for me to do so?"

"Ye think God approves of what Margaret's done?"

"No. Of course not, but we don't know just what she's done, if anything."

"That's why we have to find out." Lydia leaned forward and rested her arms on the table. "I know ye've tried to be fair. But ye can't shrink from this. It's time to do what's right."

<hr/>

Hannah, Lydia, and Dalton left the hotel with Dalton lugging the bags at his insistence. When they stepped into the boardinghouse, the woman they'd seen the night before greeted them. "Good morning. So ye've decided to stay here after all."

"That we have," Hannah said.

"It was the smell of yer cooking that convinced us," Lydia said.

The woman smiled broadly. "I'm known as a fine cook." She turned her attention to the registry. "Would ye two ladies like to share a room?"

Hannah and Lydia looked at one another. "Yes. We would," Lydia said.

"All right, then." The woman wrote in the ledger, then asked, "Your names?"

"Mrs. David Gelson."

"Hannah Talbot." Hannah's maiden name tasted like lead on her tongue.

The woman turned the ledger toward them. "Sign here."

After Hannah and Lydia had both put their signatures to the ledger, the woman said, "I'm Mrs. Jones, Elen Jones. My husband went to his eternal rest two years ago." Her eyes turned moist, but she tipped up her chin and managed to smile. "I've been running this place since. If ye have any needs, just let me know." She moved toward the entryway. "Now then, up the stairs, turn left, and go down two doors. Your room is on the right."

"Thank you," Hannah said, glancing at Dalton.

Elen turned to him. "Are you with them?"

"I am."

"All right, then, Mr. . . ." She glanced at the register. "Gelson. I'll—"

"I'm not Mr. Gelson. I'm Dalton Keen, and I'm simply accompanying the ladies."

"Oh. I do apologize." Elen blushed. "I'll put you across the hallway from them."

After signing the register, Dalton carried Hannah and Lydia's bags to their room, and then with a warning about prudence, he set off for his own.

Lydia stepped into the hallway. "Dalton. We'll be going downstairs for . . . tea." Mischief lit her eyes. "Just in case yer wondering where we got to."

His mouth tight and his brow furrowed, he said, "I'll be down shortly."

Lydia stepped back into the room. "He's not happy with us, I can see that."

"It's not us," Hannah said. "It's the circumstances. He realizes what may be at stake." She looked around the room. It was clean and tidy, with frilled curtains at the window. There were two beds with a bureau between them. A side chair sat in one corner beside an armoire. "This is nice."

"That it is." Lydia sat on one of the beds and pressed a hand into the mattress. "I believe they've used feather ticking, but it could use some new stuffing."

"Do you think we should go downstairs straightaway? I'd like to see if Mr. Douglas is among the breakfast guests."

Lydia stood and moved to the door. "We can only hope, eh."

"Lydia, this is not a game."

"I know that. Would ye prefer I wear a frown and growl at everyone?"

"No, of course not." Lydia had always been one to take life straight on without grumbling. "I'm sorry. I just have a bad feeling about all of this."

Lydia moved to Hannah and draped an arm over her shoulders. "I know. But we've got to remember God is in this with us. He'll see to it that his will is done. But we've still got to do all we can."

Hannah rested her head on Lydia's shoulder. "You're a good friend."

Lydia gave her a quick squeeze. "Come on. Let's get us some morning tea, eh."

The two made their way to the dining room. A large mahogany table nearly filled the room. A paunchy man sat at one end, a cup of coffee in hand. His face rounded when he smiled. He stood. "Good day, ladies."

"Good day," Lydia said.

"Ah, so yer going to join us, then," Elen Jones said, setting a platter of scones on the table.

"We've eaten," Hannah said. "But a cup of tea would be nice."

"Fine."

An elderly couple sat across from the man who'd greeted them. The gentleman stood. "Good day."

Lydia and Hannah both nodded and smiled.

"Mr. Booth, what can I get for you?" Elen asked.

"My wife and I would like tea to go with our scones," he said, returning to his seat.

Elen bounced as she moved about the room, filling cups and serving the morning meal of scones, eggs, and fried pork. When she came to a man sitting at the end of the table and staring into his cup, she asked, "And how 'bout you, can I get you more coffee, Mr. Douglas?"

The rhythm of Hannah's heart picked up as her eyes fell upon the man. He looked fatigued and unfriendly. *That's him.* He wasn't what she expected, not exactly unattractive but a bit pudgy and unkempt.

Lydia leaned close to Hannah and whispered, "Looks like he's been at the grog."

Hannah agreed. He'd not said a word, but she didn't like him. How could Margaret be interested in someone like him?

"Ye look a bit done in," Elen said to Mr. Douglas.

"That I am. But another cup of your fine coffee ought to perk me up."

She filled his mug and left the room.

Mr. Douglas sipped, looking over his cup at the newcomers. "Something ye need from me, ladies?" He smiled grimly.

221

"N-no," Hannah said, realizing she'd been staring.

"We'll be fine with just tea." Lydia took a place at the table.

Hannah slid into the chair beside her, wondering what she ought to say next. How did one get information out of a stranger?

"We've just checked in," Lydia said. "You?"

"I've been here a good while." He took another drink of his coffee.

"Have ye traveled a great distance?"

"Should say so—all the way from London."

"Oh, London, really? Do ye have a business establishment here, then?"

He gazed at Lydia through bloodshot eyes. "No. And I've nearly completed my affairs and will soon be sailing home."

Elen returned, carrying a tray with a teakettle and cups and saucers. Setting it on the table, she filled the cups and set one in front of Hannah and then Lydia. "Are ye sure I can't offer ye ladies something to eat?"

"Actually, I was thinking of trying one of the scones. They look grand," Lydia said.

Elen offered her the plate. Lydia took one and dipped it into her tea before taking a bite. "Mmm. This is delicious."

Elen smiled. "Thank ye. It was me mum's recipe." She looked at Hannah. "And you, would ye like something?"

"A scone will be fine." Hannah wasn't at all hungry, but she took a scone to show she had a legitimate reason for being at the table.

"All right, then. I've a pile of dishes waiting for me." Elen disappeared through a door Hannah guessed led to the kitchen.

Lydia dipped her scone again and took another bite. "What kind of business are you in, Mr. Douglas?"

He leaned his arms on the table. "Just Weston will be fine." He held his mug in both hands. "Actually, I'm here on speculation, considering just what kind of business might do well in this town. Haven't made up my mind, but I'm considering importing goods. There's a need for more suppliers, I'd say."

"So ye'd open a mercantile, then?"

"Perhaps. But more likely I'd supply the shops and mercantiles here in the local townships." He eyed Lydia more closely. "And you, where are you from?"

Hannah felt a moment of panic. What if he connected them with Margaret?

"My husband is a physician in Parramatta," Lydia said casually, her smile warm.

Hannah made note not to trust Lydia so thoroughly. She was quite a good actress.

"Ah, so you're married, then."

"I am. He's a fine man."

Weston Douglas turned his dark eyes on Hannah. "And you?"

"I work as a housemaid, nothing quite so grand as being married to a doctor." She was surprised to hear a cheery, friendly lilt to her voice.

He downed the last of his coffee. "Well, have a grand day, ladies. I've business to attend to." He pushed away from the table, picked up his hat, and with a slight bow to all gathered at the table, he walked out.

His leaving seemed to be a sign to the others. The Booths and the other gentleman rose and left the room.

Hannah pressed a hand to the base of her throat. "Oh, I just nearly fainted. I wasn't at all sure what to say."

"Ye did fine." Lydia smiled. "But we didn't learn much. I suppose we'll have to wait until dinner, eh."

"And what do we do until then?"

"I say, a day of shopping is in order. Christmas is nearly here, and I was hoping to find something for David."

"Of course . . . Christmas." Hannah had nearly forgotten. Her mind went to how this Christmas would be different than last. She pressed her palms together on the table in front of her and forced herself to think on what was at hand. "How are we going to discover anything from Mr. Douglas? We can't openly question him."

"He's sociable. Sometimes if ye just bide yer time and wait, fellas like him will tell ye all ye need to know without asking. They usually love to talk 'bout themselves."

"What is it that you need to find out? Perhaps I can be of help," Elen said.

Hannah and Lydia swung around. They'd not heard her enter the room. "We were just wondering where we might find Christmas gifts for our families," Hannah managed to say.

"Oh well, there are a couple of fine shops not far from here. Are ye shopping for yer families?"

"That we are," said Lydia.

Elen smiled. "The Johnson's have a fine store just down the street. They've toys of all sorts." She moved to the window and glanced out. "Ye just step out and turn right. It's not far."

"Thank you." Lydia dipped the last of her scone into her tea.

Elen cleared away cups and saucers and moved into the kitchen.

Lydia finished her tea. "While we're looking for gifts, we can inquire as to Weston Douglas's activities."

"We'll look suspicious."

"Not at all. People love to gossip." Lydia smiled. "Come on. It's time we were on our way."

"We ought to tell Dalton."

"My guess is he's napping. I remember when I used to work at the estate. He'd take a mid-morning nap whenever he could manage."

Hannah smiled. "He still does, if he's not needed. Still, we must tell him what we've learned—"

"Which is very little." Lydia picked up her reticule. "We can tell him later." She sounded almost giddy.

"You're enjoying this too much."

"I admit it is a bit fun. Life sometimes feels tedious. This is very much like a treasure hunt."

Hannah felt herself grow angry. She folded her arms over her chest. "We're not searching for treasure. And what we find might possibly wreak havoc on the only man I've ever loved."

Lydia gave Hannah a disdainful look. "I know. Ye've told me. But did ye ever think that he might be happy to know the truth?"

Lydia plopped down on the bed. "I think David will like his new muffler, don't ye?" She held up a dark blue scarf she'd purchased.

"It's the middle of summer, Lydia."

"Yes, but winter will come. It was a good price."

"That's because no one wants mufflers in the summer." Hannah shook her head slightly, then smiled. "It is a nice scarf."

"And I'm sure he'll enjoy the tobacco too," Lydia said.

Hannah felt melancholy. She had no husband to buy for. How nice it would be to purchase pipe tobacco for John. She'd always liked the smell of it.

"I'm sure Thomas will love his Bilbo Catcher." Lydia shook her head slightly. "How children can catch a tiny ball in a cup on top of a wooden spindle I'll never know. I can't manage it." She wrapped the scarf about her neck. "It was a fine day, but I wish we'd discovered more about Mr. Douglas."

"Maybe there's nothing to be found." Hannah sat in the side chair and stuck her legs straight out in front of her, crossing her ankles.

A knock sounded at the door. Lydia pushed herself off the bed. "Who is it?"

"Dalton Keen."

Lydia opened the door. "Why, hello. Wherever did ye get off to? We've not seen ye all day."

"I apologize. But after you left this morning, I thought I'd have a go at finding information on our Mr. Douglas."

"And did ye discover anything?" asked Lydia.

"I did, in fact."

"Ye did? Please, come in."

Dalton's face turned a slight pink. "It's not proper—a man in your room."

Lydia stepped out and glanced up and down the hallway. "No one will see. Come in."

Taking another look down the corridor, Dalton stepped inside, and Lydia closed the door behind him.

"Well, what is it?" she asked.

"It seems that Mr. Douglas hasn't been completely forthcoming about his business affairs. He professes to be contemplating opening a business here, but since his arrival, he's done nothing toward that end. Rather, he spends his time drinking and gambling."

"Really?" Hannah felt her pulse quicken. "Perhaps he truly is a scoundrel."

"Highly likely, I'd say." Dalton looked at the door, obviously feeling uneasy about being in the ladies' room.

"If he's not here on business, then what reason can he have?" Lydia asked. "What do ye think he and Margaret are up to?"

"What can they possibly want from John?" Hannah asked. "The farm is only now beginning to prosper and certainly isn't worth traveling all the way from London for."

"That's true." Lydia folded her arms over her chest. "There must be something we don't know 'bout John or the situation."

The room turned quiet. Finally, Hannah said, "There's nothing I can think of."

"He's not got a fortune hid, then?"

"No. Of course not. I'd know. He lost everything when he went to gaol—his cousin saw to that."

"There's nothing much to be done except to speak with more people and to listen," Lydia said. "Perhaps we'll discover something 'bout our Mr. Douglas at dinner."

"I'll not be there," Dalton said. "I've been invited to dine with a friend." A blush rose up from his neck and into his cheeks.

"Why, Dalton, yer blushing. Is this a special friend?"

He pressed his lips tightly together. "A lady friend of mine."

"I had no idea." Lydia clapped her hands together.

Dalton's blush deepened. "I'd best be on my way."

Hannah walked to the door, opened it, and peeked out. "No one's about." She opened the door wider. "We'll see you at breakfast, then."

"Tomorrow." He stepped outside, and Hannah closed the door behind him.

"How 'bout that, eh? Dalton has a lady friend." Lydia smiled.

"He's a good man. Whoever she is, she's lucky to have him."

"True." Lydia turned to the armoire. "We'd best get dressed for dinner. Perhaps tonight we'll learn more 'bout Mr. Douglas and Margaret."

Just as the evening meal ended, Weston Douglas swaggered into the dining room. "Good evening to ye." His words slid into each other, mangling the language. "Hope ye all had a fine day." He smiled and grabbed the back of a chair.

He's besotted! Hannah thought.

Weston moved around to the front of the chair and dropped into it. "Sorry I'm late. Just out with friends." He smirked. "Cards. Always been a good player." His smile slid sideways up his face and then turned into a sneer. "One fellow tried to cheat me." His blue eyes looked cold.

Hannah didn't much like Weston. Evidently neither did the elderly couple, the Booths. They excused themselves and left the room.

Weston called after them, "Don't leave on my account. I'll behave myself." He snickered. "Oh well." Leaning on the table, he looked at Elen. "Seems I'm in need of a meal."

"It would seem," Elen said in a disgusted tone. "Ye should have had something before ye started downing the grog."

Ignoring the comment, he looked straight at Hannah, his dark eyes penetrating. "Do I know you?"

228

"Yes. We met briefly this morning." Hannah felt her heart flutter. He couldn't possibly know her, could he?

"Ah yes. You're the quiet one with the dark eyes. Lovely eyes, I might add."

"Here ye go. Ye'll need this." Elen set a bowl of stew in front of Weston and then poured him a cup of coffee. "Ye should stay away from the spirits."

"Right you are. I lost a goodly amount of money. It matters not. Soon I'll have more than I can spend, me and my lovely lady."

"Oh, are you married?" Lydia asked.

Hannah had to admire Lydia's aplomb. Nothing seemed to unsettle her.

"No. But I've a fine lady who loves me. And she'll be coming into a goodly amount of money soon."

Alarm pulsed through Hannah. Was his lady Margaret? "Have you a business venture in the works, Mr. Douglas?"

He set his gaze on Hannah, grinned devilishly, and then leaned toward her, saying in a hushed tone, "Ah yes, I do at that. Well, Margaret and I do."

The name Margaret exploded in Hannah's mind.

"Her husband, poor soul, will soon be meeting his Maker. When he's gone, she inherits a fortune."

Hannah felt the room sway. *He can't be speaking of John!* "Is her husband ill?" she asked.

"The good Lord will be taking him home soon. But then one man's loss is another's gain, eh?" The sloppy grin returned. "Margaret and I have plans, but the first thing we'll do is sail back to London. I'll be glad to leave this vermin-infested hole." He swayed even though he was sitting. His eyes closed and his head dropped against the back of the chair. He didn't move.

"He's passed out," Lydia said.

Elen shook her head with disdain. "Not the first time. I'll have to get someone to carry him to his bed." She walked through the kitchen door.

"What do you think he was talking about?" Hannah asked, her throat tight with dread.

"Does John possess a fortune?"

"No. Not at all. You know that." Hannah looked at Weston. "Do you think he was talking about the quinsy? Perhaps he thinks John is still sick."

"That makes no sense. We'd best tell John 'bout this straightaway. Something's not right."

"I'll tell him, but not yet. I have to know more."

"What do ye have in mind?"

Hannah thought. She must find out what Margaret and Douglas's scheme was. "Perhaps he has something that would shed light on what they have planned and why. We could search his room." Hannah said it even before the idea had fully taken hold, but already she knew that's exactly what they must do.

19

Hannah paced between the window and the settee where Lydia sat looking relaxed. Dalton stood just outside the parlor door, appearing casual and unruffled. Hannah wondered how either of them could remain composed with so much at stake.

"Hannah, sit down," Lydia said. "Ye'll wear a ditch in the floor." She patted the cushion beside her.

"I can't sit." She looked from Lydia to Dalton. "I don't know how the two of you can remain so calm."

"I'm not at all, really," Lydia said. "I'd say expectation would better fit what I'm feeling. If Margaret has been up to no good, it's 'bout time she was found out. I'll be glad to expose the truth."

Dalton rested a hand on the doorframe. "The more tenuous a situation, the more tranquil I become . . . on the outside." He grinned. "Used to drive my sister to distraction."

Hannah returned to the window and gazed out. "I'm not sure I feel right about this. If we're caught breaking into someone else's room—"

"We're not breaking in. We'll just be . . . visiting and having a look 'round. And besides, it was yer idea."

Hannah turned to Lydia. "And perhaps it's not a good one. If we're caught, we could end up back in gaol."

Steps sounded on the stairs, and Dalton clasped his hands behind his back and moved into the entryway. "Good day," he said casually.

"Fine day it is too." Weston Douglas moved to the parlor door and glanced inside. "Top of the morning to you, ladies." His eyes seemed to graze as they took in Hannah and Lydia.

Hannah managed to smile and nod.

Lydia stood. "It's a grand day," she said with enthusiasm, her smile bright.

I'd have no idea she was up to something, Hannah thought, not sure she ought to be proud of Lydia or disappointed in her.

Weston tipped his hat. "Well, I'm off. I've a busy day ahead."

"We'll look for you at dinner," Lydia said as Weston walked to the door and stepped outside, seemingly oblivious to her and their encounter.

Lydia joined Hannah at the window, and the two watched him stroll down the street toward the pub. "Bit early to be imbibing. But just as well. His vice gives us better opportunity for searching his room." Lydia took Hannah's arm and started across the room.

"Lydia, I think it best if you stay," Dalton said almost apologetically.

"Me?" She stopped and stared at him.

"I know you've been waiting for this, but I ought to accompany Hannah. And if he were to return unexpectedly, you're better suited to distract him. I think it best that I be the one with Hannah, just in case he comes back without warning."

Lydia released Hannah and slapped her hands to her sides.

"I thought it was settled. Me and Hannah were to do the investigating." Her mouth turned into a pout. "I was counting on it."

"No. It's better if I go." Dalton's tone was firm.

"I'm plenty strong enough to stand up to him."

"Lydia, hush," Hannah said. "Someone will hear. And Dalton's right. You've no business confronting someone in your condition. And if Douglas comes back, you'll do wonderfully well at stalling him." She grinned. "In fact, it seems you've a talent for deception."

"I'm not sure I like that." A smiled played at Lydia's lips. "I so wanted to go. Why don't ye stay, Hannah? Ye'll do fine at distracting him if need be."

"If Douglas were to return, I'd not be able to think of a thing to say." She moved toward the door. "And John's my husband . . . I mean, he was. I should go."

Lydia folded her arms over her chest and frowned. "All right. But I'm not pleased with this, I want ye to know."

"Oh, we know," Hannah said with a small shake of the head. She glanced into the dining room to see if anyone was about. "It's time," she whispered to Dalton and led the way up the staircase to the second floor and down the hallway. Just as she and Dalton reached Weston's room, a woman stepped into the corridor.

Hannah stood with her back to the wall and looked up at Dalton, trying to think of something to say to him that sounded conversational. "Perhaps it would be a good idea to visit the wharf," she said. "They've a good selection of fresh fish."

Momentarily Dalton seemed taken aback but quickly recovered and said, "A fine idea."

The woman smiled as she passed and moved to a room at

the end of the hall where she stopped and opened the door, disappearing inside.

Hannah's heart thumped hard in her chest. She took a deep breath, checked the corridor again, and then turned and tried the door. It opened. She stepped inside with Dalton close behind.

The room stank of spirits and cigar smoke. The bed was unmade, and the only chair was nearly hidden beneath a pile of clothing. There was a desk cluttered with books and papers. Hannah moved to the window and gazed out, fearing she'd see Douglas striding up the street toward the boardinghouse. There was no sign of him.

She turned and faced the room. "He's not one for tidiness, is he?"

"I'd say not." Dalton moved to the bureau and opened the top drawer and rifled through its contents.

Hannah watched.

He looked up at her. "You'd best get to it."

"Right." Hannah decided the desk was the best place to begin. She wasn't even sure what she was looking for as she searched through a pile of papers, but hoped she'd know what it was when she found it.

Dalton pushed the top drawer closed and opened the next while Hannah thumbed through another stack of papers. "He's collected an awful lot of stuff," she said as she searched an assortment of correspondence, ink, a pen and a . . . key. She picked it up and examined it. "Could this be anything?"

"What?" Dalton crossed to Hannah. Taking the key, he examined it. "Too small for a door." He glanced around the room.

"What else could it unlock?" Hannah's eyes went to the armoire. With a pulse of excitement, she strode across the room and opened the cabinet, going through hanging shirts. Nothing. She stood on tiptoe and felt the edge of an upper shelf.

"Here, let me have a go." Dalton swept a hand across the top shelf, but found only a hat and gloves.

"It must fit something here." Hannah opened a drawer and her heart quickened. There, amidst socks and underclothes, sat a wooden box. She lifted it out and tried to open the lid. It was locked.

Dalton's eyes lit up. "So it needs a key, does it?"

Hannah carried it to the desk.

Dalton pushed the key into the lock and turned. Opening the lid, he smiled at Hannah, then looked at the contents, taking out a stack of letters.

"There's quite a lot there. It will take some time to read them all. He could come back and discover us. How would we ever explain reading his personal mail?"

"We've no justification for our presence here, no matter what he might find us doing." Dalton moved to the window and looked out. "I don't see him. He'll probably be hours, yet. Most likely in the midst of a game of cards and half inebriated already."

"Can you go down and make certain he's not back?" Hannah carried some of the letters to the desk and sat in the chair. "I'll start reading."

"If I don't return right away, then I'm probably engaged in a conversation with the chap. If so, put the box and letters back and leave." He opened the door, peered out, and stepped into the hallway.

Hannah picked up an envelope. It was postmarked from Margaret Bradshaw. Hands trembling, she opened it and pulled out a letter. It began with "My dearest Weston." Anger smoldered in Hannah.

Margaret talked about John, life on the farm, and how she hoped all went well. As Hannah read, old wounds felt as if they'd been opened and rubbed raw. She stuffed the letter back into the envelope and went on to the next. There was nothing that would create suspicion.

The door opened and Hannah's heart shot into her throat. She pressed the letter against her chest. It was Dalton. "Oh! You frightened me."

"Sorry." He closed the door. "There's no sign of him. But we'd best hurry. Have you found anything?"

"Just that Margaret was corresponding with Mr. Douglas." She handed him a stack of letters and then opened another one with the address in Margaret's handwriting. This time as she read, her interest piqued. She quickly scanned the letter. "Listen to this," she said and read, "*It won't be long now and we'll be on our way to London. I long for your arms and for the day we don't have to pretend anymore.*"

Hannah stopped reading, her ire flaring. "How dare she!" She looked at Dalton. "They *are* lovers. And she's planning to leave John! After everything he's done for her and all she's put us through she has no intention of staying."

Dalton's forehead creased. "Here's something else." He cleared his throat and read from another letter, "*We'll soon have what we came for. Only a few more weeks and we'll possess more wealth than we ever dreamed possible. Then we'll be on our way just as we planned. John has no idea.*" Dalton looked at Hannah, grief registering in his eyes.

"That woman has no heart!" Hannah could feel the threat of tears. How could anyone be so cruel?

"Do you have any notion what wealth she's referring to?" Dalton asked.

"None whatsoever. We never had much. I can't imagine."

They quickly scanned the rest of the letters, hoping to discover more specifics, but there was just more of the same. Discouraged, they returned the letters to the box and set it back in its place in the armoire.

***

"That man is a scoundrel of the worst sort," Lydia sputtered when she heard what Dalton and Hannah had discovered. "And Margaret—she's worse than a scoundrel. I can't even say what I think of her."

Hannah fumed over Margaret, but she was also angry with herself. She'd nearly done nothing. *How like me. If not for Lydia's insistence . . .*

"We've got to tell John," Lydia said.

"Yes. But they've some sort of scheme worked out," Hannah said. "We need to find out what it is."

The room turned quiet, and then a smile touched Lydia's lips. "I've an idea."

Hannah knew Lydia well enough to know it could be outrageous. "I don't know that I like your tone."

"It's nothing terrible," Lydia reassured her. "We can do to Margaret what we've done here. She may have the information we're looking for."

"What do you mean?"

"We've got to have a look at her papers as well. She may have letters from Mr. Douglas."

"And how do you propose we do that?" Dalton asked. "It's not as if we won't be noticed driving up to the farm."

"I can invite her to tea." Lydia's eyes gleamed. "It's time we got better acquainted, don't ye think?"

"She knows you don't like her."

"Yes, but she's so vain, she'll most likely believe that even I'd enjoy spending time with her." She smirked. "I can let her believe that I want to mend fences . . . since John is such a dear friend. And while we're having tea, you and Dalton can pay a visit to the farm."

Hannah could feel the muscles tighten in her abdomen. "All right. When?"

"I'll send her a note the minute we get back."

"And what of John? What if he's there?"

"He ought to appreciate our concern," Lydia retorted.

"We can't say anything, not just yet. We need to know more." Hannah rubbed her temples, hoping to massage away a throbbing headache. "He's usually somewhere on the property and not at the house."

"All right, then. Ye can go during the day . . ." Lydia smiled. "The day I'm having tea with Margaret."

John gave Margaret a hand up onto her horse and then swung into his saddle. She arranged her skirts so as not to look improper. "It's been some time since I've ridden. I feel a bit peculiar perched up here."

"Riding sidesaddle is unsuitable for this country. You can ride astride, I won't mind a bit. Hannah used to and said it made riding much easier and felt steadier."

"That may be, but it's outrageous and unladylike."

Margaret's smug tone grated on John, but he said nothing.

He remembered how he'd tried to convince Hannah to ride sidesaddle, convinced it was proper. He hadn't wanted her to appear indecent in public. His reputation is what he'd been thinking of. The memory of his egotism shamed him.

"You ride as you like, but astride is safer." He leaned forward just a bit and gently kicked his horse in the sides. As the animal broke into an easy canter, Margaret prodded her mount and moved alongside him.

"I figure it's time you saw a bit more of the farm," he said.

"Isn't it an estate? It seems quite large."

"I'd not call it something so grand as that, but I've acquired a good deal of land. One day perhaps we will be able to call it an estate."

Margaret smiled at him. "I look forward to that day. It will be grand, indeed."

They cantered across the fields, then slowed to a walk. "When Hannah and I first moved here, we had only fifty acres."

"Truly? That's all? How did you manage to acquire so much, then?"

"When I moved onto this piece, I hoped one day that the adjoining property would come up for sale, so I saved what I could. When it came available, I bought it."

"How much land is there?"

"Nearly two thousand acres. I've payments to make, but as long as the farm continues to do well, I'll have no problem with that."

"Who owned it before you?"

"A man living in Sydney Town. He never moved out here, though. Returned to England to care for ailing parents." John moved his hat so the brim shaded his eyes. "Took nearly every cent I had, but it was worth it. Without the extra ground, I'd never have been able to build the kind of farm I've always wanted." He gazed out over the open fields, golden and baking beneath the summer sun.

"It's beautiful," Margaret said. "However, I've still not adjusted to the weather. It's much hotter than England, and this time of year I'm used to it being cold. Seems strange having sweltering heat for the holidays. It shan't feel like Christmas at all."

"You'll adjust."

Margaret sighed. "I miss the green of England and the distractions of London."

"I thought you were done with all that." Disappointment and then suspicion crept inside John.

"I am. Absolutely. But sometimes a bit of revelry would be nice." She smiled sweetly and added, "You know I'd never trade the frivolous life of London for what I have now. I adore being with you."

John warmed to her affection. He and Margaret may not share the kind of love he'd had with Hannah, but given time it might grow. "We have a fine future here, together—a family and—"

"John, if you want a family, you'll have to move back into the house," Margaret said with a mischievous smile.

Embarrassment warmed John's face. "I suppose you're right." Although he knew it was time to commit fully to Margaret, the idea of it made him feel unfaithful to Hannah. "I'll be gone a few days to purchase cattle . . . when I return, I'll move back in."

Margaret reached across the space between them and took his hand. "I've so longed to hear you say that."

John felt a flicker of affection and squeezed her hand. *I've got to put Hannah out of my mind. My life is with Margaret now.*

"Will you be traveling near Sydney Town?" Margaret asked.

"It would be quite out of my way."

"Oh. I was hoping you might possibly stop at my solicitor's. It seems he has papers I need to sign. Something to do with my parents' estate. I hate to travel to Sydney Town, the road is so appalling."

"There's always the river."

"That's true. But the barges are quite primitive."

"Maybe so, but at least it's a peaceful mode of travel."

"It's dreadfully humid. And you know how bad the bugs can be." Margaret peered at him from beneath the brim of her hat, her brown eyes beseeching. "Please, would you mind?"

"I'll go, but it will have to be another day," John said. "I thought all the affairs of your parents' estate had been taken care of."

"It seems my brothers have decided to sell off more of the family property, and they are kindly sharing the profits."

"I see. And who shall I speak to?"

"Weston Douglas." She smiled. "I've inherited a tidy sum. It will be a great help to us and the farm."

"I'll speak to him, but I'd rather you accompanied me."

"Go with you to buy cattle?"

"We could drive them back together."

Margaret shook her head. "I dearly love your company, but I truly don't want to follow a mob of beef all the way from Sydney Town—the dust and flies would be frightful."

John nodded, remembering how much fun he and Hannah had when they'd herded sheep together. "Fine. You'll just have to tell me where to find him."

"I've the address. As my husband, you can sign any document for me."

"I know the law says that, but I'd rather you see what has to be signed."

"I trust you implicitly."

"All right, then. But I'll make sure you have copies so that you're abreast of what's happening with your holdings."

"Of course. That's very kind of you." She pulled back on the reins and her horse tossed its head, fighting the restriction. "When do you think you'll be going?"

"After I get back with the cattle. Possibly next week."

"Fine. That will be just fine."

20

Hannah dusted the windowsill of an upstairs bedroom, then stopped and looked out over the Atherton estate. Brown fields and hillsides cooked beneath a December sun. Her mind flashed back to London Decembers. They'd been nothing like this. Icy patterns glistened on windows and freshly fallen snow lay in mounds along the roads. Too quickly the white blanket would turn black from churning wagon wheels and the soot of countless belching chimneys.

This is better, she told herself, fighting nerves. Today Lydia would meet with Margaret while she searched John's house. When Lydia had told her it was all set, she'd seemed almost gleeful, especially over Margaret's presumption that Lydia truly desired a friendship with her. "I'd rather die," Lydia had said. Then with a smile added, "This will be a sweet revenge. I can barely wait to see the look on her face when we confront her."

Hannah hadn't said anything. She knew it was necessary to find out just what Margaret was up to. But nothing about this situation pleased her. The idea of deceiving someone, including a person like Margaret, set her on edge. It wasn't her way.

She'd always admired her mother's compassion and gentleness and wanted to be like her.

Sometimes there are circumstances that call for punitive justice, she told herself to bolster her resolve.

She opened the window, hoping a bit of air would freshen the bed chamber. It was time to go. She headed for the laundry room, where she'd leave the well-used dusting cloth.

She'd lied to Mrs. Atherton, saying she needed the day off to run errands and to visit Lydia. Catharine, in her usual way, kindly gave her permission. *I wish I were running errands.* Her stomach flip-flopped. *Perhaps this wasn't a good idea.*

What else could be done? John deserved to know the truth. If she could help to unearth it, then the risks were worth taking.

Clutching the cloth in her hands, she hurried down the staircase. Was there any possibility that Margaret was innocent? Hannah hadn't forgotten what it felt like to be unjustly charged with an offense. The thought sent shivers through her. *No. I'm right, and she doesn't deserve my pity or tolerance. And this is different. I'm not trying to do harm, I want to help.* Although she didn't know what else Margaret might be up to, at the very least, she was an adulteress. The letters to Weston Douglas proved that. Under normal circumstances, Hannah would consider it none of her concern, but this involved John, and that changed everything.

Mrs. Goudy stood at a sideboard, kneading bread dough, when Hannah walked into the kitchen. Anxious to be on her way, she moved to the washroom.

"And why are you in such a hurry this morning?" Mrs. Goudy asked.

"I'm not. Just need to make a trip into Parramatta."

"Oh, well, isn't God good?" She smiled. "I was just thinking

I needed some cinnamon. I've not enough for the apple cake I promised the Athertons. Could you pick up a bit for me?"

Hannah stopped. She'd not figured on anything like this. *I should have known to be quiet about going into town.* "I . . . I'll see if there's any available," she stuttered. "The last time I was in Parramatta, the store was waiting on a shipment of spices." Inwardly she cringed—another lie.

"No cinnamon? Hmm. That's unusual. I've never had difficulty getting it before."

Hannah shrugged. "I suppose there may be a lot of people wanting cinnamon, what with Christmas coming on."

"I suppose so."

"I'll ask for you."

"Thank you, dear." The cook left her hands in the dough but kept her eyes on Hannah. "Is something troubling you?"

Hannah stopped. "No. Nothing whatever." She tried to relax tight muscles.

Mrs. Goudy eyed her suspiciously. "I've been watching you this morning, and I'd say you're a bit tight 'bout something. In fact, you've not been yourself the last couple of weeks."

"I'm fine, truly. I just plan to meet Lydia and I've need of some sewing supplies." The lie slipped out easily, too easily for Hannah's liking.

Dalton stepped into the kitchen and stood just inside the door. "Can I be of assistance?"

"Thank you, Dalton. I'll have need of the buggy."

"Certainly. I'll get it ready for you." With a knowing look, he walked through the kitchen and the back porch.

Mrs. Goudy returned to her bread dough, pressing the heels of her hands into the mound and then rolling it back onto itself. Without looking at Hannah, she said, "Something's going on. I can feel it." Her hands rested. "Of course, if you'd rather not share, I'm fine with that. But I'll be praying for you all the same."

Hannah wished she could tell the kindly woman the truth, but she dare not. For now, no one could know. "Everything's fine, Mrs. Goudy. But thank you." She left the kitchen and headed for her cottage. She'd need to take something as a gift for Margaret, just in case she was home.

After laying a dish towel in a basket, she took three jars of preserves down from a shelf and put them in the container. At least this way, if need be, it would appear she'd had no ill intent.

With the basket over her arm, she set off for the tool shop. When she stepped inside, Thomas stood watching Perry at the kiln. Another man worked the bellows. Smoke and the smell of burning metal filled the room. Hannah moved toward them. "What an awful stink."

"Perry's teaching me to cook metal," Thomas said.

"He's a bit young for that, don't you think?"

Perry straightened. "He's just watching, is all."

"All right. But stay clear, mind you." Hannah tousled Thomas's hair.

"Aren't ye going to town?"

"Yes. I'm just leaving and wanted to say good-bye. You mind Perry, now."

"I will."

"No worries, Hannah. He's a good lad," Perry said.

"Thank you for looking after him."

Perry set long metal tongs on the hearth. "I like spending time with him. He's a fine lad and a help to me."

"I shan't be long. Just there and back."

Hannah dropped a kiss on Thomas's forehead. "Well then, I'll be off. Dalton will have the buggy ready for me," she said, her nerves popping.

She left the shop and hurried to the carriage house. Dalton already had the horses in harness and the buggy set to go.

"Thank you." Hannah moved to the buggy and placed the basket on the seat.

"I ought to go with you."

"I understand your concern, but I shan't be long. And if John or Margaret do happen to be home, how will I explain your driving me? I've made the trip on my own many times. I don't want to raise questions."

"Do be careful." He gave her a hand up. "If John is about, what will you tell him?"

"I doubt he'll be there. This time of day he's always working on the property somewhere. And if for some reason he's home, I'll simply tell him I've come to visit Margaret."

"And will you tell him what we've discovered?"

"At the proper time."

"And that will be . . . ?"

"I'm not certain, but I'll know when the time comes." The idea of John discovering that she'd been sneaking about and snooping into his life made her tremble inside. Would he understand that she'd done it *for* him and not *to* him?

"If it was me, I'd want to know the truth. And the sooner the better."

"I've thought of that." Hannah settled on the seat. Just the idea of speaking to John about all this ugliness made her stomach tighten into knots. "Pray that I find the truth."

"I'll do that."

Hannah lifted the reins, clicked her tongue, and the horses

set off. Choking dust billowed up around the buggy and settled on the seat and Hannah's skirt. Her mouth and throat became dry, and she couldn't keep from coughing. Slowing the buggy, she reached down, picked up a canteen, and took a soothing drink. After replacing the lid and putting it back on the floor beside her feet, she looked at the cloudless sky and longed for rain to dampen the dry earth and cool the air.

Hannah urged the horses to a fast gait. She wanted to get this thing done. Soon the geldings shimmered with sweat, and lather appeared between their hind legs. Hannah knew she needed to drive more slowly. It was too hot to hurry the poor beasts. "Sorry, lads," she said, pulling back on the traces until the team's trot became a walk.

The world moved by at a leisurely pace, but Hannah's nerves thrummed. Would she discover Margaret's intentions? And just what was she up to? Was John in any danger? *Oh, Lord, I pray not.* She decided that if she found something dreadful, she'd speak to John straightaway. Still, the idea of facing him with a terrible truth horrified her.

Lord, I need your guidance. I'm not sure what I'm to do. I don't know what to expect, but whatever may come, please protect John's heart. It's already been heavily tread upon.

Hannah approached the track leading to the house. She stopped the team and looked all around to see if anyone was about. She saw no one so moved forward, her hands gripping the reins so tightly her fingers ached. The muscles in her neck were tight, so she rolled her shoulders back to release some of the tightness. She needed to appear relaxed in case she met up with Margaret or John.

She steered the team to the front of the house, almost expecting to see Margaret step onto the porch. Unconsciously, she touched the basket next to her, preparing a speech of well wishes. No one appeared. All remained quiet.

She stopped, tied off the reins, and climbed down. Lifting the basket of preserves from the seat, she faced the house. Memories of how it had been built came in a torrent. Friends and neighbors arrived with materials and strong backs, and the house had seemed to rise from the land. She remembered the party after the house was finished—she and John had danced, and life seemed perfect. *None of that matters now,* she told herself, forcing the pictures from her mind.

Moving up the steps, she made her way to the door and knocked. There was no answer. She knocked again; still no answer. To make certain no one was about, she set the basket on a table and walked to the barn.

"Hello," she called and stepped inside, the shadows making it hard to see. The smell of heated hay and grain calmed Hannah's nerves slightly.

"John? Margaret? Is anyone here?" There was no answer. Hannah moved to the back stalls. Her mare stood in the shadows, munching hay. Hannah pressed a hand to her face and stroked her. "I've missed you." The horse seemed to remember Hannah and nuzzled her shoulder. With a pat, Hannah moved to the shed to make sure it was empty. When she found no one, she returned to the house. *I'd best hurry before John or Margaret return,* she thought, quickly taking the steps.

Fear of being discovered bristled within Hannah as she opened the door and walked inside. She was an intruder.

"Hello. Anyone here?" Silence answered. She shut the door. It wasn't the same as she remembered. A different tablecloth covered the simple table, lace curtains framed the windows, and a brocade mantle had been draped over the chair that had once been Hannah's. The changes seemed to mock her, shouting that she no longer belonged here. *Strange I didn't notice any of this when John was sick,* she thought, then shrugged it off, realizing she'd been thinking only of John and his welfare. Her eyes followed the rungs of the ladder up to the loft. Tender memories of Thomas met her there.

It was peculiar to stand in this house. She and John had shared so much here. Now it was Margaret's—she didn't deserve this nor a man like John. And if all they'd discovered thus far was true, she would lose it all and again John would lose his wife. The thought cut through Hannah. *Lord, he deserves better.* "Enough," she told herself swiping away unbidden tears.

She moved to the bedroom. It seemed the most likely place for Margaret to hide something. When Hannah reached the door, she stopped and stared inside. Unprepared for the power of her past, she gripped the doorframe and fought a tide of heartache. So much love had been shared within these walls.

She willed away the memories and stepped into the room, moving to the bureau. Pulling open the top drawer, she searched through Margaret's handkerchiefs, stockings, hats and gloves, a corset—nothing remarkable. She quickly looked through the other two drawers, but still nothing.

With a glance out the window to make sure she was still alone, she moved to the armoire and ran a hand over the top shelf. Her fingers found an envelope and her heart quickened. Was this what she was searching for? With trembling hands, she opened it and scanned the papers inside. She swallowed disappointment when she realized it only had to do with Margaret's parents' estate. She returned the papers to the envelope and set it back on the shelf.

After that, she looked through the clothing hanging in the cabinet, and searched the drawers, but found nothing.

Frustrated and afraid that she was running out of time, she surveyed the room. There was nowhere else to look. Hannah moved to the kitchen and explored the cabinets, but found only commonplace items. She made a quick trip up the ladder and inspected the loft. Thomas's bed was still there, unmade since his last visit.

Descending the steps, her eyes found Margaret's sewing basket. It sat beside the chair just the way Hannah's had. *Perhaps she's hidden something in it.* Afraid Margaret would return and feeling as if she were being chased by the woman's very spirit, she hurried down the steps and to the basket. Opening it, she found the mundane—scissors, pieces of trim, needles, and thread. Closing the lid, she asked, *Lord, what am I looking for? Show me.*

She returned to the bedroom and stood just inside the door, her gaze roaming over the room. *If I were going to hide something, where would it be?* Her eyes moved to the bed. What about underneath it? In three steps she reached the bed and dropped to her hands and knees for a good look but found only a bit of dust. Disappointed, she rested on her arms, allowing her stomach to press against the floor. She could feel the presence of her child and with renewed vigor pushed to her knees. Just as she was about to stand, Hannah's eyes went to the bedcovers. They were snugged in beneath the mattress. It seemed a bit untidy, odd for someone like Margaret who was obviously a meticulous housekeeper. Hannah pushed to her feet and lifted the mattress. A large folder had been stuffed beneath it. Taking it out, she could barely catch her breath as she sat on the edge of the bed. She knew she'd found what she'd been looking for. Closing her eyes, she took a deep breath, then untied the laces and opened it.

A stack of legal papers lay inside. Her eyes went to the top of the first page. It read "Last Will and Testament of John Bradshaw."

John had a will written up? But why hide it beneath the mattress?

She read on. "Signed and witnessed 4 February 1804 together with Joseph Taylor and signed into probate on 10 January 1806." *This can't be John's will.*

Confused, she read more.

In the name of God I, John Bradshaw, of the city of Marseille, being of sound mind, memory and understanding do make and declare this to be my Last Will and Testament thereby revoking all former wills by me made.

First, I resign my Soul to Almighty God, trusting solely through the merit of our blessed Lord and Savior Jesus Christ to have a Joyful resurrection to eternal life and my body.

Secondly, I bequeath all my worldly goods to my nephew John Bradshaw, my country mansion house and my city home, including all of the effects therein. I give also all the sums and dividends held in trust at the bank of England and . . .

Hannah's head swirled. She scanned the following pages, which included land holdings, lists of furniture, jewelry, dishes, and other property. There was also a public notice that Mr. Bradshaw had died on 10 January 1806.

With a gasp, Hannah pressed the papers against her chest. *This must be John's uncle.* She remembered him mentioning his uncle and said he'd liked the man but that he hadn't seen him since he was a boy.

John is wealthy beyond belief. Hannah's mind clicked back over the past months. This must be why Margaret had come to

New South Wales. She wanted to share John's inheritance. *Why would she say nothing about it? What good is a hidden will?*

Suddenly Weston Douglas's words returned to her. *"He'll soon be meeting his Maker."* A shiver went through Hannah. When he'd said it, she'd thought he was talking about John's illness. That hadn't been it at all.

Weston Douglas and Margaret meant to kill John.

21

He'll soon be meeting his Maker. He'll soon be meeting his Maker. Douglas's words echoed in Hannah's mind like a taunting lyric. Alarm shouted at her. If John were dead, Margaret would receive his inheritance, unencumbered.

Hannah pressed down rising panic. She had to do something—now.

I should have known. There were signs. Oh Lord, why didn't I see?

Rage momentarily replaced Hannah's panic as she envisioned Margaret and her cruel plan. It was unspeakable. How could anyone do something so heinous? She gripped the papers so tightly she crumpled them. Loosening her hold, she tried to read the top document again, but tears blurred her vision and dread, like a rogue wave, washed over her.

I've got to find John.

Hannah shoved the papers back into the packet. *I won't let them hurt him. I won't.* She tied the string, nearly snapping it as she pulled it tight. *Douglas and Margaret are odious human beings. Monstrous. John is a good, kind man. How can that woman even consider doing such evil against him?*

Clutching the packet against her chest, Hannah pushed off the bed. Margaret couldn't know she'd been here. Fighting against an urge to hurry, she set the documents on the table, then moved through the house, checking each room to make certain it looked just as it had before she'd arrived.

She'd left the sewing basket on the chair. Putting it to rights, she set it on the floor where she'd found it, then returned to the bedroom. The bedspread was rumpled. Had it been that way before she sat on it? Most likely not. She smoothed it and then moved to the bureau and the armoire, tidying the clothing so they looked untouched. With one last look about, she grabbed the packet off the table and hurried to the front door, nearly at a run.

Stepping onto the porch, her eyes went to the road, afraid she'd see Margaret's buggy. It was empty. *Praise you, Lydia.* She knew her friend was working hard to give her as much time as possible.

There was no activity at all. Hannah grabbed the basket of preserves from the table and hurried down the steps. *Where would John be? Most likely he's somewhere on the property.*

Hannah turned her gaze to the pastures. Was it possible he was close by? After placing the basket in the buggy, she headed toward the barn. "John! John!" she called. There was no response. There were so many places he could be, where should she look? How would she ever find him? *If only he'd come home.*

Not sure just what to do, Hannah fought against rising panic. She couldn't take the buggy. It wasn't made to travel the hilly, uneven grasslands. *I can't wait for him, either. I've got to speak to him before Margaret returns.* She could imagine the scene between her and Margaret should the despicable woman come home now. She wasn't sure she could trust herself not to retaliate right on the spot. *If only I had a pistol.* The thought stunned Hannah. She'd actually considered murdering Margaret. She'd never felt that way about anyone. *Lord, forgive me. And help me leave Margaret to you.*

Forcing thoughts of retribution from her mind, she shaded her eyes against the sun and wondered if Quincy might be nearby. "Quincy!" She scanned the property.

When there was no reply, she lifted her skirts and ran to his cottage. She knocked once, and when there was no answer, she opened the door and looked inside. The small house was surprisingly tidy, though sparsely furnished. There was no sign of Quincy. Closing the door, she sprinted to the barn. She could take Claire. Stepping through the open doors, darkness and the smell of hay enveloped her as she strode toward the stalls. Her mare stood in the darkness.

"Oh, Claire." The cinnamon-colored horse looked hot and miserable. Hannah ran a hand down the front of her face. "Would you like to go for a ride?"

The horse nickered as if understanding the invitation.

Hannah ran back to the buggy, climbed in, and drove it to the barn, pulling it to a stop in the shade behind the building. Hopefully, if Margaret returned before she found John, she wouldn't see it.

Leaving the horses in their harnesses, she filled a pail with water and gave them each a good drink, then went to the tack room and grabbed a blanket and a bridle off a hook on the wall.

When she returned to Claire, memories of outings she and the horse had taken assailed her. Until this moment, she didn't realize how much she'd missed riding. The mare tossed her head in greeting. "It's so grand to see you again," Hannah said, stroking the side of the animal's face, then caressing her soft lips. "You'll help me find John, won't you?"

After placing the bit in the mare's mouth and settling the bridle over her face and ears, she draped the blanket across her back and then hurried to get the saddle. It was heavy, but Hannah managed to lug it from the tack room to the stall and then hefted it onto Claire's back. She hooked the left stirrup over the saddle horn, and then, winded, she leaned against the horse to rest. She could feel her child kicking its protest at so much activity. Knowing she'd been pushing herself harder than she ought, she pressed a hand to her abdomen. Was she risking this child's life? Closing her eyes in prayer, she beseeched God, *Please help me, Father. I must find John. Don't let any harm come to this baby.* Taking a deep breath, she straightened. *Everything will work out fine. I'm not alone.*

Pressing against Claire's side, she pulled the cinch tight, then dropped the stirrup back in place. She led the mare to the barn door and peered out, afraid she'd see Margaret driving up the lane. How much time before she returned? How would she ever find John and get back without being discovered? She knew Lydia planned to extend the visit as long as possible, but even Lydia had her limits. *Please, friend, work your wonders and keep her busy a good long while.*

After making sure Claire had a drink from the trough, Hannah pushed into the saddle, more easily than she'd expected, and nearly toppled off the other side. It had been too long since she'd ridden. Adrenaline hummed through her. With no thought to whether her skirts looked decent or not, she set out. Her mind was on John. Where would he most likely be?

Lord, tell me where to go, she prayed, her eyes roaming over nearby pastures and hillsides. *Where are you, John? Where?*

The stock pens lay to the west. He might be there. She turned Claire in that direction and gave her a gentle kick, holding the reins loosely. The horse was ready to go and with a flick of her tail loped off, finally settling into an easy rhythmic gallop.

The minutes passed, but Hannah saw no one. *Where are you?*

Soon Claire was in a lather and Hannah's skin and clothing were wet with perspiration. The sun's heat cooked the earth and every living thing on it. Hannah soon realized she'd made a terrible mistake. She'd seen to watering the horses but had overlooked her own needs. She'd forgotten to bring water. With each passing minute, she felt hotter and her thirst intensified. Her head throbbed and she longed for something cooling. Still, she continued on.

Even though the urgency to find John had not diminished, Hannah knew she must slow to a walk. She couldn't risk damaging Claire or even killing her by pushing too hard.

In the distance, she thought she saw something through the haze. Two men worked at a stock pen. *Oh, let it be them!* In the rising heat waves they were only shadows, but who else could it be?

With a click of her tongue, Hannah leaned forward in the saddle and Claire stepped into a lope. As she approached the men, Hannah could see it wasn't John and Quincy. She didn't recognize them. They looked like they could be prisoners, with their tattered clothing and suspicious gaze. Why had John hired such impoverished men? Could she trust them?

They might know where John is. She gently kicked Claire and moved forward, fear feeling like prickles of cold in the heat. *What if they were escaped prisoners?* She kept moving. She had to know if they'd seen John. She studied them, looking to see if they had weapons.

As she approached, the men stopped their work and watched her approach. Neither of them spoke. Alarm clanging in her mind, she moved toward them.

When she was only a few yards from them, she reined in Claire. Her mouth nearly too dry to speak, she said, "I . . . I'm looking for John Bradshaw. Have you seen him?"

The shorter of the two asked, "John Bradshaw?" He tipped his hat up. "Don't think I've met him."

"What about Quincy? Have you seen him?"

"Quincy." The man nodded and his posture relaxed. "Yeah."

Hannah was encouraged. "So, you've seen him," she said, her voice laced with anticipation. He didn't reply. "Quincy, you've seen him, then? Where?"

The other man spoke up. "He put us to work and then rode off."

"Do you know where he was going?"

"Said he had to check on a mob of sheep up that way." He pointed to the north. "Figured he'd be back by now." He wiped his shirtsleeve across his wet forehead.

Hannah felt jubilant. At least she knew what direction to head. "Thank you. Thank you so much."

"Don't know if I'd take off in this heat, ma'am, if you don't mind my saying. It's real hot."

"Thank you for your concern. I could use something to drink."

"Wish we had something. But we finished off the last of our water awhile ago."

Hannah brushed aside disappointment. "I'm sure I'll be fine." She turned Claire toward the north and rode on.

Although she knew what direction to head, the open land-scape was frighteningly empty. Hannah glanced at the sun, hoping it would help her keep her bearings and continue in the right direction. *I'll come upon him soon,* she told herself, trying to quiet her uneasiness.

Her thoughts turned to Margaret's betrayal. *How will I tell John?* She could imagine what she'd see in his eyes—another wound to tear him down. *Margaret must have no heart,* she thought, hatred for the woman burning like a hot coal in the pit of her stomach. *She was so convincing.*

Hannah contemplated what she'd say to Margaret when she had the opportunity. In her mind, she could see how she would approach her and exactly what she would say. Resentment and rage flamed, becoming more powerful as the image took hold. It would be gratifying to tell her what she thought. *I won't harm her, Lord, but I need to speak my mind.*

The truth of God's Word penetrated Hannah's loathing. She understood that when bitterness was allowed to fester, it could become a vicious and devastating disease of the heart. She knew she should forgive Margaret and Douglas. But for now she relished the hatred and held onto it and wondered what Margaret might be capable of if she'd planned her own husband's murder.

Thomas! The little boy's trusting face came to Hannah's mind. Was he in danger? If Margaret didn't love John, how must she feel about Thomas?

Like a fire out of control, fury burned hot in Hannah. It raced through her. She'd tried to be kind; she'd accepted Margaret and had graciously given the woman what she thought was her rightful place at John's side. And she'd fought against hatred, but now . . . now she had reason. *This is righteous anger,* she told herself. *Even God allows righteous anger.*

The sun's heat grew more intense, but Hannah kept searching. Each acacia, each gum tree beckoned her to seek refuge in the shade of its limbs, but she forced herself to continue. Her mouth and throat were so dry that each time she swallowed it felt as if dust coated her throat. The pounding in her head grew worse, but she dare not stop.

Hannah stared at burnt fields with rising waves of heat dancing above the cooking grasses. *Show me where he is,* she prayed. *Help me find him. Please.*

She kept moving, wondering if she was still heading in the right direction. Was she lost?

A new kind of fear set in. Would she perish on the empty grasslands? No one knew she was here.

Water. If only I had a bit of water. Verses from Psalm 42 meandered through her mind. *"As the deer pants for the water brooks, so pants my soul for You, O God. My soul thirsts for God, for the living God."*

Hannah closed her eyes. Had she ever sought God as intensely as she now longed for water? No. Until now she'd not fully understood the magnitude of the image of thirsting for God.

Forgive me, Father. She smiled. *And now that I understand the meaning of the Scripture more clearly, please show me a way to safety.*

Her head pounding and feeling faint, she stopped and patted Claire's neck. "I haven't done us in, have I? I'm so sorry. I didn't mean to get us lost."

It was then that she saw a dust cloud in the distance. Could it be a mob of sheep? Perhaps John was there. With renewed hope, she moved toward it.

Soon she heard the bleating of sheep and watched as bundles

of moving wool appeared from the cloud. In the midst was a man on horseback. "John! Thank the Lord!"

She hurried toward him, but it wasn't John. It was Quincy. Was John with him? She peered through the dust and dirt, hoping to see him, but he wasn't there. Disappointment washed over Hannah, but only for a moment. At least she'd found someone. She and Claire wouldn't perish, not today anyway.

Quincy cantered toward her. "Hannah, what are ye doing all the way out here?" he asked, hauling back on the reins. "Ye look done in. Ye've had too much sun." He climbed down from his horse, lifted a flask that had been draped over the saddle horn, and opened it. "Here, ye best have a drink."

Hannah took a big gulp, then another.

"Not too much, now. Ye'll make yerself sick." Quincy took the canteen. "Let me help ye down." He draped the flask over his shoulder and assisted Hannah from her horse. "Ye come out 'ere with no water? Ye daft?"

"Evidently so," she answered, then explained, "I was so distraught that I forgot. I didn't think of it."

Nearly overcome by the heat, she swayed and kept hold of Quincy's hand. "Thank you. I'm not sure what I would have done if I'd not found you."

"'Ere, let's get ye out of the sun." Quincy held her arm and guided her toward a lone acacia.

Still hanging onto his hand, Hannah sat and leaned against the rough bark of the tree. "Thank you. I'm obliged." She closed her eyes, savoring the relative coolness of the shade.

Quincy gave her horse a drink, then sat across from Hannah. He lifted off his hat, and swiped back damp hair. "Now, tell me why yer out 'ere by yerself. It's a foolish thing to do."

"I know that now, but I thought John might be with you."

"Ye came all the way out 'ere looking for John?"

"Yes. I must speak to him. I've discovered something, something horrible." She pointed at the horse. "In the pack . . . there are documents." Her voice cracked.

Quincy offered her another drink and she took it, the wetness soothing her parched throat.

"What papers could be so important that ye couldn't wait 'til he got back?"

"Where is he?"

"Sydney Town."

"Sydney Town?"

"Don't look so panicked. He'll be back tomorrow. Ye can talk with him then." Quincy eyed Hannah. "What is it? Ye look scared out of yer wits."

"They're going to kill him."

"Who?"

"Margaret and that Mr. Douglas."

"Weston Douglas?"

"Yes. Do you know him?"

"Never met him. But that's who John went to see."

22

The world spun, and Hannah thought she might be sick.

"Hannah, ye all right? Yer white as a ghost."

Fighting nausea, she tried to focus on Quincy. "We've got to find John! They're going to kill him! They might . . ." She pressed her hand to her mouth. "Oh Lord, they might have done something already." Saying it out loud made the reality all the more horrifying. What if John was already dead? *Stop thinking like that! He's fine. He's fine.*

"John left a couple of hours ago. Said he had errands in Parramatta and then he'd be heading for Sydney Town. Yer saying Margaret and this Mr. Douglas want to kill him? Why?"

"They want his money."

"What? He's got little of that."

"No. That's not true. John's wealthy. And he doesn't even know it yet. That's what I was saying about the documents. I found them in Margaret's room. It's a will from his uncle who died. He gave John everything. From what I can see of the property listed, he was an extremely wealthy man."

"Why would Margaret want to kill him? She's his wife. She'll share in the prosperity."

"Yes, but she's in love with Weston Douglas, or it seems she is. They want the money for themselves."

Understanding dawned in Quincy's eyes. "Lord, no. Yer sure?"

"I am." Hannah pushed to her feet. The world tipped, and she pressed a hand against the tree. "Did he say why he was seeing Mr. Douglas?"

"No, just something about legal papers—for Margaret, something to do with her family inheritance. I think he was going to sign some documents."

"They're going to kill him. I know it." Hannah's head throbbed. She couldn't think clearly. She moved toward Claire. "We've got to go. We've got to tell him. Before he . . ." Hannah swallowed, unable to say more. *Lord, save him. Please save him.*

"Calm down, Hannah. I'm sure John's fine." Concern furrowed his brow. "I'll go after him. And see that he's all right. We'll sort this out."

Hannah nodded, but her heart still battered beneath her ribs.

"I might be able to catch him on the road—depends on how long he was in Parramatta. He wanted to make it into Sydney Town before the sun set, so I figure he's got a good head start."

"I'm going with you." Hannah grabbed hold of the saddle horn, shoved her foot into the stirrup, and pushed herself up and into the saddle. "We can't wait a moment longer. He could be heading straight into trouble."

"I'll go. You stay with Lydia. I can ride faster alone."

"I can keep up, don't you worry about that." Tears burned. "And I have to go. John will need me. When he hears . . ." She blinked back the tears. "How will he abide more treachery?"

"Figure if what ye say is true, he'll be glad to be rid of her."

"Maybe so." Hannah felt a spark of hope. Perhaps John would see it as a reprieve rather than betrayal.

"I left the Athertons' buggy behind the barn at the house. Margaret will see it when she returns. She's probably there already. She'll know that we know."

"We'll think of something." Quincy climbed into the saddle and turned his horse toward the house. He glanced at Hannah. "We'll say ye came for the mare. Margaret won't take that news well." He grinned.

"Does she ride?"

"Almost never. But I figure knowing that ye've got something she sees as hers will get under her skin. I'll be glad to see that."

"Will she believe you?"

"Don't see why not. And what does it matter? Even if she suspects something, she's got no place to go. She's not going to set off for Sydney Town on her own. And where can she go that the law can't find her?" He picked up his pace. "Right now, all we need think 'bout is finding John before he meets up with Douglas. And I'll be happy to deal with that man."

Urgency pushed Hannah. All thoughts of the heat forgotten, she leaned forward and gave Claire her head. *Help us find him, Lord. Give us wings like eagles that we might run and not grow weary.*

<hr />

When they approached the house, Hannah saw that Margaret had returned. She'd left her buggy next to the house at the front steps, allowing the horses to bake in the sun. *She has no consideration for anyone or anything.* Her stomach tightened. She hated the woman. *I'll not be able to hide it from her. She'll see.* "So, we'll tell her I came for the mare and that I wanted to speak to John about it?"

"Right. But let me talk to her," said Quincy. "It could be fun." He grinned, a gleam in his eye.

"Gladly," Hannah said. "I'm too angry. And I'm sure I'll say something to give us away." She took a deep breath and tried to relax tight muscles, but she felt as tense as a drawn bow. "She deserves what she gets."

"That she does. But for now, we'll have to hold our tongues, eh?"

As they approached, Margaret stepped onto the porch. Arms folded over her chest, she waited, unable to disguise her rancor. Coolly she assessed them. Gone was her friendly smile.

Her eyes settled on Hannah. "I've been wondering just where you'd gone to. I saw the buggy. When I looked about, you were nowhere to be found." She looked at the mare. "And I see you're riding Claire. What was so urgent you couldn't wait for me or John?" Margaret's nostrils flared slightly.

"She didn't mean to worry ye," Quincy said. "She's been longing for her mare and came to see if she might take her back to the Athertons' with her. When she found no one home, she figured a ride would do her and the mare good, and then it was just natural to look for John. After all, she'd have to ask him if she could take the animal."

"The horse doesn't belong to her. It's mine. She has no right to it."

"Well now, I'm not sure that's quite right." Quincy nudged his hat up slightly. "John gave the horse to Hannah. I figure Claire belongs to her."

Margaret clenched her jaw. "Well, we'll have to ask John about that . . . when he returns."

There was something in her eyes that alarmed Hannah. Margaret didn't expect John to return. When Margaret looked at her, Hannah met the brazen gaze with one of her own, unable to keep her anger completely in check.

"Hannah wants to take the horse to the Athertons' and I think she should."

"No. Not until she speaks to John."

Quincy pushed up in the stirrups. "She has a right to her. And I know John would agree."

Margaret's lips became a tight line. "That animal belongs to this farm. And I shan't have someone . . ." Momentarily she seemed lost for words. "I shan't have someone coming up here and taking whatever they wish."

Margaret eyed Hannah, her look suspicious. "Strange you'd come today and then go looking for John in this heat."

Fury boiled inside Hannah so intensely she feared she'd erupt. "I had the day off," she said tersely.

"Well, look at the poor animal. You've nearly run her to death. Why are you in such a hurry anyway?"

Quincy quickly replied, "The horses wanted to run, so we gave them their head. I expect poor Claire's tired of being locked in the barn."

"She's not much of a horse anyway. You can have her." Margaret waved them off. "I have a headache. I'm going to lie down."

She's certainly dropped her sweet act. Claire blew a blast of air from her nostrils and stomped her foot. Hannah patted her neck. "She's a fine horse. I'll be glad to have her back." She met Margaret's dark eyes. "I'll ask John, though, the next time I see him. And if he doesn't feel right about it, I'll return her."

Margaret lifted her chin a bit and looked down at Hannah. "Fine. You ask him, then."

"Good. It's all settled." Quincy's tone was friendly and relaxed. "In the meanwhile, I'll see that Hannah gets home safely."

Margaret turned, then looked at Hannah, her gaze probing. "I'm sorry you missed John. He's not due home until tomorrow. He has business in Sydney Town."

"Yes. I heard," Hannah said, surprised to hear her voice sound untroubled.

"Oh, Quincy, before you go, could you put the buggy and horses away? I hate to leave them out here in the sun. It's terribly hot."

"No trouble at all," he said. "I'll take care of it straightaway."

Inwardly, Hannah groaned. They needed to leave. Each minute that passed put John in more danger.

"Good day, then." Margaret walked inside the house.

Quincy dismounted, handing the reins to Hannah. "Take the horses to the barn, give them a good drink, then tie them to the back of the buggy." He glanced at the house and lowered his voice. "We'll leave the buggy in Parramatta."

"All right. But we've got to hurry."

"I know. I'll put these animals away, and then we'll be off." He climbed into the buggy and drove it to the barn.

Hannah trotted alongside, leading his gelding and all the time wishing she could set out for Sydney Town immediately. Her heart thrummed and her mind was awhirl with all that might happen. What if John were facing some terrible danger right now?

After the horses each had a drink from the trough, she tied Claire and Quincy's gelding to the back of the buggy. When she finished, she watched Quincy stride toward his cottage, disappear inside, then return with a bag in hand. Determination lined his face.

When he approached, he said quietly, "Makes no sense, yer going. I can find him faster on me own."

Keeping her voice hushed, Hannah said, "I don't agree. I'm a good horsewoman. I'll not slow you down." Even as Hannah said it, she knew it wasn't true. Quincy could get to John more quickly without her.

He studied her, his eyes challenging the statement.

"You're right," Hannah conceded. "You can travel faster on your own. But I don't know how I'll bear the waiting, not knowing if something terrible has happened."

"Ye can do what ye have to."

Grudgingly, she said, "I'll stay at Lydia's." Hannah placed a hand on his arm. "Please tell me as soon as you know. Come straight to Lydia's as soon as you can."

"I will. I promise." Quincy helped Hannah into the buggy, and then they set off, careful not to look like they were in a hurry.

The moment they were out of view of the house, Hannah took the documents out of the saddlebag and handed them to him. "You'll need these. John will want proof. He's been betrayed by Margaret once before, I don't want him anguishing about whether this scheme is true or not."

Quincy stuffed the papers into his pack. "He'll believe ye, but I'll take them all the same." He pulled the horses to a stop, handed Hannah the reins, and climbed down. "I'm off, then. I'll stop at the Gelsons' when I get back to Parramatta." He pushed into the saddle and then added, "I'll bring him back. Ye can count on it."

"Thank you." Hannah stared after him as he galloped down the road. *Lord, be with him. And keep John safe. I couldn't bear it if something happened to him.*

A late afternoon breeze stirred heated air, carrying a damp, musky odor from the slow-moving Parramatta River. The wind brought some relief from the oppressive heat and cooled John's damp skin. He stopped and drank from his water flask. Replacing the lid, he draped it over the saddle horn and glanced at the sky. The sun was still high. He should easily make it to Sydney Town before nightfall.

He'd hoped to get into town early enough to meet with Weston Douglas. He'd rather get that piece of business out of the way so tomorrow he'd be free to have a look at some cattle. *Perhaps Margaret's right and I ought to think about expanding.* If he could get a good price, he'd purchase a few head and start for home. It would be an easier trip back, though, if Quincy had come along. *I need another hand to help out 'round the place.*

As usual, Margaret hadn't joined him. She had no interest in anything that was the least bit unpleasant, not even if it meant they could spend time together.

She's nothing like Hannah. Hannah would gladly have ridden with me.

That kind of thinking served no purpose, so John turned his mind to the business at hand. Before having a look at the cattle, he had stops to make at a couple of businesses in town. His last visit to the port city, he'd had several inquiries about tools. He could do with a bit of extra cash, so he hoped to make some deals before returning home.

This close to the ocean, the river widened into several tributaries, wandering and making it less defined. His mind wandered as well, to Thomas and the quiet afternoons they'd spent fishing. He hadn't seen him as often as he'd like, not since Hannah had moved to the Athertons'. He missed the lad and often wished he still lived at the farm.

He couldn't bring himself to take Thomas from Hannah. She had so little. And Thomas loved living at the Athertons'. He and Perry had become good friends, and Thomas was proud of his toolmaking skills. Jealousy jabbed at John. It was foolishness, he knew, but emotions were sometimes hard to manage.

When John approached Sydney Town, he urged his horse to a faster pace. He didn't want to miss his meeting with Weston Douglas. If he didn't hurry, the man would have gone home for the evening and John would miss him. He kicked his mount in the sides and settled into a relaxed gallop.

His eyes moved to the hill above the port and stopped at the prison. His stomach tightened. He remembered it all—the food deprivation, illness, brutality, and the fear that he'd never share his life with Hannah. And now, even with all of God's blessings, his greatest fear had come to pass. He'd lost her.

Heavy of heart, he turned his eyes to the port. Two ships lay at anchor, and for a moment, he wished he were setting sail, going anywhere except here, someplace where he didn't have to think about Hannah and didn't have to try to love Margaret.

Like a dark mist, sorrow settled about him. There was no place he could go that his love for Hannah wouldn't go with him.

He turned his focus to the road leading into town. It was lined with simple homes, some of them barely more than hovels. He slowed to a walk. A little girl worked beside her mother in a garden patch. Dirt smudged her face and her hair was a tangle, but her blue eyes were vivid and they widened innocently as she watched him pass. John smiled and tipped his hat. She hurried to hide behind her mother's skirts. Gazing out at him from safety, she smiled and her blue eyes danced with delight.

Perhaps I'll have a daughter one day. The idea pleased him. With Margaret it would be possible. He envisioned what his daughter might look like, then realized the picture in his mind was one of a tiny Hannah. Misery tightened like a band about his chest. He and Hannah would never have a child.

"John! John!" a voice called from behind him.

He turned to see someone coming toward him, riding hard. As he drew closer, he realized it was Quincy—his horse was in a lather, and its sides heaved as it sucked in oxygen. *He'd never run a horse so hard without just cause.*

Quincy pulled up alongside John. "I'd started to think I'd never catch ye. Ye've come a good long way since I saw ye this morning."

"What's wrong? Has something happened at the farm?"

"No." Quincy was breathing hard as well. "Not easy to catch up to ye." He lifted his hat and wiped his face with his shirt sleeve. "Thank God I found ye and yer all right." He resettled the hat.

"What do you mean? Thank God I'm all right?"

"Hannah came to the farm today . . . looking for ye. Said that Douglas is planning to kill ye."

"What? Why would he kill me? I don't even know the man."

Quincy reached into his pack and took out the documents Hannah had given him. "Hannah found these. Ye best read them." He handed them to him.

John opened the envelope and scanned the contents while Quincy gulped water from his flask. Screwing the cap back on, he said, "Seems yer wealthy, but what good is money if yer dead, eh?"

John's heart quickened. He glanced at Quincy, not yet ready to discuss theories. His uncle had died. He'd not seen him since he was a boy. A flash of memory brought back an afternoon picnic and a new fishing pole he'd been allowed to use. At the end of the day, his uncle had given him the pole.

John looked at Quincy. "I haven't seen my uncle since he moved to France. I was just a lad." He felt a pang of loss. "He was a good man."

He looked at the documents. "Where did Hannah get these?"

"They were in Margaret's room."

John considered that, then asked, "How did Hannah get them?"

"It seems she and Lydia had some misgivings about Margaret and Mr. Douglas, so they did some checking and found out that . . . well, that yer wife and him are . . . very well acquainted."

John knew the implication and could feel the familiar heat of betrayal. "What do you mean?"

"They've been seeing each other in a familiar way."

"You know this for a fact?"

"I do. I trust Hannah. And she said that she, Lydia, and Dalton went to Sydney Town and found letters written between the two. And it was clear they were up to more than just business. It also seems they figured on coming into a good deal of money . . . just as soon as Margaret's husband died."

The words didn't penetrate at first, but when they did, John felt a tremor of shock move through him, and then the old bitterness and hatred erupted. "Not again. I let her do this to

274

me once. What a fool I am." A malevolent rage took hold of him.

"You're not a fool. She was convincing. Even I thought her a good sort."

Slapping the papers against his leg, John rumbled, "I should have known."

"Well, yer a wealthy man, that's a good thing, eh." Quincy offered him a slanted grin.

"Wealth has nothing to do with money." He gritted his teeth. "That's all she wanted—the money. Get rid of me, and she and her Mr. Douglas can have the whole lot to themselves. That's it, isn't it?"

"Would seem so."

John shoved the papers back into the envelope, tied it off, and pushed it into his satchel. "We'll just see how Mr. Douglas figured on doing me in. I'm sure he has a plan."

Wearing a vicious smile, John added, "We'll give him his chance, eh?"

23

"I'll be here, if ye've a need," Quincy said. "Ye can count on me."

John knew he was walking into trouble, but he relished the coming conflict. Weston Douglas needed to be put in his place, and he was the one who should do it. He'd deal with Margaret later.

Hoping not to attract attention to himself, he walked casually across the street and headed toward Weston's office. The interior was dark, but something had been posted on the door.

A note, instead of Weston Douglas, waited for John. He snatched it from the peg that held it in place, then read, *I apologize, John, but I was called away. I'll be at the Reardon warehouse at the wharf. You can find me there. I'll be working late, so come by anytime.*

He's waiting for me. A deserted warehouse is as good a place as any to do me in.

The murkiness of dusk settled over the town. John looked at Quincy, then glanced up and down the street. Was Douglas watching? Was he waiting to ambush him as he made his way to the warehouse?

Crumpling the note, he threw it to the ground and walked back to Quincy. "He's not in the office."

"Where's he gone to?"

"He's at the Reardon warehouse. And that I'm to meet him there."

"Strange place to be doing business, especially at this time of night."

"My guess is he's up to some kind of dirty business. Something he'd like to keep hidden." John pushed his hat up with his thumb. "He's waiting for me. And the warehouse is part of the plan. No one about down there this time of night and nothing to tie him to me. It's the perfect place for murder—no witnesses."

Quincy rubbed at a two-day stubble. "This is getting out of hand. We need to get a constable."

John worked the idea around his mind. Quincy was right, but he wanted a face-off with Douglas—without the law looking on. "We don't need the constable just yet."

"I understand yer need for revenge, and Douglas deserves it, but it'll only bring more trouble. Ye'll not get satisfaction. If ye don't end up dead, yer likely to end up back in gaol." He glanced up the street, shrouded by shadows. "Let the law take care of it."

John looked straight at Quincy. "I'm going. Are you coming with me?"

Quincy swept his hat off and slapped it against his thigh. "I believe in ye, John, but Douglas could do ye in before ye even catch sight of him." He looked at the darkening street. "There's no reason to risk yer life. Don't be a fool."

John's irritation spiked. "I've been a fool. Now it's time I gave Douglas what he deserves. I'm going whether you like it or not."

"And if ye die? What about Hannah and Thomas?"

"I've got to do this if I'm to face them. He's a snake who's done his best to tear my life and my wife and son's apart. Now he plans to kill me. What kind of man would I be to back down from the likes of him? I'll not add more shame to what I already carry. I'm dealing with him . . . and then Margaret. They'll both get what they deserve." As John spoke, rage stormed inside of him.

"The hate in ye is powerful, it's lying to ye and it'll destroy ye." Quincy laid a hand on John's shoulder.

"That may be, but I'm not ready to let it go. This is mine to do." A wave of memories of wrongs done assaulted John—betrayal, degradation, hope, and then more treachery. "I've no choice. I've been a gentleman long enough." *It's time I take my revenge.* "I can't let go, not tonight. Retribution is mine. I'll be going with or without you."

A candlelighter moved toward them, illuminating the main street of Sydney Town as he went.

"All right, then. I'm with ye." Quincy's eyes narrowed. "Have to admit I wouldn't mind having a go at him myself." He glanced toward the wharf. "What's yer plan?"

"I'd like to get my hands about his neck, but as much as I'd find pleasure in killing him, I won't . . . not unless I've no other choice." He grinned mirthlessly. "I've a few things to say to him. And I'll be glad to give him the scare of his life." John's voice was terrifyingly cold.

"I'll go ahead of ye and do my best to see that yer not ambushed."

"No. I go first. If he sees you, we'll give ourselves away. He knows you work for me." John looked toward the quay. "Leave enough space between us so if he's watching he won't see you." He gripped Quincy's forearm. "I'll know you're there."

John set off down the street, Quincy lagging behind. More than once John's hand found his pistol, tucked into its holster. The feel of the wooden handle strengthened his resolve. *I'll kill him only if I have to,* he told himself, but he couldn't rid his mind of the idea of retribution. He craved it.

Each step brought a reminder of a wrong done, and his rage grew. He and Hannah had endured months of anguish because of Margaret and Douglas. And Margaret had taken him for a fool—again. *She'll not get away with it this time. I'll see to it.*

His mind flashed on Hannah. Margaret had not only misused him but her as well. The thought turned his stomach; he could taste the bitterness of her deceit. And poor Hannah, she didn't deserve such treatment. She'd done nothing but love him. She'd even risked her life by staying beside him when the quinsy struck. Where had Margaret been? The truth hit him. She'd been with Weston Douglas.

Thomas came to mind. *I should have listened to him. He knew.*

In his mind, he could see Margaret's brown eyes and auburn hair that had once so beguiled; they were no longer alluring. *She's hideous, evil, heinous.*

Moving down empty streets, John continued toward the quay and whatever lay in wait for him. Darkness shrouded him. There were few streetlamps in this section of town. As he approached the port, a hot wind carried the odor of raw fish and of the foul mud left behind as the tide receded.

Glad for the darkness, John walked with confidence, outrage fueling his need for a confrontation. Approaching the warehouse, he slowed his steps. Lantern light glowed from inside. *Douglas must be here.*

He moved to the door, then stopped and listened. No sound

came from inside. He glanced up the street, but couldn't see anything, not even Quincy. Still, he was confident his friend was there, ready to help if needed.

He put his hand on the doorknob and felt a flush of fear. His life might end here. His hand found his pistol and rested there a moment while he contemplated whether to withdraw the weapon or not. *No*, he decided. *I don't want to give away what I know too soon.*

He let his hand drop from the pistol, turned the doorknob, and pushed the door open. It creaked on rusted hinges.

He peered inside. There was no sign of Douglas. A table sat on the wharf side of the large warehouse. A lantern flickered in the middle, its light casting shadows over stacked crates and bags of grain and other goods. John stepped into the room and pulled the door closed. Its complaining rasp echoed.

Most of the warehouse lay in darkness. Douglas, most likely, hid somewhere inside. John's skin prickled with gooseflesh and his hand returned to his pistol for a moment. Where was the man? John edged in, looking about, his eyes probing dark corners.

"Weston Douglas?" His voice echoed. He glanced up at a ceiling two stories above him. "Mr. Douglas. You here?" No answer. John moved to the table, wondering if Douglas might have left a note of some kind. There was nothing. *He's here . . . somewhere.* "Douglas!" he shouted.

In the silence, the click of a pistol hammer being drawn back reverberated throughout the huge chamber. Every nerve in John went taut. He forced himself not to grab his own pistol and slowly turned toward the sound.

"I've been waiting for you." The man's voice sounded malevolent.

John's eyes probed the dimness. He moved toward a stack of crates, thinking they might provide cover in case he needed it.

"Stay put," the voice demanded.

John stopped, and deciding he ought to play dumb, asked, "Mr. Douglas? It's just me, John Bradshaw. No reason to fear. I'm not an intruder. I've come to sign the papers for Margaret." He took a step away from the table and its light.

The sound of his footfalls echoed, and Weston Douglas stepped out of the shadows. He held a pistol in each hand, both pointed at John.

"I daresay, firearms aren't required," John said.

Weston smirked, his dark eyes reflecting the flicker of the lantern light. "You're here to sign papers, eh?" He chuckled. "You've no idea, do you? Margaret told me what a fool you are. I didn't believe her." He grinned. "After what happened in London, you ought to know better."

John's ire blazed. "What is it you want?"

"I've already got what I want."

"And that is?" John wondered where Quincy was and hoped he was close. He forced himself not to look for him and kept his eyes on Douglas.

Douglas moved a step closer. "Well, there's Margaret. She's mine, along with her assets and properties." He tightened his hold on the pistols. "That fool cousin of yours left her. Didn't have a brain, couldn't see what a prize he had." He grinned. "Not that she can't be difficult from time to time, yet what a beautiful trial she is."

John's wrath raged inside him, but he maintained a calm exterior. "She's my wife, so you have no claim to her assets. And I'm not a wealthy man, so there's very little to fight over on any account."

A shadow fell across Douglas's face and his eyes narrowed. "She's your wife in name only. She doesn't care a whit about you, never did. She was happy when you were thrown into prison and happier yet when you were transported, figured she'd be rid of you."

One lip lifted in derision. "'Course when she found the posting, that changed everything." His expression took on the look of someone remembering a special event. "She came home that day beside herself and in a rage. You were so far away. But then we came up with a plan that would give her what was rightfully hers." He looked straight at John.

"What are you talking about? What posting?" John continued his ruse, hoping he and Quincy could still catch Douglas off guard.

"The old man's death and the notice of an inheritance for his long-lost nephew, John Bradshaw."

"My uncle? He's dead?"

Douglas laughed with mirth. "He's in the ground all right. And he left everything to you."

John could feel blood pulsing through his head. He wanted to pummel the man standing across from him. Where was Quincy? "So, that's what Margaret wanted. All this time?"

"What else would she want from a man like you? You're nothing but a farmer who lives at the end of the world." He sniggered. "She's been counting the days until she can sail for London. In less than a fortnight, we'll be departing, she a grieving widow and me . . . well, I'll be comforting her."

"You think so, eh?" John's rage grew. "So, with all you know of her, you think you can trust her? Why would she share her fortune with you, eh?" A flicker of doubt crossed Weston's face, and John grinned.

He squared his jaw. "She loves me."

"She's fooled others, why not you?"

Douglas glared at John. "We're two of a kind. We understand one another—we'd never swindle the other."

"You're sure of that, eh?" John allowed a taunting smile to touch his lips.

A muscle twitched above Douglas's left eye. "I'm sure."

John shrugged. "I'd say you're a fool, then."

"Shut up! Just shut up!"

John stared at his adversary. "And what do you have in mind for me, eh?"

"You'll be found along the wharf . . . the victim of some drunken sot looking for a few pence to pay for his grog. Margaret and me will be free to enjoy your uncle's fortune. Might even be able to get a few pounds out of that miserable farm of yours."

"You're despicable, the both of you."

"That we are." Weston laughed and then stopped suddenly, moving his guns higher and looking down the barrel of one of them. "Now move to the door. Can't have your blood making a mess in here." He motioned toward the door. "Move."

John walked slowly toward the door, berating himself at having let Douglas better him. He hoped Quincy was close by.

"I'll take real pleasure in this. I've given up a good deal—left my home, crossed more than one ocean, lived in this stinkhole of a—"

"And yer 'bout to be even more miserable," Quincy said, stepping into the light, his pistol trained on Douglas. "Just as soon as we turn ye in to the authorities." He grinned.

Shock registered on Weston's face as he looked at Quincy. "What are you doing here?"

John pulled his pistol out of its holster and aimed it at Douglas. "I may be a fool, but you're a horse's behind. You think I'd meet with the likes of you without a plan? I knew what you and Margaret were up to."

Weston kept his weapon pointed at John. "You'll be dead before your friend can fire his weapon."

"Maybe so, but then you will be too. Quincy's a fine shot. You'll meet your Maker, that I can guarantee."

John took pleasure in the fear he saw in Douglas's eyes. "I'm looking forward to seeing Margaret when she finds out just where you two are truly heading in less than a fortnight. It won't be London, I can assure you."

Weston licked his lips and glanced at Quincy, then back at John. "It was all her idea. I never meant you any harm. I was just going along with her. You know how she can be."

Beads of perspiration popped up on his forehead and upper lip. "What if we make a deal? You keep your fortune and Margaret. And I'll be on my way—no harm done, eh?"

"No harm done?" A guttural sound came from deep in John's throat. "If you think I want her, you're daft." Fury came from inside, and his voice dripped with venom. "You'll be going nowhere, except prison."

His eyes glinting in the lantern light, Douglas glared at John. He fired one of the pistols. Something struck John's left arm. Pain seared his flesh. Douglas turned toward Quincy, but before he could discharge the second gun, Quincy shot him in one knee. Douglas dropped to the floor, hollering and holding on to his blood-soaked limb.

Quincy closed the space between him and Douglas and grabbed the man's pistol. Moving to John, he asked, "Ye all right?"

"I am." Still gripping his pistol, John moved to his opponent.

Writhing on the floor and clutching his leg, Douglas looked at Quincy. "You blew my knee apart."

"And I'll do more than that," John said, standing over the contemptible man. He pointed his pistol at his head. "I've a shot left." He savored the terror on Douglas's face.

"Don't shoot me. You're a decent chap. I know your kind. Killing a defenseless man will haunt you."

"You don't know me. And the death of a man like you would never haunt me."

"Have mercy. I beg you. Margaret beguiled me. She has power over men. You know how she is."

"John, leave this to the authorities," Quincy said.

"He deserves death."

"He does at that . . . but not at your hands."

"Please. Don't kill me." Douglas's face dripped with sweat and his eyes bulged with horror.

"Why should I let you live?" John pulled the hammer back.

"I . . . I have some holdings of my own. I'll sign them over to you."

"I'm wealthy beyond my dreams. I've no need of your money."

"John," Quincy said. "Turn him over to the constabulary."

John's wrath billowed like gathering storm clouds as he stared at Douglas. He pressed his finger against the trigger. "He's done enough harm. No reason to leave him to do to someone else what he planned for me." Wanting to fire the weapon, he kept the gun pointed at Douglas, but finally lowered the pistol, unwilling to let this man hurt him or Hannah any further. "No one will take me for a fool again. Not ever."

Douglas let out a breath and closed his eyes.

"Ye'll be all right while I get the constable?" Quincy asked.

"Yeah." John sat on a crate, cradling his wounded arm.

"I'll bring a doctor for ye," Quincy told John.

"Don't leave me with him," Weston begged.

Quincy stared at Douglas and shook his head. "I can't control him, whether I'm here or not." He grinned at John. "And I can't report what I don't see." He walked out.

<hr>

With Douglas in the Sydney Town gaol, John still had Margaret to deal with. The doctor had seen to his arm and suggested he rest, but John couldn't wait. He and Quincy had set out immediately for Parramatta.

Using his good arm, John turned his horse toward the center of town. "I've got to see Hannah." *Lord, forgive me, but I'm happy. I'm thankful to be free of Margaret. Now Hannah and I can begin again.* His mind worked over the previous months. He'd shut Hannah out of his home and out of his life. Now could they truly begin again? *Things will be set right once I deal with Margaret.*

<hr>

He'd had time to consider his circumstances, and John's anger had dissipated. The humiliation needled him, but he knew that would fade. All he needed was a few minutes with Margaret to give her a piece of his mind and he'd be right as rain, especially once she was on her way to gaol.

He moved up the main street of Parramatta, his anticipation growing. Hannah was waiting for him. He imagined what lay ahead for them; they'd be together again. He could already see the relief on her face when he told her all was well. He looked at Quincy. "So, you're sure Hannah's at Lydia's?"

"She is." Quincy grinned. "She'll not move until she hears word of your well-being."

"I have to see her before we go to the farm."

"Figured so. And Hannah will be glad for it." Quincy pulled back on the reins. "I'll see that a constable goes to the house with us. He can bring Margaret back."

"I won't be long," John said. He rode on to David and Lydia's. As he got closer, the pain in his arm eased. All he could think about was seeing Hannah—his wife, Hannah.

She must have been watching for him, because she ran onto the street before he even made it to the apothecary. Her eyes went immediately to his bandaged arm. "Oh John, are you all right?" She hurried to him.

"It's nothing." He smiled, his insides warming at the sight of her. She was his.

"What happened?" Lydia asked, joining Hannah.

"Quincy and I had a meeting with a weasel." John grinned and climbed out of the saddle, careful not to use the injured arm.

"Oh John. Did he shoot you?" Hannah moved closer.

"He did. But the doctor took care of it. I'll be fine, no damage really." He longed to put an arm about Hannah and pull her close. He dared not. They weren't legally husband and wife, and no one in town had any idea of what had happened. "He'll not give us any more trouble. He's in gaol. We're on our way to see Margaret. It's time she paid consequences for her sins, as well." He caressed Hannah's cheek. "I'm sorry for all she's done to you and to Thomas."

For a moment Hannah leaned into his hand, and then stepped back. "So our fears were true, then?"

"Yes. All of it. The plan was to kill me and take the inheritance. But it's over now. Everything will be fine." Love shone in Hannah's eyes. He took her hand. "We can be together again."

"John, we're not married."

"We'll find a way." He smiled. "Soon we'll be together."

Hannah's chin quivered and her eyes brimmed with tears as she gave him a nod.

"Now, I've got business at the farm. Margaret's been free long enough."

24

Uncertain of how she ought to feel, Hannah glanced at John, who sat beside her. Everything was different now.

He smiled at her and she could feel a blush heat her face. He lifted the reins and hurried the horses along. She liked the strength in his hands. *What am I to do, Lord? What does all this mean? Are we to go back to what we had? John was making a go of it with Margaret. He must have loved her, at least a little.*

Quincy rode alongside the buggy, a smile on his lips. Hannah wanted to rejoice, but so much had happened between her and John that she doubted stepping back into a life together would be easy.

The miles passed slowly and yet too quickly. It was time to end this ordeal, but was there any possibility of a truly happy conclusion? What if Margaret refused to go? What if she fought arrest? Hannah imagined the ugly scene and felt weary. She was tired of the struggle and no longer had the energy to hate. She'd had enough of that.

She gazed at the river. It flowed quietly toward the ocean without struggle, accepting its course. It didn't rail against the choice made for it but instead accepted and even relished its path.

Hannah knew that's what God had wanted for her—to trust him and the direction he'd taken her. Instead, she'd fought to hang on to what she'd had, fought despair, and fought the hatred she felt for Margaret. Now . . . she was simply worn out. She knew what waited for Margaret, but surprisingly felt no satisfaction.

Anyone locked away in a New South Wales gaol was to be pitied. She glanced back at the wagon driven by a constable. He'd be the one taking Margaret back to Sydney Town. Hannah remembered the beastly conditions—filth and fear and no end to hopelessness. Like a heavy weight, sorrow pressed down on her. She took in a slow deep breath. She may have walked away from prison, but it had not left her.

As she thought about all that had transpired and about Margaret, she realized the woman must be terribly unhappy. *She can't possibly possess a shred of peace. Has she ever known tranquility?*

John turned to Hannah. "You look troubled. Perhaps you should have stayed at Lydia's." He rested a hand on Hannah's. "I can take you to the Athertons."

The baby kicked, as if knowing its father was near. "I'm fine," she said, laying a hand on her abdomen. Was it truly possible that she and John would once again be a family? *It feels like a dream*, she thought, a shiver of joy touching her heart.

The wagon following groaned and rasped as it dropped into a hole and then found its way out. What would become of Margaret once she was locked behind the gates of prison? *Perhaps I should talk to her, remind her of God's love.* Even as the thought came to her, Hannah knew Margaret would never listen to her. Still, the idea lingered. Without hope in Christ, Margaret had no hope at all.

"John, I've been thinking . . . would you mind if I spoke to Margaret before you do?"

"Why would you want to do that?" Before Hannah could answer, he continued, "I completely understand your need to tell her how you feel. What she did was beyond reproach. And I'm sorry for what happened. But I don't think it would be a good idea. It will only make everything uglier." He grasped her hand. "I don't want you to go through any more."

She liked the feel of his callused palm. It was strong and sturdy.

"However, if you must do this, I understand and support you."

"I hated her, especially when I found out she wanted to kill you." She glanced at their clasped hands. "And I'm within my rights to speak my mind. But that's not what I want."

John gave her a puzzled look.

"I'm not angry anymore. I know it's hard to believe—I'm not sure even I believe it—but I feel pity for her more than anything. Not just about what's ahead for Margaret but for how wretched her life must have been, how she must feel inside. I can't imagine living without love. I doubt she knows what it is."

John looked stunned. "She doesn't deserve your pity, Hannah. I expect she keeps company with the devil himself," he sputtered.

Hannah knew he was right, but God was doing something inside her, and she dare not ignore his leading. "Can you imagine how lonely she must be? And afraid."

"Margaret afraid?"

"Even the most brutal are frightened by life. Possibly more than the rest of us." Hannah gazed at the hills rolling away from the road. "God loves Margaret. I'd forgotten that." She squeezed his hand. "If he does, shouldn't we?"

John gazed at a small bird flitting among dry grasses. With a shake of his head, he said, "You take all the fun out of retaliation." He grinned. "I had a tongue lashing all prepared." His tone turned serious. "She deserves hell, you know."

Hannah rested a hand on his arm. "We all deserve death and hades."

John nodded solemnly. "All right. You can talk to her, but I'm going with you."

"No. I have to speak with her alone. If we go together, she'll know her plot has been discovered, and she'll instantly get her back up. If that happens, I won't have an opportunity. She won't hear a thing I have to say."

"I don't know, Hannah. I understand your heart, but she could do most anything. I don't want you in danger."

"Please, John. There may be no other opportunity. We can trust God. He's never let us down before."

John raised an eyebrow. "No, but he's allowed a lot of . . . growing pains in our lives."

"And has always seen us through every trial."

John lightly slapped the reins. "All right, but I'll be nearby. I'll ride up the side field, out of sight but close to the house. That way I can hear if there's trouble." He cupped Hannah's cheek in his hand. "I don't want you hurt."

"I'll be fine. Everything will be just how it was meant to be."

When they neared the farm, the constable pulled the wagon to the side of the road, stopping beneath a eucalypt. He took out a flask of water and gulped down a long drink. "I'll wait until ye call me, but don't be too long, eh. It's hot."

"It won't take long," John said. He turned to Hannah. "You sure you want to do this?"

"Yes." Hannah felt inexplicable peace. She knew it was God-given. She felt no anger, nor fear. "Margaret is no less deserving of God's truth than you or I."

"I know. I'm just not as generous as you." Handing the reins to Hannah, he said, "All right, then." He climbed out of the buggy and untied his horse from the back. "Quincy and I will ride up along the draw. We'll wait there."

"I'll be fine. Don't worry." Hannah lifted the reins and clicked her tongue. The horses moved forward, carrying her up the drive to the house.

She stopped in front of the veranda. There was no sign of anyone about, and Hannah had a flash of fear. What if Margaret had left? What if she knew?

She tied off the reins and stepped to the ground. Walking toward the veranda, she saw Margaret's face in the window for a brief moment. Afraid Margaret would spot John, Hannah forced herself not to look to see if he was in sight and walked up the steps. *Lord, tell me what to say.*

She stood quietly for a moment and took a deep breath. *Help me love her. Let there be no malice in my heart.* She knocked lightly.

Margaret didn't answer right away. Hannah waited. Finally, the latch lifted and the door opened.

Margaret stood just inside looking confused. At the sight of her, Hannah felt a prickle of the old hatred. *Trust in the Lord. Serve him only.*

"Hannah, what a surprise." Margaret's voice sounded strained.

"I should have sent word. But I needed to speak with you right away."

Margaret glanced outside as if expecting someone. "Well then, do come in."

Hannah stepped into the house. After the bright light of outdoors, it seemed dark. And it smelled of fetid pork. Two bags sat just inside.

Margaret closed the door and crossed the room. "I'm sorry everything is a bit of a mess. I wasn't expecting a caller." She sat in the chair Hannah had once called hers. "Please. Sit." She nodded at a cushioned armchair.

Hannah sat. She pressed her hands together in her lap and couldn't keep from looking at the bags by the door.

"I'm preparing for a short trip to Sydney Town, just a few days. John is meeting me there." She tried to smile, but it came out more like a grimace.

Feeling a flicker of contempt, Hannah accepted the lie and sought a higher place. She took in a breath. "Margaret, I know your life has not always been what you'd hoped it would be."

"My life is fine, good, in fact." Her eyes flickered with irritation. "You needn't worry about me."

Hannah wet her lips. This wasn't going to be easy. "All of us have hardships, and we may act as if life is satisfactory, even when it's not."

"What are you implying? That I'm unhappy? I can assure you, I'm quite delighted with my life."

"I just want to say that . . . God loves you. Just as you are."

"Well, of course he does. He loves everyone." She studied Hannah. "Why would you feel a need to give me religious counsel? Isn't that the reverend's responsibility?"

"Yes. It is. But there are times when the Lord asks others to speak up. And he expects us to come alongside one another to help in times of trouble."

Margaret fiddled with her collar. "I know all I need to know. I've been going to church since I was a child. There's nothing you need tell me, and I have no need of your help."

"Yes, of course. But do you know the Savior?"

"Whatever are you talking about?"

"Do you know Jesus Christ? The Word says he wants to know us intimately . . . as our Lord. He calls us to spend time with him, in prayer and in worship. He loves us."

"I know that." Margaret stood. "What is this? What do you want?"

Hannah expected irritation; instead she felt God's presence. "I don't want anything except that you know that even in the gravest of circumstances, God's love never fails. He knows who we are, even on the inside, and still loves us. And he'd like to be our friend."

"God a friend?" Margaret pursed her lips. "Whoever heard such nonsense? God is God, and he's no one's chum."

"Christ called his followers friends. We're his friends too. And he longs for us to know his love and to soothe our hurts."

"I'm just fine as I am." Margaret moved to the door. "You should go." She opened the door. "I must be on my way. I've no time for this foolishness."

Hannah knew she wasn't going to change Margaret's mind. She wasn't ready to hear. For now, there was nothing more to be done. She met Margaret's dark eyes. "Margaret, I know."

"You know what?"

"About the inheritance, Weston Douglas . . . and your plan . . . to kill John."

Margaret let out a small gasp and pressed a hand to her chest. "Whatever are you talking about?"

"I know you wanted the inheritance and that you had a lover—Weston Douglas. And that you and he wanted the inheritance for yourselves . . . no matter what it took to get it."

"You're not making sense. I can't believe you'd have such vile thoughts about me. It's time you left. Please go."

Her voice was hard, but Hannah heard panic. She was tempted to walk away, but wasn't willing to give up without one more try. "Please, Margaret, hear me. You need the Lord, now more than ever."

Margaret glared at Hannah. "You think you're all high and mighty? One of God's servants carrying his Word to the lost? Well, you're no better than the rest of us. And you know nothing about me. Nothing. Get out!"

Hannah moved toward the door, then stopped. "I want you to know that I hold no ill will toward you. I forgive you, and so does the Lord—all you need do is to seek forgiveness, and he will hear your heart."

"I've done nothing wrong! Get out!" She swung the door wide. "Get out! Get out!"

Hannah stepped onto the veranda, and Margaret slammed the door behind her. Looking at the hillside, she saw John. With a heavy heart, she lifted a hand in a defeated wave.

Hannah watched as the constable steered Margaret toward the wagon with a heavy hand. She felt no joy or satisfaction over the arrest. Rather, she felt sorrow at a life lost. *Lord, may she remember your words and find you, even in prison.*

Margaret didn't go easily. The constable was forced to bind her hands.

When she reached the wagon, she looked at him. "This isn't right. I've done nothing wrong." She turned to John. "Please, tell this man that I've done nothing. If Weston tried to kill you, it was his idea. He was jealous and wanted me for himself. I had nothing to do with it."

"All that will be decided in court," John said, his voice regretful.

"You'll let me go to prison for something I didn't do?"

John didn't answer.

"Fine, then. I wish he had killed you. You deserve to die. I've never loved you. Never!"

Quincy helped the constable heft Margaret into the back of the wagon, then tied her cuffs to an inside loop. He stepped back and watched the constable climb onto the front seat. With a nod, the man lifted the reins, turned the wagon toward the road, and rumbled away. Margaret no longer looked belligerent. Sitting hunched over, she stared at the floor of the wagon bed.

Hannah leaned against John, unable to stop a flow of tears. No matter what Margaret had done, Hannah felt the woman's wounded spirit. "I wish she would have listened to me."

John put his arm about Hannah and squeezed gently. "Me too."

Hannah looked up at him. "Do you mean that?"

"Yes. I do."

Quincy strolled toward Hannah and John. "Well, I've work to do. In the midst of all the excitement, I've neglected the place."

"Yes. And I'd best get back to the Athertons'. They must be worried about me and you. I saw Perry in town yesterday, so I'm sure he and all the rest are waiting on word of you."

"Stay," John said. "Please. Let's just sit on the veranda for a bit, eh?"

"It's getting late."

"Just for a few minutes."

"I guess it would be all right." Hannah walked up the steps and sat in one of the cane-backed chairs. "You know I can't stay. We're not legally married. And a lot has happened. We'll need time."

"I know. And we have time." John reached across the space between the chairs and took her hand. "I want to spend the rest of my life with you, Hannah. I have since I first saw you on board that foul ship." He gazed out over the farm. "And now, with my inheritance, we can have the estate we've always dreamed of."

"I don't care about that. I'm just thankful for you." Hannah pressed his hand to her cheek.

"It will be just as it was—you, me, and Thomas. It'll be grand."

"That it will be." Hannah knew now was the time to tell him. She'd been waiting for the right moment, but never imagined circumstance would be so perfect. She allowed her eyes to rest on the golden haze in the sky. "It won't be just the same."

"Well, of course things will change—"

"Yes." Hannah smiled, enjoying hanging on to her secret for one more moment. "Our family will be bigger."

"What do you . . ." John's eyes got wide, and he looked more closely at Hannah.

"I'm going to have a baby, our baby, John."

His shocked expression was replaced by a broad smile. "I thought it looked as if you'd put on a bit of weight. And when you started wearing those shifts, I wondered why . . . but I never imagined." He kissed her hand. "When?"

"In March sometime."

John's eyes pooled with tears. "I thought I'd lost you . . . forever. And now . . . this is more grand than I could imagine." His eyes turned serious. "I've been lost without you, Hannah." He cupped her cheek with his hand. "I feel I shall burst with joy."

"I was afraid for you. Thinking that this horrible thing with Margaret would destroy you. I knew you must love her . . ."

"I haven't loved her for a long time. I tried because of the circumstances, but . . . no. I couldn't. I loved you."

He moved to Hannah and pulled her to her feet. "God brought us together. No man can separate us. We shall be together always." He drew her to him. "Always."

ACKNOWLEDGMENTS

I owe Cheryl Van Andel, who works with a superb team of artists, a huge thank-you. Each book in the Sydney Cove series has had a fabulous cover. I also appreciate your allowing me to be part of the process. I deeply admire your work and although we know that "you can't judge a book by its cover," your covers have offered great introductions to my stories.

I must thank my usual group of cohorts. Your contributions have helped me create a story I can be proud of. To my critique group, Ann, Billy, Diane, Julia, and Sarah—thank you for working with me through every line of this book. I am truly grateful for each and every one of you and for the expertise you lent to this project.

Once again I must thank Jayne Collins, my research partner who lives in Queensland, Australia. It has been great fun working together, and I'll miss tossing ideas and questions back and forth across the pond. Although you live far from Oregon, I consider you my friend. Thanks so much.

And to Mary Hawkins, an Australian author who actually

lives in Australia, I appreciate your taking the time to read the manuscript of *Enduring Love* and helping to catch the goofy things that sometimes show up in a book.

And a thank-you also to Lonnie Hull Dupont, senior editor for Revell. Knowing that you've read through my manuscript and given it your stamp of approval gives me confidence. I trust your knowledge and your instincts for what's right and for what's not.

And to Barb Barnes. Thanks for taking care with my projects. You can't know how much I appreciate your quality editing and your respect for my story, plus the soft touch you use that allows my writing to be mine and still shine.

Bonnie Leon dabbled in writing for many years but never set it in a place of priority until an accident in 1991 left her unable to work. She is now the author of several historical fiction series, including the Queensland Chronicles, the Matanuska series, the Sowers Trilogy, and the Northern Lights series. She also stays busy teaching women's Bible studies, speaking, and teaching at writing seminars and conventions and women's gatherings. Bonnie and her husband, Greg, live in Southern Oregon. They have three grown children and four grandchildren.

Visit Bonnie's website at www.bonnieleon.com.

Go back to where
it all began . . .

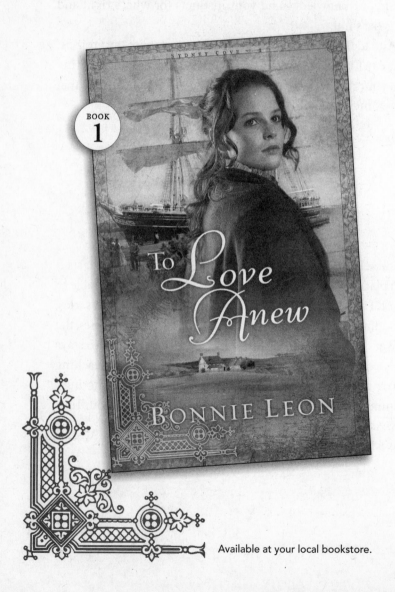

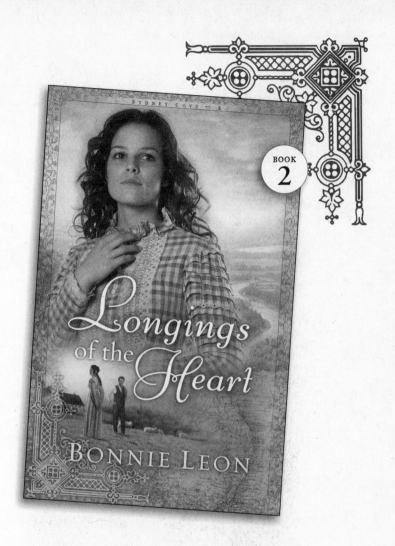

Discover the Sydney Cove series.

Get lost in these heart-gripping stories about
two people journeying toward forgiveness and love.

Revell
a division of Baker Publishing Group
www.RevellBooks.com